All that Sparkles

The Texan Quartet #2

Claire Boston

BANTILLY
PUBLISHING

First published by Momentum in 2015
This edition published by Bantilly Publishing in 2017

All that Sparkles: The Texan Quartet 2

EPUB format: 978-1-925696-00-4
Mobi format: 978-1-925696-01-1
Print format: 978-1-925696-02-8

Cover design by XOU Creative
Edited by Kate O'Donnell
Proofread by Thomasin Litchfield

About the Author

Claire Boston is a contemporary romance author who enjoys exploring real life issues on her way to the happily-ever-after. She writes heart-warming stories, with resilient heroines and heroes you'll love. In 2014 she was nominated for an Australian Romance Readers Award for Favourite New Romance Author.

When Claire's not writing she can be found creating her own handmade journals, swinging on a sidecar, or in the garden attempting to grow something other than weeds.

Claire lives in Western Australia with her husband, who loves even her most annoying quirks, and her grubby, but adorable Australian bulldog.

You can connect with Claire through Facebook (https://www.facebook.com/clairebostonauthor) and Twitter (https://www.twitter.com/clairebauthor), or join her reader group (http://www.claireboston.com/reader-group/).

Also by Claire Boston

<u>The Texan Quartet</u>
What Goes on Tour
All that Sparkles
Under the Covers
Into the Fire

<u>The Flanagan Sisters</u>
Break the Rules
Change of Heart
Blaze a Trail
Place to Belong

<u>The Blackbridge Series</u>
Nothing to Fear – coming November 2017

<u>The Beginner Writer's Toolkit</u>
Self-Editing

DEDICATION

This book is dedicated to my critique group both past and present; Anna, Juanita, Leonie, Lorraine, Susy and Teena. Your insightful feedback, enthusiastic encouragement and general comradery are a huge support to me and I look forward to our meetings each month.

Chapter 1

"Imogen, *darling*, I need you to check through the collection for fashion week."

Imogen Fontaine suppressed a groan. She did *not* need this now. Not when she was already running late. The day was turning in to one big did-not-finish and Libby was meeting her to try on her wedding dress in a few short hours.

She turned, pasting a smile on her face. "Why don't you do it, Jacques? Just this once?"

She didn't dislike many people, but Jacques was the top of the list of those she did. He had a chip on his shoulder the size of Mount Rushmore. It wasn't Imogen's fault her father was determined she should take over the company one day.

Jacques shook his head, tutting. "I don't have that kind of authority. Only a Fontaine can sign off on the line, and your father is away on business."

It was days like this she wished her father would trust someone else enough to give them approval rights, but he didn't think anyone knew his way of doing things like Imogen did.

He was wrong. Jacques was probably a worse stickler for quality than Imogen was, and he lived and breathed Tour de Force just as much as Remy Fontaine, whereas Imogen didn't always agree with some of her father's designs.

Imogen sighed. "Where is it?"

"Where it always is, *darling*. In the finishing hall."

Imogen accompanied him downstairs to the big ballroom-sized space where all completed garments ended up. She walked through the door and pushed down her anger. All the outfits were enclosed in their garment bags, lined up one after the other on special hooks against the wall. It would take her ages to take everything out of the bags, check it all and put it back in – and Jacques knew it.

"How about you unzip the outfits over there?" she said.

"Oh *darling*, I would *love* to, but I must leave early today to watch my daughter's school ballet concert. Your father has already approved it. Toodles." With a little wave and a smirk, he left the room.

Imogen wanted to swear, but it would do no good. Instead she walked over to the first garment in the line, unzipped the bag and started her checks.

***

It was several hours before she was finished and she hurried back upstairs to her office, doing her best to avoid running into anyone else. It was almost the end of the day so most people were in go-home mode anyway, but Imogen didn't want to take the chance. She closed the door behind her and let out a deep breath. She was tired. Tired of snide remarks from people like Jacques and tired of the haute couture outfits her father loved. She wanted to design something real, something stylish, but a little bit different, that the person on the street could afford. It was one of the reasons she'd been so thrilled when Libby had asked her to design her wedding dress.

The thought of Libby's dress spurred Imogen into action. She had to get home to finish the beading.

She grabbed her purse, shut down her computer and headed home.

***

Imogen parked next to her cottage and got out of the car. Breathing deeply, she inhaled the fragrance of the nearby magnolia blooms and stretched to release some of her tension. She glanced down the path which led to her secret garden. She didn't have time to go to her tree house, to remember that summer with Christian, but just the thought of it made her smile, made her relax. She headed inside.

In no time at all she found herself sewing the final bead onto the wedding dress and tying off the thread, snipping it close to the knot. She straightened out the gown and got to her feet, slipping the dress onto its hanger, and stood back to get a good look.

It was gorgeous.

The line would subtly define Libby's small curves and float down to her ankles, turning her into a princess for the day.

She hoped Libby still liked it.

Nerves skittered over her skin. She didn't normally design wedding dresses, had never done so in fact, but when Libby had described the type of dress she wanted, Imogen had unconsciously sketched it on the paper in front of her. Libby had been blown away by the drawing and Imogen had been so caught up in her friend's excitement that she'd agreed to make it before she'd considered the consequences.

But really, there was no way she could have refused. When her closest friend, Piper, had introduced her to Libby a few months earlier, they'd become fast friends.

The clock on the wall caught her attention. She didn't have time to sit contemplating. She jumped to her feet, pressed the dress and enclosed it in a garment bag before dashing into the kitchen to get the champagne she'd left chilling.

As she turned back toward her sewing room, there was a knock on her kitchen door and her father walked in. She groaned inwardly. He was supposed to be in LA.

"*Ma bichette*, I am home." He kissed both of her cheeks.

It was one disadvantage of living at the guesthouse of Chateau Fontaine: her father never called before walking over. She rubbed her arms. She didn't want him there when Libby and Piper arrived. "Hi, Papa. I didn't think you were going to be back until tomorrow."

"I missed you too much," he said. "Now, what are you doing with champagne? Have you friends around?"

Imogen hesitated. "Libby's coming for a dress fitting."

"Ah, the mysterious wedding dress you will not show me. I must examine it if it is to have the Tour de Force name on it."

His French accent was more pronounced than usual: a sign he wanted to persuade her.

"Papa, I wasn't going to put Tour de Force on it. It's a favor for a friend."

"Nonsense! This friend is marrying the most famous rock star in the world. She must have an outfit worthy of her."

Imogen thought frantically about how to distract him but he moved purposefully toward her sewing room.

"Ah, there it is!" He stalked over to the garment bag and unzipped it. "Let's have a look."

"It's what Libby wanted," Imogen said as he removed the bag to reveal the outfit.

Silence.

Remy Fontaine, founder of Tour de Force, one of the most prestigious clothing brands in the world, examined the dress Imogen had designed and made.

Imogen clasped her hands tightly in front of herself. When the silence became too much to bear, she asked, "What do you think?"

He made a noise, a hum, and stroked his thumb over his lip. Finally he said, "It has potential." He scrunched up a section on the side. "If we pin this here, put a red bow there, add some different colored beading and mess up the hem a bit, we could call it a Tour de Force."

Imogen let out an exasperated squeak and rushed over to take her father's hand off the dress, before trying to smooth out the wrinkles. "Libby doesn't want color."

"Nonsense. Every woman who wants a Tour de Force wants color."

Before Imogen could reiterate that Libby didn't want a Tour de Force dress, the gate intercom buzzed. Her friends had arrived.

"Wait here." She hurried to press the gate release and waited by the front door, hoping her father wouldn't touch the dress again.

Piper and Libby drove up and got out of their cars. Imogen forced a smile. "Hi! Come in."

"I can't wait to see the dress," Libby said as she hugged Imogen.

"Come through," Imogen said and rushed back to her sewing room, where her father was still examining the garment.

Libby noticed Imogen's father first. "Mr. Fontaine, I'm sorry. Are we disturbing something?"

"No. He wanted to view your dress," Imogen said before her father could reply, and then remembered Remy had unzipped the garment bag, which meant Libby and Piper could see it too.

Libby gasped and her hands went to her mouth.

Imogen cringed. The dress was crinkled now and all she could see was what her father did: plain and boring.

"It's perfect," Libby breathed. She hurried over and reached out a hand to the dress and then paused and turned to Imogen. "Can I touch it?"

Imogen nodded.

Reverently Libby touched the beading and ran her hand down the smooth satin. "It's just what I imagined." She turned back to Imogen, tears in her eyes. "Thank you." She hugged her tightly again and all Imogen's nerves melted away. It didn't matter what her father thought of the dress; what mattered was Libby loved it.

"Are you sure you don't want a little color?" her father asked, seemingly intrigued.

"No. It's perfect."

He huffed out a breath. "I'll leave you girls to it," he said and walked out of the sewing room.

Imogen breathed a sigh of relief.

"You have to try it on," Piper said, moving over to them now Remy had left the room.

"Can I?" Libby asked Imogen.

"Of course. That's what you're here for." Imogen unzipped the gown while Libby undressed to her underwear and then together she and Piper helped her into the dress.

"Close your eyes," Piper ordered as she zipped up the dress. "Imogen, pass the bag over there."

Imogen fetched the bag, which contained a shoebox. Piper opened the box and pulled out the perfect pair of gorgeous white strappy high heels. Imogen helped Libby balance while Piper put the shoes on her feet and then together they led her to the full-length mirror hung behind the door.

Imogen fussed around making sure the dress sat perfectly and then stood back.

"Open your eyes," Piper said.

Slowly Libby opened her eyes and they widened as she viewed her reflection. "Oh." She put a hand up to her mouth as if she couldn't believe what she saw.

Imogen felt a surge of pride. The dress *was* perfect for Libby; it didn't need any of the extra fussiness her father wanted.

"You look beautiful," Piper said with a hitch in her voice. Imogen's eyes watered as well. She'd only known Libby for a few months but it didn't matter. This was her friend in the dress she was going to wear to marry the man she loved. Imogen grabbed the box of tissues from her table and passed them around.

Piper dabbed her eyes and cleared her throat. "How do you want to do your hair?" she asked and went to stand behind Libby, whose straight brown hair was falling loose down her back.

"I'm hopeless with hairstyles." She examined herself. "Maybe up?"

"Definitely," Imogen said, standing next to Piper and taking a handful of Libby's hair, piling it on top of her head. "If you pin it up loosely, so it's a bit messy but exposes your neck, you can then wear dangling earrings, which will balance the dress perfectly." She handed Piper some sample earrings then started pinning the hair. "Those are an example," she said. "So if you hate them it's fine." She grinned at Libby in the mirror.

Imogen had spent enough time helping out backstage at fashion shows, so she had Libby's hair in an artfully messy arrangement in about a minute.

She stepped back. "What do you think?"

Libby was silent for long enough for Imogen to start to worry. Then she said, "You need to take a picture. This is exactly what I want."

Imogen let out a breath as Piper laughed and retrieved her phone from her bag. "Hold still."

Piper took a few photos of Libby and then of the three of

them. Imogen grinned at their differences. Libby was tall and slim with that long chocolate hair; Piper was average height and her honey-blond hair was short and stylish; and then there was Imogen. She'd always been short, petite, her father said, and her black hair was cropped into a pixie cut.

She turned and helped Libby out of her dress and then opened the bottle of champagne she had placed on her table. "Here's to Libby and Adrian."

They drank the toast and then Libby said, "I'm so lucky to have you both. I can't believe I met the man of my dreams, reconnected with Piper and met you, Imogen. I'm so happy."

The man of her dreams. Christian's face immediately appeared in Imogen's mind and she blinked it away. She beamed. *She* was the lucky one, finally meeting Piper's Australian friend. "You deserve to be. Has Kate chosen her flower-girl dress yet?"

Libby exchanged a glance with Piper. "When we showed her the dresses you designed for us, she said she wanted you to design her something."

"Really?" The sketches she'd made for Libby and Piper had just been doodles. She was amazed that her friends had seen their potential.

"You don't have to," Libby said in a rush.

"No, I'd love to," Imogen assured her. "I'm just surprised. Bridal clothing isn't my specialty."

"You have a way of listening to what people want and making it a reality," Piper told her.

It was the nicest thing anyone had ever said to her. "Do you have plans tomorrow?" Imogen asked. "We could have a girls' day with Kate."

"She'd love that," Libby said. "Let me call and ask her."

Libby called Kate and after she explained Imogen and Piper could both hear the squeal of delight from the other end of the phone.

"I think that's a yes," Imogen said.

Piper chuckled and put down her champagne glass. "Have you got anything to eat? The champagne has gone right to my head."

"Sure."

Libby hung up the phone and Imogen said, "Do you want

to stay for dinner?"

She shook her head. "Adrian's got a thing this evening. I need to head home to look after Kate."

"No problem. We'll pick you two up tomorrow at nine."

"Sounds great."

Imogen and Piper walked Libby to the door and waved goodbye. Then they returned to the kitchen where Imogen searched for something to feed Piper. The one thing she always had was crackers and cheese. It was a start.

Placing the collection of nibbles on the table, she asked, "Libby doesn't want a hens' night, does she?"

"No. She doesn't see much point to the traditional go out and get drunk."

"What about a hens' day?" Imogen suggested, the idea she'd had beginning to grow. "I'll check if Papa's limo is free and we can do the full pamper package: massage, spa, nails, hair. I'll talk to Kate about her dress and we can have lunch in town."

Piper grinned. "Sounds fantastic."

Imogen grabbed her phone out of her bag and started making calls. She wanted to make her friend's day as special as possible.

***

When the limo picked Libby and Kate up the next morning, the little girl nearly pulled Libby over in her excitement. The chauffeur opened the door and she bounded in. "Hi Piper. Hi Imogen! This is so exciting! Where are we going? What are we doing?"

Imogen laughed. "You'll find out when we get there."

Outside the car, Adrian gave Libby a goodbye kiss. Imogen felt a twinge of envy as they reluctantly parted. What would it be like to have that kind of love?

Imogen greeted Libby as she climbed into the car and waved to Adrian. He was dressed casually today, his black cargo shorts and T-shirt sitting loose on his tall, rangy frame and his short black hair mussed stylishly.

"Y'all have a great day and take care of my girls."

"Will do," Piper called and then the chauffeur closed the door leaving the four of them in the back seat of the limo.

Imogen pressed play on the stereo and some quiet jazz played in the background. Then she got out her sketchbook and turned to Kate. "What kind of dress do you want, Kate?"

Her eyes widened. "I don't know. Something pretty." She clasped her hands together.

Imogen began with the easiest decision. "Short or long?"

"Short. Kind of knee length."

The speed with which Kate replied made Imogen think she had a good idea of what she wanted.

"Long sleeves, short sleeves, straps or nothing?"

"Short sleeves or maybe straps."

Imogen asked more questions, taking notes, and then started sketching. By the time they arrived at the spa, she had a rough draft. She showed it to Kate.

Kate was quiet for a long moment and then asked, "Could you maybe make the skirt bigger?"

Imogen smiled and made some adjustments. "Like this?"

Kate nodded. "And maybe the sleeves smaller?"

Imogen took in the sleeves.

"Perfect," Kate breathed. "Can you really make it?"

"Sure. Are you going to have the same fabric as Piper?"

Kate turned to Libby.

"If you want, Kate. You can choose the color and fabric."

"I'd love to have the same as Piper." Kate beamed.

"Easy. I'll do a toile next week and you can decide if you like it."

"A what?"

Imogen grinned. "A toile is a sample of the dress in a cheap fabric to make sure the pattern is right before doing the real thing."

"Great!" Kate said. "You're the best." She threw her arms around Imogen.

Surprised, Imogen hugged the girl back. Her heart tugged at the enthusiasm and affection of Kate. She wanted to have children, a whole tribe of them, but she'd never met a guy she wanted to have them with.

The men she met were more interested in her money than in her.

Except Christian. That summer when she was fifteen had

been one of the best times of her life. He was often in her thoughts. If only he hadn't disappeared without a trace.

"Earth to Imogen!"

Piper's voice shook her back into the present. The others were waiting for her on the pavement. Quickly she got out, thanked their driver and smiled at the others. "Let's go get pampered!

***

A week later Imogen was putting the finishing touches on Piper's bridesmaid dress when Libby called.

"Are you free for dinner tonight?" she asked.

"Sure."

"Our place at seven. Adrian and George's friend from school has arrived back from overseas and needs to be filled in on the wedding plans. He's going to be the usher."

George was Adrian's manager and best man. "So it's going to be a wedding review?"

"Yeah."

"I'll bring Piper's and Kate's dresses around."

"That'd be great. See you then."

***

By the end of the day she was running late. This time it had been Lacey, one of the seamstresses, who needed a hand completing a garment for an awards show. It needed to be couriered overnight, so it had to be finished.

Imogen could never refuse the frequent requests for help. She had spent almost every school break at the business since she was fifteen, and because she loved it, she'd made sure she learned about every stage of the clothing process; from design, to sample-making, to manufacture, to selling. Besides if it were for the good of the company, her father would want her to do it.

When Imogen finished the dress, she checked the time, cursed in her head and then rushed out to the parking lot to her little yellow sports car.

***

Houston traffic was always hell at rush hour. She rang Libby to tell her she was running late.

When finally she arrived, Imogen was ready to explode. She'd tried to take a different route but a car had broken down, making it twice as bad as the original route. She took a minute to calm her breathing, saw that Piper's car was already in the drive along with another couple of cars and then got out and took the garment bag from the back seat. At least she had something to offer tonight.

Kate opened the door and ushered her inside. "We waited for you," she said as she showed Imogen into the living area.

"Sorry I'm late," she said as she gravitated toward Libby and Piper with the garment bag over her shoulder. She laid it over the back of one of the empty chairs before she turned to greet Adrian, George and the friend she hadn't met yet.

He was facing away from her, dressed in jeans and a casual blue shirt.

Adrian smiled at Imogen and interrupted the conversation. "Chris, you haven't met Imogen yet."

Chris turned as Adrian said, "Chris Barker, this is Imogen Fontaine."

Imogen stared at the face of the man who turned around. The blue eyes and the neat brown hair were the same as those of the teenaged guy she'd known.

The guy who had disappeared after the most perfect few weeks of summer.

The guy she'd imagined meeting again in a million different ways.

Her heart stuttered and her breath caught.

After all this time.

It was Christian.

Chapter 2

"Christian." The name came out of Imogen's mouth without her meaning to.

Adrian glanced between them and asked, "Do you two know each other?"

"We met as kids," Imogen said, smiling at Chris. "But we haven't seen each other in years."

There wasn't even a flicker of recognition on his face. He frowned for a moment as if trying to place her. This was nothing like the reunion she'd fantasized about. Her excitement faded as fast as the wrong dye in a synthetic fabric.

He didn't remember her.

Her throat closed but she forced a smile back onto her face and to fill the awkward silence she added, "Christian's father was the head gardener at our house for a few years." Until they'd suddenly disappeared one weekend, never to be heard of again.

"The girl with the tree house," Christian said, snapping his fingers together.

"Yes," Imogen said, nodding. Was that all those weeks had been to him? A novelty tree house?

He turned to Adrian and George. "She had this two-story tree house in her garden with a slide that wrapped around the trunk."

"Sounds awesome," Kate piped up.

"You'll have to come over and check it out one day," Imogen said, glad to move the conversation forward.

"You still live there?" Christian asked, surprised.

Imogen nodded. "At the guesthouse." Her father had kicked up such a fuss when she suggested moving out the first time that she'd agreed to stay, but only if she could have her own place; the disused guesthouse was the perfect compromise.

He didn't comment further but she could tell he was judging her.

It was hardly any of his business. She didn't know why she even cared what he thought.

"Imogen, is my dress in there?" Kate asked, pointing to the garment bag.

"There's a mock-up."

"We'll have a look after dinner," Libby promised and called them all to the table.

Relieved by the change of topic, Imogen followed them into the dining room.

***

Dinner was difficult.

Imogen sat between Christian and Piper, and Christian – or Chris as it appeared he was called now – ignored her, instead talking to Adrian, Kate and George, catching up on news he'd missed during his time overseas. Imogen tried not to take it to heart, but it wasn't often she was completely ignored. Usually people wanted to know all about her father and Tour de Force. She had to admit it hurt Christian didn't remember their summer together. It had been the highlight of her teenage years – a couple of weeks when she'd felt so daring and naughty and alive, when meeting up with Christian had been her little secret – but it appeared it had been just another summer break to him.

She sighed quietly.

No matter how she tried to focus on the conversation Libby and Piper were having, she couldn't shake off the awareness of Christian beside her. He radiated heat and her skin prickled.

"Imogen. Do you want to do the dresses now?" Libby asked.

Imogen blinked and realized everyone was watching her.

"Of course," she said and pushed back her seat. She brushed by Christian and he jerked away, while a zing raced up her arm.

He couldn't be clearer he wanted nothing to do with her.

She held her head high and walked into the living room to pick up the dresses and then followed Libby, Piper and Kate into Kate's bedroom for the fitting.

She didn't need him.

She had friends who needed her.

***

Chris let out the breath he'd been holding when Imogen walked out of the room. God, he hadn't been expecting to meet her again, ever.

The shock of seeing her, the instant delight on her face when she recognized him, had been so hard not to respond to.

But he'd always promised himself he wouldn't give her the time of day after what she'd done.

After what her father had done.

"So Chris, you don't remember the lovely Imogen?" George asked with a grin on his face. "I can't imagine she was ever the ugly duckling."

She hadn't been. He'd thought she was a pixie when he'd first seen her up in her tree house, all short black hair, tiny frame and a pink dress with jagged hem, the type that Tinkerbell and other fairies wore.

He had to say something. He shrugged. "It was only a couple of weeks."

"You sure made an impression on her," George said.

It appeared he had, and Chris didn't know how to feel about that. He'd convinced himself she'd been playing with him, setting him up to get his father fired. The fact she would even acknowledge that time surprised him.

Before he was forced to comment, Kate came running into the room. "Uncle Ade, check out my dress!"

It was bright yellow and set her dark red hair aflame. "It's a practice copy," she explained as she twirled to show it off.

"Damn good practice," Adrian said. "Stand still, kiddo, so we can have a look."

Chris knew very little about dresses but even he could tell it was not something you'd buy off the rack. The straps were wide and the top section fitted, but in a way that suited a nearly eleven-year-old, and the skirt flared out to knee length. A great combination of sophistication, but with a childish flair.

"Did Imogen design this?" George asked.

Kate nodded. "I told her what I wanted and she drew it up. She's going to make it in the same color as Piper's dress." She twirled again, obviously enamored with her new dress.

So Imogen had inherited her father's talent for design.

"Kate, come back here. Imogen wants to check the fit," Libby called.

The little girl waved and raced away down the corridor.

"Must be costing a pretty penny to get dresses designed by Tour de Force," Chris commented, unable to stay silent.

Adrian shook his head. "It's not costing us anything. Imogen said the designs were doodles and didn't want to charge for them. She and Piper have been friends for years and Libby just slipped in with them." His voice was warm and full of praise for Imogen. "Piper and Imogen have made the move to the US so much easier for Libby."

Adrian had met his fiancée, Libby, while on tour in Australia. They'd fallen in love and Libby had moved countries to be with him. Chris had met her before heading overseas and he could see why his friend loved her. She was so down-to-earth, and a genuinely nice person who cared about those around her.

He'd once thought Imogen was like that.

He forced away the thought. It was obvious why Imogen would accept Libby. Libby was in the right social circle, marrying a rock star. "What does Piper do?"

"She's a journalist," George told him.

"Fashion pages?" There had to be a reason Imogen would associate with someone so middle class.

"No. She's an investigative journalist." George said.

"Piper and Imogen have been friends since middle grade and Libby and Piper were friends in Australia during elementary school," Adrian explained.

Piper's father must be important for Imogen's father to allow them to associate with one another.

What did he care? It really didn't matter. After the wedding he wouldn't have anything more to do with Imogen.

"We need a male opinion," Piper announced from the doorway. She wore a royal blue dress that at first glance appeared a bit risqué – there was a lot of skin showing – but on further examination was completely decent and very elegant.

It had to be one of Imogen's designs.

George gave a low wolf-whistle.

"It's not too much?" Piper asked, plucking at the sides and moving forward. "I love it but do you think it's all right for a wedding?"

"It seems decent," Chris said. As the words came out of his mouth he noticed Imogen behind Piper and her face fell. What did she want, her friend to look indecent at the wedding? Mind you, the designs of Tour de Force were all rather out there so maybe that was what she was going for.

He didn't understand fashion and he had no desire to understand Imogen.

He'd get through this wedding and then he wouldn't need to see her again.

Absentmindedly he rubbed at a twinge in his chest.

Piper and Imogen disappeared down the hallway again and Chris turned his attention to Adrian. "I still can't believe you're getting married, man." His friend had always been shy and Chris hadn't thought he'd ever find a match.

Adrian turned his head in the direction of Libby's voice and smiled. "I can't imagine life without Libby in it." His tone was full of love.

Chris was pleased. When he discovered his friend was getting married he'd been worried the woman would be taking advantage of him, marrying Adrian because he was also Kent Downer, rock star. But one meeting with Libby had put those worries to bed. It was obvious the two were deeply in love and she loved Adrian's niece, Kate as well.

He, on the other hand, had no time for women – no time for anything much but work at the moment. He'd just returned from a three-month tour of his company's operations, ensuring their legal teams were ready for upcoming legislation changes and prepping for a big merger. His role on the trip had been to meet people and learn from one of the senior lawyers, who was setting up for retirement.

It was an amazing opportunity for a thirty-year-old but the company had decided they needed to invest in talent early in order to keep them. Having said that, he'd seen nothing but hotels, boardrooms and airport lounges for close to three months. Sitting here in his friends' dining room having a home-cooked meal was his idea of luxury. He hoped to have the whole weekend to recover and relax.

When the women returned from their dress fitting, Libby directed them all into the living room so they could talk weddings.

By the time he wandered in, there was only a seat next to Imogen. He checked again and then sat on the couch next to her, keeping as much distance between them as possible. He was annoyed at himself. He shouldn't feel this much emotion – anger, annoyance, attraction – for someone he'd spent part of a summer with almost fifteen years ago. He was determined not to let her affect him in any way. He ignored her and turned his attention to Libby.

Libby had a notebook, which appeared to be full of lists. Chris didn't know how she could have so many. From what Adrian had told him it was going to be a small wedding in their backyard with fewer than thirty guests. There couldn't be too much to organize.

He only half listened as Libby rattled off details of caterers, decorators, clothing needs, and cake requirements. She had everything under control. Next to him, Imogen fidgeted, playing with a bead that hung off the bottom of her orange top.

He wanted to grab her hand and tell her to hold still. This kind of small-scale wedding might not interest her but it meant something to their friends.

She really was a posh princess.

"To avoid the paparazzi we've chosen three potential dates, all within the time Mum and Dad will be out from Australia," Libby said. "You guys will know the correct date but the different suppliers will have all three dates."

Seemed like a lot of work, but Chris had seen all the photos in the gossip magazines when Adrian's identity had been revealed. The paparazzi had been relentless, hounding them for weeks. It appeared to have died down now though, but they couldn't be too careful. "Book anything in my name if it will help," he said. "There aren't many people who will link me with Adrian."

"Really? That would be great," Libby gushed and made a note on her notebook. "Are you still happy to be MC as well?"

He nodded. Talking was something he was good at.

"Imogen is on for hair and makeup?" Libby phrased it as a question.

"Of course. I can't wait." Imogen smiled and seemed genuinely excited.

Chris frowned. Shouldn't she have 'people' to do that kind of thing for her?

Before he could comment, Libby had already gone on to the next point on her list. He snuck a look at Imogen and caught her watching him. He put on his best disinterested negotiation expression and turned back to the conversation, but not before he saw the flit of hurt across Imogen's face.

He felt like a jerk, but he reminded himself that innocence was Imogen's game. She liked to pretend to be something she wasn't. He'd been so convinced she'd meant what she'd said about wanting to see him again that he hadn't believed her father when he'd said she wanted him to leave her alone. That he'd crossed some boundary and his father would need to find another job. That they weren't welcome at Chateau Fontaine any longer.

He'd been a fool of a kid, but he'd learned his lesson. No one would fool him again.

Especially not Imogen.

***

Imogen drove away from the dinner, her cheeks aching from pretending to be happy all evening. All she wanted to do was crawl under a mat and hide, but appearances mattered. She couldn't let Christian know she was bothered by his disinterest.

But now, alone in her car, driving along the lit streets, she could stop smiling, she could let out her pain and she could cry.

As tears ran down her face she brushed them away, annoyed

at herself. It was her own fault. Over the years she'd built Christian up on to a pedestal, comparing every date to what she remembered as the perfect time in her fifteen-year-old life. The excitement, the adventure, the love. He'd become her happy thought. She'd often go out to her tree house and remember that summer.

And didn't that say a whole lot about her maturity and lack of close friends?

Of course he would be different. Of course he couldn't live up to the character she'd built for him. It was foolish of her to even be disappointed.

But for him to remember *nothing* of that summer, to not even remember her – well that stung.

She let out a shaky breath.

It didn't matter. Since then she'd found new friends with Libby and developed a place for herself at Tour de Force.

She was happy.

She just needed to find a new happy thought.

***

When she pulled through the gates of Chateau Fontaine, and saw the lights on in the main house, she debated briefly whether to go and visit her father. She didn't really want company, so she continued down the drive to where it split to the guesthouse. Normally when she felt this way she'd wander through the gardens to her tree house, but Christian had ruined it for her. She wouldn't be able to go back there until she'd reconciled herself to the fact her memory had played her false.

Instead she took a long shower and climbed into bed with her sketchbook. This was her guilty pleasure, sketching clothing ideas more suited to the street than to the runway. When she'd put enough good designs together, she would pitch the idea to her father and he would let her develop her own line of clothing, allowing everyone to have the kind of style and trend that were usually unaffordable. Adding it to the Tour de Force range would give it instant brand recognition and she was sure it would be a success.

She just had to convince her father of it.

So far, whenever she'd brought up the idea of branching

out, her father had laughed and waved her off. The next time she suggested it, she'd have a full business plan and proposal to back her up.

Happy to have something to focus on other than Christian, she worked until late.

***

The next week started much like the week before had ended—with Imogen running late. She really had to learn to say no to people, but Lacey always helped *her* when she needed it. By the time she'd finished hand-stitching lace on the latest haute couture outfit she was so stressed about being late that she had to take a second to calm herself before she hurried into the room where the weekly meeting was already underway. She mouthed 'sorry' to her father and slid into the empty seat at the back of the room. Jacques smirked at her from the other side of the table but she ignored him and concentrated on what her father was saying.

He was reviewing the previous month's sales figures. They weren't as good as the previous month; in fact they'd dropped significantly. It was good the Fall/Winter fashion show was right around the corner and that starlet Nikki Jameson had worn a Tour de Force dress to the Oscars.

Remy went through the usual items on the agenda before he raised the subject of the next year's fall collection.

"We need something really outstanding. Something that is fresh and new." Remy looked around the room at the people in there. "I think it is time to give Imogen a chance to be head designer on a collection."

Imogen gasped as her father beamed at her. She glanced around the room to be met with a killer glare from Jacques, who had designed that year's collection, a surprised expression from Abigail, who was the production manager, and a big grin from Derek, who made the patterns and toiles. This was not going to endear her to those aiming for a spot in Remy's inner circle, but she couldn't prevent the rush of excitement through her body. Papa had seen her wedding dress design and maybe he'd changed his mind, decided her changes were the way Tour de Force should be headed. This was her opportunity to finally show him what she could do.

"Abigail and Jacques will of course be consultants and designers on the project as well." He turned to his daughter. "I expect great things from you, *ma bichette.*"

Imogen smiled, but cringed on the inside. She hated when her father used her pet name in the office. It made everyone so much more aware that she was his daughter and she had enough trouble avoiding the jealousies. She picked up her notebook as the meeting ended and everyone left the room.

"What do you think, *ma bichette?* Are you up for the task?" her father teased.

"Of course. I've got some great ideas for fall."

"Wonderful. I shall expect to review the first concepts next week." He patted her hand and walked out of the room.

Imogen headed around the corner to her office to plan. She'd hoped to catch Abigail and Jacques but they had disappeared, so she sent them a meeting invite for tomorrow to discuss their suggestions. She wanted to make sure they had their say and were able to offer their opinions. Then with her head spinning with ideas she shut the door and drew.

*****

Imogen had arranged the meeting for mid-afternoon to give Jacques time to get his notes in order. She'd arranged afternoon tea and booked a meeting room rather than hold it in her office, knowing Jacques at least would view it as a territory issue.

Making sure she arrived early, she arranged her designs on the board ready to show when the time was right.

Abigail greeted her politely and set her notebook on the table. She was closer to her father's age than Imogen's and they had a respectful business relationship.

"Help yourself to a muffin," Imogen told her and checked her watch. Jacques was late.

She didn't want to start without him.

The two of them sat in silence, eating the muffins while they waited for Jacques. Jacques sauntered in ten minutes late, and grabbed a muffin. "Sorry, *darling*. It's been one of those days. I'm *dying* to see what you have to show us."

"Jacques you might not have anything better to do, but I

certainly do," Abigail said.

He shrugged. "I thought you'd begin without me."

Imogen squirmed. The rule at Tour de Force was meetings started on time no matter if people were late but Imogen hadn't seen the point without Jacques. She hadn't considered she was wasting Abigail's time.

Jacques hadn't brought anything with him. "Where are your ideas, Jacques?"

"Oh, shoot. I knew I forgot something. They're down in my office. Why don't we view your designs since you're ready to go?" He indicated the display board.

Imogen hesitated. She'd wanted to see the other ideas first, explain how she wanted to tone down some of the ultra-quirky to a more acceptable range. She took a deep breath to calm the nerves ping-ponging in her stomach.

"All right. Remy wants fresh and new. I've taken a slightly different approach from normal and I'd value your feedback." She took the cover off her first design and started to talk.

When she got to the end of the presentation there was silence for a long time. Abigail appeared to be considering something but Jacques had a dumbfounded expression on his face.

"Do you want to ruin the brand?" he asked, his voice pitched high and incredulous.

Imogen blinked. "Excuse me?"

"Tour de Force is the number-one haute couture and pret-a-porter label in the world. We are color, we are quirky, we are different." He waved a hand at her designs. "These are incredibly dull. This is what other designers with no imagination would come up with. This is not Tour de Force." He stood. "You've wasted enough of my time. Your father will never approve any of that." He walked out of the room.

Imogen stared after him in shock. He didn't like her, sure, but she never would have expected him to put down her designs so cruelly in front of another staff member. She swallowed and turned to Abigail.

"He is right about one thing," the older woman said. "Remy will not approve those for Tour de Force." Her tone was gentle. "You know that, Imogen. You know what Tour de Force is all about. This – " she pointed to the boards " – is not it."

Imogen opened her mouth to speak.

"But," Abigail continued, "it is *good*. In actual fact I think those are some of the freshest designs I've seen in a long time. You should be proud of your work."

Imogen shut her mouth with a snap. Abigail was not the type to say things she didn't mean.

"I suggest you talk to your father before next week's meeting. Show him your designs and tell him what you want to do. He may have a different outlet for you."

Imogen considered her advice. If she got the same reaction from her father in the weekly meeting that she'd got from Jacques, it would be horrific. She nodded. "Thank you for your advice." She ended the meeting and Abigail left.

Imogen lowered her head onto the table. Was Abigail right? Would her father reject her designs, or did he *really* want something new and fresh? There was only one way to find out. She had to ask him.

Pushing to her feet, she gathered her designs and walked back toward her office. There was still a mountain of things she had to do today but she had no energy with which to do it. She needed to get this sorted first.

She detoured upstairs to her father's domain. He sat behind his large oak desk, pencil in hand, sketching on the notepad in front of him. Imogen stood at the doorway for a moment to study him. His hair was more gray than brown these days, but that was the only way you would be able to tell he was in his seventies. His face had very few lines and his body was that of a fit fifty-year-old. As usual he wore one of his own designs: a shirt with more colors than a rainbow.

She tapped on the door.

"*Entrez.*" He kept sketching as Imogen walked into the room.

She waited until he looked up. "*Ma bichette.* Have you some designs for me?" he asked, indicating the portfolio she carried.

"Yes, Papa." She hesitated. "They are different from Tour de Force's normal designs."

"Different can be good," he said, putting down his pencil and giving her his full attention.

It was one thing Imogen loved about her father, one thing he was admired for by others: when you got his attention, you had his full attention. Right now that wasn't very comforting though.

Imogen paused before she opened the folder. "You will be honest with me, Papa? If they are no good, then I need to know, so I can improve."

"Of course, Imogen. I will always tell you the truth."

Imogen flipped over the folder and waited while her father examined the designs, one by one. Finally he glanced up, confusion on his face. "These designs are not seriously for next fall's collection?"

The hope fluttering nervously in her stomach went splat.

"You said you wanted something new, something fresh."

"New and fresh, yes, but boring, no." He picked up a drawing. "Where is the flair, where is the color, where is the *Tour de Force*? This may be suitable for the average person but our customers are not your average person. Our clients want special, they want spectacular, they want pizazz."

Which meant her designs were none of that.

Regrouping, she asked, "What about if we create a new line – something affordable for the average person – these designs could be used that way."

She might have told her father she wanted to move to the moon for the reaction he gave her.

"The average person?" he repeated. "We do not deal with the average person. We make art, for people who appreciate it!" His voice rose in volume and lost some of its French cadence.

Imogen stared at her father's reddening face. "You won't consider a new line?"

His mouth set in a grim line. "No. Tour de Force is about people who can afford us. They do not want something anyone can have. We will not be doing a line for the *average* person." His mouth twisted in distaste.

Imogen's and her dreams tumbled down like a child's building blocks. "But – "

"I will have no more talk of it." He closed the folder and pushed it away from him. "If this is the best you can do, I shall make Jacques head designer for the collection."

Imogen stared at him, astounded by his refusal to listen to her. She drew her folder to her. This was what she wanted to do. She didn't want to design things that were ridiculous for the sake of it; she wanted to do real things.

Making her decision she stood. "I'll tell Jacques he's been promoted."

Her father gaped at her. Imogen turned and left the room. Nausea rolled in her stomach but she was determined not to run to the toilet to be sick.

She wouldn't give in to the disappointment.

She just had to get it under control.

Chapter 3

Imogen spent the weekend drafting a business plan. It was obvious her father wasn't going to let her have the opportunity she wanted, so she would have to make it herself.

The more she wrote, the more daunting the idea became. It wasn't just about designing clothing, it was about making sure those designs could be transferred to pattern, about sourcing the right fabrics and factories to make the clothing, finding shops who would agree to stock her label and working out how much the setup of the business was going to cost.

The idea terrified her.

She would be announcing herself to the world, saying, 'here I am' and everyone would compare her to her father. They had such different styles. Would her designs be enough to keep people interested past the initial gawking stage?

Abigail had said they were good, but she was one person. Imogen really wanted to have others review them. If no one else liked the designs there was no point going forward. Before she could talk herself out of it, she dialed Piper's number.

"Hi, I was about to call you," Piper said after Imogen had said hello. "Libby's invited us around for dinner. Do you want to come?"

Imogen wanted to show her designs to Libby and Piper and if Adrian was there, she could get a male perspective as well.

"Sure. There's something I want to ask your opinion about."

"Sounds very mysterious. What is it?"

Imogen hesitated. "I can't explain over the phone, I need to show you."

"You're going to keep me in suspense all afternoon?"

Imogen laughed at Piper's mock outrage. "You'll live."

"All right. I'll meet you there about six."

Imogen hung up the phone and tucked her designs back into her portfolio holder and put her business plan notes together in a binder. It was far from finished but the bones were there. She swallowed down her nausea. Everything would be fine.

Her friends would be truthful but kind in their comments even if they didn't like the designs.

But if she was going to dinner, she wanted to get Kate's flower-girl dress completed. Walking into her sewing room was like walking into her own comfortable lair. This was where she could create, this was where she had no restrictions, this was her workshop. She spotted Kate's dress over the mannequin and some of the tension left her.

She *was* good at this, no matter what her father said.

Hitting play on the stereo, the room filled with one of Kent Downer's rock songs. The energy of the music surrounded her, and she nodded her head to the beat as she got to work on Kate's dress.

*****

At six sharp, Imogen knocked on the door to Libby and Adrian's house.

"I'll get it!" Kate called and Imogen heard thundering footsteps to the door.

As the door opened, Imogen said, "Hi, Kate."

"Hi, Imogen. Is that my dress?" Kate opened her eyes wide.

"Sure is. I'll get you to try it on later to make sure it fits properly." She followed Kate into the open-plan kitchen and her footsteps faltered.

Christian.

He was delightfully casual in a green collared shirt and denim shorts, with low-slung sneakers on his feet. Even his profile was enough to make her heart go into a rock-and-roll beat.

She wasn't supposed to be having this kind of reaction to him. He wasn't interested in her in the slightest.

Bumping her huge portfolio against the doorway she had the sudden urge to hide it, but it was too late.

Christian glanced over. "Bringing a little work with you?"

"Something I wanted to show Libby and Piper," Imogen said brightly, trying to make it sound like the dreams for the rest of her life weren't hanging from her shoulder.

Christian nodded and went back to his drink.

Libby glanced over from the kitchen island where she was chopping up a salad. "Put it in the living room if you want."

Grateful for a reason to exit, Imogen moved through to the living room and propped her portfolio against the couch. As she turned to return, Piper came through the door.

"Is that what you want to talk to us about?" She indicated the folder.

Imogen nodded as the swirly, icky sensation in her stomach returned.

"Great. I've been in suspense all afternoon. Let's grab some drinks and go through it now."

"Oh, no. I don't want to hold up dinner." The doubts came crushing around her.

Piper studied her. "It's serious, isn't it?"

Imogen waved her off, but Piper didn't change her gaze. That gaze was one reason her friend was such a good journalist. Imogen examined the ground. "It is to me."

"Stay there. Let me check how long dinner will be." Piper left the room, returning only a minute later with Libby and a bottle of wine.

"We're having a barbeque," Libby said. "The guys are happy with their chips for the moment. What gives?"

Imogen sat on one of the couches and then, too agitated to stay put, got to her feet again. "I've got this idea," she began. "Papa doesn't like it, won't let me do it at Tour de Force, but I could maybe do it myself. But I don't know. Maybe it's too much; maybe I'm kidding myself."

"Slow down, Imogen," Piper said, watching her pace.

"What's the idea?"

Imogen took a deep breath. "My own clothing label," she said in a rush. "I haven't figured out a name yet, but it would be clothes for everyone. Stylish clothes anyone could afford." Now she'd started, she had to explain it all. She opened the portfolio and spread out designs on the coffee table. "These are my ideas for a winter collection. Coats, scarves, hats, pants, jumpers – maybe even boots down the track. I've drafted a business plan and was going to show Papa but he's not interested. I needed a second opinion." Imogen stopped talking as Libby and Piper passed her sketches to each other.

"I love that," Piper said, pointing to one of the coats.

"Those pants are gorgeous," Libby said, holding one of the drawings for longer.

"Is it seriously something you would buy, though?"

Both women looked up at her with similar expressions of disbelief. "Of course. This stuff is fabulous," Piper said.

Some of the nerves settled. "What about the men's clothing?"

"Why don't you ask the guys?" Libby asked.

It was a huge step for Imogen. Still, she wanted an honest opinion, and she needed it from people other than her best friends.

"All right. Should I take it in to them?"

"No, I'll go get them." Libby jumped to her feet and left the room.

Imogen clenched her hands and then sorted through the designs to put the men's ones on top.

Piper put a hand out to still Imogen's fidgeting. "These are really great," she said.

Imogen closed her eyes. It meant a lot for her to say that, but it didn't stop the doubt.

Adrian, George and Christian walked into the room with Libby and Kate right behind them.

Imogen stood up again, unable to sit.

"Libby said you wanted our opinion on something," George said.

Imogen nodded, and then cleared her throat. "I'm considering my own clothing label and wanted to find out whether my designs for men were any good." She picked them up and passed them over. "Would you wear anything like this?"

Christian didn't even glance at the paper. "Could we afford to wear this?"

Imogen bristled, but kept her expression pleasant. "My aim is to have an affordable clothing line that the average person can afford."

"So you'll get it manufactured in some Asian sweatshop?"

Imogen gaped at him. "No! I'll do my research and find out where I can have the line made. It's all part of my business plan." Or would be when she got to that stage in it.

"You do realize most of the people working in manufacturing plants in Asia earn less per year than what one of Tour de Force's shirts would cost?"

She didn't, but she wasn't going to admit that to him. "As I said, I'll do my research."

Before Christian could say anything else, George nudged him in the ribs. "I think this is something you'd wear." He showed him a picture and then winked at Imogen. "He studies labor rights as a hobby." He turned back to Chris. "Maybe you could advise her on the better places to go."

Christian looked directly at Imogen, a dare in his eyes. "If she's really interested."

The last person she wanted to be taking advice from was Christian but she couldn't say that here. "I'd appreciate it."

"Imogen, there are outfits here I'd wear and definitely stuff Kent would wear. Are you going to start manufacturing soon?" Adrian glanced at George. "We could use this stuff for the next tour."

Imogen sucked in a breath. To have Kent Downer wear her clothing line would be a massive coup. "Really?" She didn't mean to sound quite so pathetically hopeful.

Adrian smiled at her. "Yeah."

"There's a lot to do before I can start production. I have to register a business, and a label, I need to source fabrics, manufacturers, find some funding and shops to sell the line ..." Listing them out sounded so daunting.

George picked up her business plan and flicked it open.

Imogen resisted the urge to grab it off him. "It's not

finished yet."

"You've covered all the bases." He passed it to Christian. "What do you think?"

Christian scowled but spent more time reading through her plan.

Kate piped up. "Are you doing a kids' range too?"

Imogen blinked. She hadn't got that far. "I might, when I get settled. Do you like these designs?"

"Yep. I could be your research assistant if you like. Tell you what kids want."

Imogen smiled. "That would be great. You'll be the first person I call when I'm ready."

"Can I try my dress on now?" Kate asked.

Imogen laughed. She'd forgotten about the flower-girl dress but it was obvious Kate hadn't. Christian was still reading the plan so she said, "Sure."

"I'll light the grill," Adrian said.

Piper and Libby followed Kate into her bedroom. Imogen fussed around when Kate was wearing the royal blue dress, checking the seams, making sure everything sat right. "How do you want your hair?"

"I don't know."

Imogen rummaged in her bag and produced the couple of barrette options she'd brought with her. "I think it should be down, or partially up. Your hair is too beautiful to be restrained."

Kate beamed at her.

"So we could clip it here …" Imogen slid in a clip to show Kate what she meant. "Or we could pin the front up like this." She demonstrated.

"Like this," Kate said when she saw the final version. "I look like a princess."

Imogen's heart warmed.

Piper whipped out her phone and took a picture.

"Shoes?"

"She's allowed a small heel," Libby said and retrieved the shoes, pretty black strappy sandals with a tiny heel on the back. Kate slipped them on and preened in the mirror.

"Do you want to show your uncle?" Libby asked.

"Yeah." She walked demurely out of the door.

Imogen smiled. It was the slowest she'd ever seen Kate go.

"I think it's a hit," Piper commented.

Down the corridor the men told Kate how beautiful she looked.

"*Ma belle, tu es très chic.*" It was Christian's voice, in perfectly accented French, telling Kate she was gorgeous.

Imogen ignored the shiver his voice caused and wondered how much French he spoke.

Kate returned to the room, her cheeks flushed red. "Chris spoke French to me," she said, blushing brighter.

"Do you know what he said?" Imogen asked.

Kate shook her head.

Imogen translated for her and Kate shut her eyes in delight.

"He's a bit of a hunk, isn't he?" Piper asked.

Imogen glanced at her friend, wondering if she was going to make a move on him. Wondering why it mattered so much if she did.

"Yep."

"Was he cute as a boy?" Piper asked Imogen.

Startled, Imogen stared at her. She'd never mentioned Christian's name to anyone.

"You mentioned his dad used to be your gardener," Piper prompted.

Of course. "I didn't see him much," she said, busying herself putting Kate's dress back in its bag. Piper waited for an answer but Imogen ignored her. "Shall we check if dinner's ready yet?"

Piper gave her a look that said she wasn't finished with this, but didn't stop Imogen as she left the room.

Back in the kitchen Imogen immediately noticed her business plan sitting on the table. Both Christian and George were standing by the barbeque on the patio with Adrian, so Imogen grasped the opportunity to retrieve it. She was at the doorway when Piper said, "Don't you want to know what Chris thought?"

"I'm sure he read it because George handed it to him. I don't want to put him on the spot."

Piper raised an eyebrow and called, "Chris, what did you

think of Imogen's business plan?"

Piper had no such qualms.

Imogen cringed.

***

Hearing his name called, Chris turned from the conversation he was having with George. His gaze immediately found Imogen, but from the expression on her face, he didn't think it was she who had called him. It was Piper who was waiting for an answer.

Beside him, Adrian was piling up the meat in a dish to carry inside, so Chris wandered in. "What did you say?" he asked Piper.

"What did you think of Imogen's plan?"

He'd been impressed but he wasn't going to admit it. Imogen's father's company would have plenty of people to write that kind of thing. "It's a good start. Did one of Tour de Force's business managers write it?" There was no way she'd know how the real world worked. People as rich as the Fontaines had minions to do all the hard work.

Fire flashed in Imogen's brown eyes, an intriguing contrast to the smile on her face and her pleasant tone as she replied, "I wrote it. It has nothing to do with Tour de Force."

He believed Imogen was a harder woman than she pretended. That fire proved it. It was a good reminder not to trust her. "They're not footing the bill?"

"No."

Chris was intrigued but he didn't want to seem too interested. Luckily George was curious as well.

"Your label isn't going to be part of Tour de Force's empire?"

Imogen shook her head. "It's not a good fit," she said, only hesitating slightly. "I'll be doing this on my own."

With Daddy's support, Chris was sure. "How are you funding it?"

Her cheeks flushed red and she lifted her chin. "I have money."

Probably a trust fund.

"How can the plan be improved?" Piper asked him.

"Find a good lawyer to draw up the documents and if

you're serious about manufacturing overseas *and* you care about your workers, make sure you visit the factory before you make a decision."

Imogen nodded. "Thank you." She sounded like she meant it.

"Chris can probably recommend a few lawyers," George said. "They're his species."

Chris smiled but he wasn't happy. He wanted to have as little to do with Imogen as possible, not help her build a business that would enable her to do whatever she liked with people's lives, like her father.

Luckily at dinner he sat next to Kate, who kept him entertained chatting about all manner of things, including the new book she was writing. She also complained bitterly that Libby wouldn't let her read any of the next Jessop Chronicles book.

Libby heard her. "You know full well it's in dirty draft stage. It's not ready for human consumption yet."

Kate laughed. "I know, but I so can't wait." She turned back to Chris. "What do you like to read?"

Chris couldn't remember the last time he read for enjoyment. There were always reams of contracts, legalese documents and background papers he had to read and he often fell asleep with one on his lap. "I love adventure series." At least he had as a kid.

"Have you read the Jessop Chronicles?" she asked.

He glanced at Libby, acknowledging the twinge of guilt. "No, I haven't."

"You must," Kate declared. "I'll lend you my copy."

Before he could refuse, she left the table and ran down the hallway toward her room. She returned with a stack of books, which she placed next to Chris on the table.

"Here's the first four. Once you start reading, you're going to want to read the lot and then we can talk about them."

Chris swallowed his grin as Adrian said, "Kiddo, he might not want to read them all."

Kate gave her uncle a disbelieving look and then turned to Chris. "Trust me. They're addictive."

"Thanks, Kate."

Libby looked mortified.

He grinned at her. "Can't wait."

Though kids' books weren't his thing, he'd make an effort to read at least the first one, so if Kate grilled him later, he'd have answers. He liked the young girl and was pleased to see her cheerful and happy. He remembered too well what she'd been like after the car accident that had killed both her parents. He and George had helped Adrian get through those first few months, one of them always being there as his sounding board when things got too much. It had been rough.

He got to his feet to help clear the table and stack the dishwasher.

"Any more wedding lists, Libby?" George asked.

Libby shook her head. "I think everything's organized. My parents arrive next week and then we just need to pick up the cake on the day."

The wedding was the following weekend and Chris was glad. There would be no more planning dinners and he wouldn't need to see Imogen again. Her presence made him antsy.

He'd got over her a very long time ago. Right after her father had said she never wanted to see him again and threatened to take out a restraining order on him if he came anywhere near his daughter.

When Kate made noises about playing a board game, Chris knew it was time to leave. "I've got some briefs to read through," he said by way of explanation.

"And the Jessop Chronicles too," Kate said, handing him the pile from the table.

He took the books and smiled. "And those."

Adrian walked him out. "Libby will give you the rundown on her stories if you don't want to read them."

Chris glanced at him. "I'll read the first one. I promised Kate."

"We both know she can be tenacious at times."

Chris grinned. "But so loveable. It's probably about time I gave myself some downtime. This will force me to do it."

"Just as long as you don't feel obligated."

"Not a chance." He hesitated, debating whether he should ask Adrian the question he'd been wondering all night. "Do you really think Imogen can get this label thing off the ground?" he asked as he reached his car.

Adrian turned to him in surprise. "Yeah. Don't you?"

Chris shrugged. He didn't know the person Imogen had become. "Setting up a business is difficult."

Adrian shifted. "She's dedicated. That's one thing I've learned about her in the last six months. Dedicated to her friends and to her work. I think she'll make it work." He was quiet a second and then asked, "What's your issue with her?"

Should he tell Adrian?

Today wasn't the time to go into it. "It's nothing. I'll see you next week."

He drove home to his apartment. Once inside he dumped the books on his kitchen bench and walked over to his office, which was stacked with neat piles of papers he needed to go through. He flicked open his calendar to check what he had on tomorrow, even though he had a fair idea.

The last thing he felt like doing was reading through more dry documents.

But that was what he was paid to do.

He made a coffee and sat down to read.

An hour later he was confident he had all the information he needed for the next day. It was getting late and he should head to bed. An image of a smiling Imogen popped into his head but he shook it away. She was not what he needed to be thinking about.

Still, his fingers typed *Tour de Force* into his laptop's search engine.

The website was bright but stylish. Chris clicked through buttons to check the latest range and snorted.

It was ridiculous. They weren't the types of clothes people would actually wear in public, unless going to a fancy-dress party. No wonder Imogen's father hadn't liked her designs.

He paused, not sure why he'd assumed Remy Fontaine hadn't liked Imogen's work. Probably because he wasn't willing to make it part of the Tour de Force brand. Still, from what he knew of the man's love for his daughter, Chris was surprised. He would have expected Remy to give Imogen the moon if she'd asked him for it.

He sighed and shut off his computer. He didn't want to think about Imogen. He'd spent far too many years obsessing over her when he was younger.

Standing up, he picked up the books Kate had loaned him and found the first in the series. He flicked over and read the blurb on the back. It sounded all right.

He'd read the first chapter and then go to sleep.

It would keep his thoughts away from the girl who'd taught him not to trust.

Chapter 4

When Christian arrived at Adrian's house the next weekend for the wedding he carried all four of Libby's books with him. Kate answered the door wearing a blue kimono, her hair half up and the lightest hint of makeup on her face.

"All ready to go?" he asked as he handed back the books.

"We're on schedule," Kate answered. "Did you read them?"

Chris grimaced. "It is entirely your fault I've had little to no sleep this week," he said. "Yours and Libby's."

"I knew you'd like them!" Kate crowed.

He followed her down the corridor. She was right. The books were well written and had reminded him why he'd loved to read action adventure as a kid. "So when's the next one out?"

"Libby got her author copies this week," Kate said, smiling slyly at him. "If you're nice to me, I might be able to swing you a copy."

He laughed. "I'll be super nice then."

Kate stopped him at the kitchen. "Guys are that way," she said, pointing down a passageway. "Guests should arrive in about half an hour and then you need to take them through there." She pointed again.

Chris smiled. It seemed Kate had taken on the role of wedding organizer. He glanced outside. The garden had been decorated in swathes of white and blue fabrics, lanterns and other pretty decorations. He had to admit it looked pretty good.

Leaving Kate, he wandered down to the groom's end. He wasn't sure what state he'd find Adrian in. His friend had had anxiety attacks when they were younger – even through his early twenties – but the attacks were less frequent now.

When he walked into the room he found both George and Adrian sitting in lounge chairs sipping mint juleps.

"You've got the alcoholic version and the non-alcoholic version," George said by way of a greeting.

"Non-alcoholic," he answered, not wanting to mess up his role as master of ceremonies and usher. There'd be time for drinking later. He took the drink George handed him and sat down. "No nerves?"

Adrian shook his head. "None at all." He held out a steady hand. "Asking Libby to marry me was the best decision of my life."

George laughed. "Even if it took a bit of prompting."

Adrian shrugged. "I got there in the end."

Chris sipped his drink, happy to have the chance to sit and chat to his mates.

"You looked wiped," George said.

Chris opened the eyes he hadn't realized he closed. "It's his niece's and fiancée's fault," Chris said. "I started Libby's damn book and couldn't put it down."

Adrian beamed at him. "She'll love to hear that."

Chris grunted. "So anyone I need to keep an eye on today? Anyone likely to misbehave?"

George passed him a folder. "Photos of the guests," he said. "For those you don't know."

Chris opened it and read through. He didn't want to be responsible for letting paparazzi in. There was a face he recognized somewhere. He checked the name, Michael Atkinson – Piper's father. He was a vice president at an oil and gas company that Chris occasionally had to do business with. It made sense that Remy let Imogen be friends with her. Piper was in the right social sphere.

Closing the folder, he was pleased. There weren't too many guests he didn't personally know.

"I'm not sure about Libby's parents," Adrian said. "They're

here, but I got the feeling when I met them that it's more because it's expected of them than from any real love for Libby. They don't understand her." He scowled.

"Her father walking her down the aisle?"

"No. No one is," Adrian said. "She agonized over it for weeks. I think she would have asked Piper's father if her own parents weren't coming but she didn't want to snub her father. And he would have made it seem like a chore so she went without."

Families could be hard work at times. He was lucky he and his dad always got along.

"Does she want someone to walk her down the aisle?" George asked.

Adrian hesitated. "I think she would, but really there's no one she could ask without causing offense to her parents."

"What about me?" The offer was out before Chris considered it.

Both George and Adrian looked at him.

He shrugged. "We're about the same age so you can't call me a father figure." He liked Libby. They'd got along really well since they first met. "We could say the usher doing it is a Texas tradition. Her parents aren't likely to check."

"I'll ask her." Adrian reached for his cell and dialed. When he hung up he said, "Imogen's cross with you for making Libby cry and ruining the makeup. She'd love you to."

Chris's chest tightened, but he smiled. "I'd better go check my amended schedule then." He placed his glass on the table. "I'll see you guys out there."

Down the other end of the house he caught a glimpse of Piper running between rooms.

"Male entering," he called as he entered the female zone.

Kate raced out. "You're the best, Chris." She threw her arms around him and hugged him tightly.

Chris hugged her back. The kid could always make him feel good about himself. He walked with her into the room where Libby, Piper and Imogen were getting ready. His step faltered as the first person he saw was Imogen, or rather her firm, rounded bottom pointing toward him, covered in nothing but a nearly see-through slip, as she bent toward Libby to fix her makeup.

His body stiffened and he glanced away, clearing his throat.

"Come in, Chris. We're all decent," Piper said.

Chris wasn't sure he agreed with her. There was nothing decent about the sheerness of Imogen's slip. He avoided looking at her and instead focused on Libby. "Reporting for duty," he said.

She laughed and stood up. Like Kate and Piper, she was wearing a kimono, hers white and silver. "I hear you haven't had much sleep lately. I could say I'm sorry, but I'm glad you enjoyed the books."

"They were great," he said honestly. "Kate tells me the next in the series arrived this week."

"And you definitely deserve an early copy," Libby said. She took his hands. "Thank you for offering to walk me down the aisle." Her eyes watered.

"Oh, no. Don't you cry. Any crying and I walk – not to mention Imogen will kill me." He smiled as he said it and it had the desired effect of making her laugh. Over Libby's shoulder Imogen gave him a smile like a supernova. His heart thudded painfully in his chest.

The doorbell rang.

"That would be my cue to leave," Chris said, giving Libby a hug. "I'll see you later."

He disappeared before his body could have any other inappropriate responses to the woman he was determined not to like.

***

Doorman duty was a piece of cake. By the time everyone had arrived, there was no hint of a photographer – aside from the one Libby had hired to shoot the wedding.

Chris locked the front door and went to check on Libby. "Everyone's arrived," he said as he walked through the door, but any other words he could have said, died in his throat. Imogen had turned around and Chris saw what was now covering the decent slip. It was a dress of the palest pink, and it floated around her as though there was a constant gentle breeze in the room. Her matching pink heels gave her an extra two inches in height and she'd done something to her face to accentuate those dark brown eyes.

It was the pixie brought to life again.

She was beautiful.

Her lips moved but Chris had no idea what she said. Mentally shaking himself he said, "What?"

"We need another five minutes. Are the guys ready?"

"I'll check." Eager to be out of there, he fled the room.

Adrian and George were still sitting where he'd left them but there was some evidence they'd moved because George was hoeing into a packet of chips.

"They'll be ready in five," Chris said as he walked in.

Adrian shot to his feet. "Great. Let's go."

George put down the bag of food. "Hang on, let me clean up."

Adrian tapped his hand on his thigh. "How does she look?" he asked.

Chris had no idea. He'd not noticed Libby or Piper when he'd been in the room, only Imogen.

"No, don't tell me. I'll see for myself in a minute."

George came out of the bathroom. "Let's play ball."

***

Imogen took her seat next to Piper's family. She wasn't sure what to make of Christian's offer to walk Libby down the aisle. It was a beautiful gesture and it made it difficult for her to stay indifferent to him. She knew Libby equated walking down the aisle by herself with no one loving her. Piper had told Imogen about Libby's parents and their lack of affection for their youngest child as well as the issues with Libby's previous boyfriend. Imogen could understand her friend's feelings even though she'd been lucky. Her father might frustrate her at times, but Imogen never felt as if she were unloved.

As the music began, everyone turned to watch Kate walk down the aisle. She positively beamed as she demurely sprinkled red rose petals along the path. Following her came Piper, absolutely stunning in the blue dress Imogen had designed for her. Then finally Libby entered with Christian by her side.

Imogen had never seen a bride so lovely. Libby glowed with happiness as she walked down the aisle.

Christian smiled as he walked and whispered something to Libby to make her grin. At that moment he captured Imogen's attention. His smile reminded her of their time together as teens, the way she'd felt so special to have his focus on her and how she was sure this boy was going to be the one.

He looked stylish in a charcoal suit with a crisp white shirt underneath and a matching charcoal tie. A small fluttering started in the bottom of her stomach and she squashed it down. She couldn't have nice feelings about Christian: he'd proven he wasn't the least bit interested in her.

Christian and Libby had reached the front, where Adrian was waiting. Adrian's gaze was fixed on Libby and he had the biggest smile across his face.

Imogen's heart squeezed, and as they swapped their vows she reached for a tissue, but realized she'd left them inside.

"Here," Piper's mother whispered and handed her one.

"Thank you," Imogen mouthed back and dabbed at her eyes.

This was the type of love she secretly longed for. The type that made you smile, and feel secure, and made you realize you were never truly alone. The type where the person you married was also your best friend.

She imagined her parents had had that kind of love, because after her mother had died, her father had never found anyone else. It was as if he could never love another woman as much as he had her mother.

The celebrant announced Libby and Adrian as husband and wife and they kissed while the crowd cheered. Imogen got to her feet as Adrian and Libby walked past, both of them grinning from ear to ear. While the others joined the receiving line to congratulate the happy couple, Imogen whisked around to make sure the caterers had everything organized. There were going to be canapés and finger food while the bridal party had some photos and then a sit-down meal at tables set up around the garden.

As she reached the catering section her footsteps slowed. It appeared Christian had had the same idea. He was already talking to the head chef.

Imogen hesitated a moment too long and the caterer

noticed her and smiled, which caused Christian to turn around.

He scowled. "Checking I'm doing my job?"

"What? No, I was going to check the caterers had everything they needed."

"Which is what Libby asked me to do." The look he gave her was pure contempt.

It hit her in the chest like an arrow. Did he have to be so different from the boy she remembered? "I'm sorry. I didn't realize. I'll leave you to it." She turned and hurried away, joining the line to congratulate her friends. She needed to remember he was not the boy she'd met; he was a man who had had experiences in the time since that had changed him.

When Libby and Adrian had gone to have photos, Imogen glanced around for a place to sit. There was an older man standing apart from everyone, as if he didn't know anyone. Something about him was familiar and Imogen tried to think where she'd seen him before. He wandered over to admire a flower in the garden and that's when it hit her. Mr. Barker.

Christian's father.

Delight filled her and she rushed across the grass, slowing as she got nearer to him, wondering whether she would get the same reaction from him as she had from his son.

There was only one way to find out.

"Mr. Barker?" she asked.

The man turned and frowned and then recognition lit his face. "Little Imogen!" He stepped back to have a better look. "You've grown up."

There was something about his manner, something about the way he said her name that brought memories flooding back, of all those days as a child when she'd snuck out to the garden to follow him around and learn about plants. She threw her arms around him and gave him a hug. "It's so good to see you."

He seemed shocked at first and then hugged her back. "Well now," he said when she let go. "It's mighty fine to see you too."

Imogen wanted to pepper him with questions, ask him where he'd been, why they'd left in a hurry, why her father's private investigator hadn't been able to find them, but now was not the time.

"Do you know many people here? I can introduce you to

Piper's family."

"That'd be swell. Chris is busy helping out."

At that moment Christian appeared next to her.

"Chris, you remember Imogen Fontaine?"

He nodded curtly. "We met the other day."

His father frowned and Imogen didn't want him to make things worse so she said lightly, "I had to remind him who I was. It's been a long time. When you left so suddenly I thought you must have been abducted by aliens." She laughed to keep the mood friendly.

Christian grunted. "Calling your father an alien now?"

Mr. Barker shot Christian a warning look that told him to shut up and Imogen frowned. "What do you mean?"

Christian shook his head. "It doesn't matter."

Her brain tried to make the connection. Her eyes widened. "Are you saying Papa had something to do with your disappearance?"

"It's not important, Imogen," Mr. Barker said. "It's water under the bridge."

The hair rose on the back of Imogen's neck. There was clearly something important that she didn't know. "Not to me it isn't," Imogen replied. "I want to know what happened."

Christian's face turned a dull shade of red. "Don't pretend you don't know. Your father sacked Dad and kicked us off the property because you didn't want us there."

He might as well have punched her in the stomach. All her breath left her. "That's not true."

"It is," Christian said angrily. "Your father came over and gave me a letter from you saying you didn't want to see me again."

Imogen could see pain in his eyes.

"Chris – " his father began.

"He kicked us out, left Dad without a job or references."

Imogen shook her head. "No. I cried for weeks after you left. I made him hire a private investigator to search for you. He wouldn't have done that to me."

Christian gaped at her. "A private investigator?"

She nodded. "I wanted to find you, to make sure you were all right. You left so quickly I thought something terrible must have happened."

"Imogen, your father loves you very much," Mr. Barker said, stepping forward and placing a hand on her arm. "He didn't think we were a good influence on you so he sent us away."

The man didn't appear to hold any grudge against her father.

"But why?"

"We were too poor for you," Christian said quietly. "He said no one of my status would ever be acceptable for his daughter."

There was something in his tone, some hint of caring.

Confusion flooded her mind. All this time she'd thought Christian had disappeared and it turned out her father had caused it?

She had to find somewhere quiet to sit. Somewhere she could think things through. She didn't want to ruin Libby's wedding by causing a scene.

"If you'll excuse me," she said. "I need a minute." Her voice caught on the last word.

"Imogen." Chris put a hand out to stop her but she shrugged him off.

"Give me a *minute*," she whispered and headed toward the house, smiling and waving hello at guests but making sure she looked like she was on a mission. Which she was.

A mission to get the hell out of there without crying.

She headed to the room where they'd got ready and closed the door behind her. There were clothes strewn about the place and her makeup kit was spread over one of the tables. Needing something to do with her hands she tidied up, picking up clothes and folding them.

Her father had sent Christian away.

She couldn't quite comprehend it but yet it rang true. Her father had always approved the friends she was allowed to socialize with. It was one of the reasons her clandestine meetings with Christian had been so exciting – her father hadn't known.

Now it made sense that the private investigator had turned up no trace of Christian and his father: he had been paid not to. Or not hired at all. Imogen had wondered how they could have disappeared so completely, and now it appeared they were living in the same city all of this time.

How could he have done that to her?

When Christian had disappeared she'd run to her father, telling him about their time together and telling him he needed to find her friend. Her father had listened and been oh so sympathetic and promised to do whatever he could for his *bichette*.

He'd lied to her.

She wanted to call him immediately, accuse him of this crime and discover what he had to say for himself, but there was no point. Her father did not respond to accusations, tantrums or temper. Not from her.

She would have to speak to him when she was calmer.

But God, it hurt.

She'd trusted him. She snatched a tissue from the dressing table and dabbed at her eyes. She was a mess. Her eyes were red and her cheeks streaked with tears.

Outside she heard cheers and it reminded her she was at a wedding. She had no time for self-pity.

Determined to put it aside, she took a couple of breaths and then cleaned up her face, reapplying makeup where she needed to. She walked back out of the house and spotted Christian immediately. It was as if he'd been watching for her and he headed her way, but she shook her head and went to talk to Piper's brother and parents.

She wasn't ready to face him yet.

***

Imogen managed to avoid Christian until after dinner, which she considered to be a success. She'd had photos with the bridal party and been introduced to George's family and Kate's aunt, uncle and cousins, and had even had a conversation with Libby's parents, though that hadn't been much fun. As soon as they had realized she was the daughter of Remy Fontaine, founder of Tour de Force, they were all over her, asking whether she'd like to donate something for a charity auction they were organizing. Imogen promised to discuss it with her father and excused herself with a lie about having to check on dinner preparations.

Now, however, the mood was relaxed. The sun had gone

down and thousands of fairy lights lit the garden with a flickering elegance. Everyone had eaten and the band was playing mellow tunes.

Adrian and Libby got to their feet and had the first dance. It was lovely to watch them sway to the music, caught up in the moment and each other.

When the song was done, Piper and George joined them and then Kate and Christian danced together. It brought a smile to Imogen's face to see them dance, with the big difference in their heights, but Kate was obviously having a ball, and so, it appeared, was Christian.

Someone sat down next to her and she turned to Mr. Barker. She smiled. "I apologize for my behavior earlier," she said. "I was surprised about what Christian said."

"You have nothing to apologize for," Mr. Barker said. "I'm sorry the news upset you." He sighed. "You were such a lonely child."

Imogen stared at him. She'd never really considered herself lonely. There was always plenty to do at Chateau Fontaine, from the tree house, to the gardens, to the pool, and the cinema inside the house. But then she hadn't had anyone aside from her father to share those things with, which was possibly one of the reasons she'd enjoyed spending time with Mr. Barker in the garden.

"I argued with your father when he wanted to send us away. Fought not just for my job, but also for your right to choose who your friends were. Your father did not listen. He threw money at me to make me go away and never return." His expression was sad. "I took the money from him, even though you and Christian had something special. I had to think of my own child. The money put him through his undergraduate degree and his first year at law school."

Imogen gaped at him. She didn't blame him for taking the money, but the fact her father had been willing to pay so much so she didn't see Christian again was unbelievable. Did she know her father at all?

Christian was suddenly at her side and from the shock on his face, he'd heard what his father had said. "You took money from him to go away?"

His father sighed and nodded. "I knew it would be difficult to get a job afterward, and that you were smart enough to get to college, so I did something to ensure you'd get there."

Christian frowned. "I never realized."

"You didn't need to."

Christian was obviously still processing the information, figuring out if he was all right with that. It was then Imogen realized Christian had been as betrayed as she had. His attitude toward her made sense now. Perhaps she could help to right things.

She got to her feet, deciding to take a risk. "Would you like to dance?" she asked Christian.

He blinked at the hand she held out. Then a smile crossed his face. A smile she remembered from that summer; her heart warmed.

"Sure."

His palm enveloped hers as she led him to the dance floor. The music was soft and slow, almost dreamy. It soothed Imogen as Christian pulled her into his arms and they too swayed together, not speaking.

Christian was taller than she was, and even with her two-inch heels she had to tilt her head a little to look him in the eye. She wrapped an arm around his neck and clasped his other hand in hers. His arm encircled her, drawing her close enough for her to brush the lapels on his jacket.

They fit together well, not talking, lost in their own thoughts. What would things have been like if her father hadn't sent Christian away, if they'd been allowed to continue a friendship that had held so much promise?

She sighed. As Mr. Barker had said, it was all water under the bridge now. There was no point thinking about could-have-been.

Christian chuckled.

Imogen glanced up. "What's so funny?"

"You still have the same sigh," he said. "I remember you sighing like that when I told you I didn't like the boy band you were so keen on."

Imogen smiled at the memory and then realized what he'd admitted to. "You do remember!"

He spun her around but his smile was tinged with sadness. "Yeah. It was the best summer."

Imogen stopped swaying and stared at him. "But you pretended you didn't remember me when we met."

"Hardest thing I've ever done. I was still mad at you for dumping me, even after all these years."

Her heart quickened at the confession. "And all I wanted to do was fling my arms around you, because I was so happy you were still alive."

"We had fun, didn't we?" he said.

"Yeah, we did."

The song finished and they stood there, looking at each other. Imogen didn't want to let him go. It was so comforting to be held in his arms, so right. She'd dreamed about feeling his body against hers for years and now it was a reality. She was close enough that if she just moved a tiny bit, her lips would meet his. As she took a breath to do just that, a loud rock song kicked in, startling her and breaking the spell. She stepped away and Christian led her off the dance floor, back to where his father was sitting.

It was for the best really.

Imogen was keen to catch up with Mr. Barker, find out what he'd been up to over the last fourteen years, maybe ask for his advice on the roses she'd planted that weren't doing so well. He'd be pleased she'd kept up her gardening after he'd left, though she'd had to resort to books as the new gardener had made it clear he wanted nothing to do with her.

They chatted well into the evening until it was time for Libby and Adrian to leave to catch their flight to Hawaii. Kate was staying with her aunt, Susan, for the week.

When all the guests had left, Imogen sat down at the kitchen table, where Christian, Piper and George had all flopped.

"What a fabulous day," Piper said, sighing.

"It was always going to be, especially with Libby organizing it," George said, chuckling.

Imogen relaxed and kicked off her shoes, groaning as they escaped their torture device. "Are we cleaning up now?" she asked, hoping the answer was going to be no.

"I'm too tired to deal with this mess tonight," Piper

declared.

"I agree. Shall we reconvene tomorrow?" George suggested.

What a relief. "How about lunch time? I'll bring pizza."

"It's a date," George said, getting to his feet. "I'm going to crash here. There's plenty of room if you want to stay," he offered.

"Sounds good to me," Christian said.

Imogen hesitated. Sunday morning was her normal brunch appointment with her father and there were some things she wanted to discuss with him.

"I'd love to, but I have a cat that needs to be fed in the morning. I can only ask my neighbor to help out so many times," Piper said.

"I'll head off as well," Imogen said. "I've got some things I need to do tomorrow morning."

She and Piper walked out together. Imogen yawned. Right now, all she wanted to do was sleep.

"I'll catch you tomorrow," she called to Piper and drove home.

She had to work out how she was going to confront her father in the morning.

Chapter 5

Imogen's first thought upon waking was of Christian. She smiled as she remembered their dance and how, when the truth had come out, they had immediately been able to talk the way they had talked as teenagers.

Then she frowned. The truth about Christian's disappearance was something Imogen had to address with her father that morning. She swept back her bedsheets and padded into the bathroom.

She had no idea how to broach the subject. She couldn't very well accuse Remy outright. He probably wouldn't remember Christian or Mr. Barker and never responded well to accusations in any case. Imogen would have to find a way to bring the topic up gently. Even though there was no way to change the past, she wanted to understand why he'd done it. Why he'd lied to her.

Imogen switched off the water, toweled herself dry before dressing in jeans and a T-shirt. She'd head around to Libby and Adrian's straight after brunch.

Then she hesitated in front of the mirror. Her father hated to see her in anything that wasn't designer label. It was the reason why her work clothes were so different from her weekend clothes. She debated how much her outfit would affect the way her father responded to her, versus the convenience of being able to leave from brunch to go and clean at Libby's.

She really wanted her father to listen to her.

Sighing, she changed into something he would approve of – a full knee-length skirt in a bright crimson, with a matching jacket and a white shirt – leaving the jeans and T-shirt out on the bed so she could change on her return. Then slipping on a pair of comfortable but high-end flats, she swiped on some lip gloss and checked her reflection again in the long mirror in her room. Stylish chic.

Imogen trotted along the path that ran from the guesthouse to Chateau Fontaine. At the break in the trees she stopped to admire the house she'd grown up in. House was probably too mild a word. It was really a mansion designed like a French chateau with its big brick chimneys, pointed slate roof and long windows. Her father had designed it for her mother, who had loved the chateaus she'd seen when traveling in France, where she'd met Imogen's father.

To Imogen it was just the place where she'd grown up, where she'd laughed and cried, and been treated as older than her years.

With a sigh she continued walking up the steps to the terrace and around the corner; her father was seated at the outdoor setting waiting for her.

"Morning, Papa," she said, leaning over to kiss his cheek.

"*Ma bichette*. How was the wedding?"

"Beautiful. Adrian and Libby are so happy together. I'm heading over there later to help clean up."

Her father frowned. "Surely the rock star can afford people to clean up for him?"

Imogen smiled at his surprise. "Adrian doesn't like strangers in his space. Besides, it will give me a chance to catch up with Piper, George and Christian."

She waited for the question she knew would come.

"And who are these George and Christian?"

"They're friends of Adrian's. Went to school with him." This was her chance. "Actually you probably know Christian, Papa. Remember Mr. Barker who used to be our gardener? Christian is his son. I caught up with Mr. Barker last night as well."

Her father shrugged. "I do not recall him."

"Don't you remember the summer Piper went back to Australia, I made friends with Christian and then they left without warning? I got you to hire a private investigator to search for him but they were never found."

"Vaguely." Her father waved his hand before picking up his coffee and taking a sip.

Either he really had no recollection of the incident, which painted him as the most self-absorbed person, or he was pretending. Imogen decided to push the point.

"Oh, Papa, you must. You were the one who asked them to leave."

His eyes flitted up to hers in shock before he composed himself. "What nonsense. Who told you that?" The shock and hurt on her father's face made Imogen glance at her hands.

"They did."

"Well of course those type of people would tell such lies. I am surprised you would believe them, *ma bichette*." His tone was disapproving.

Imogen bit her lip. It hadn't occurred to her they could be lying. She forced herself to look at her father. "It's strange a private investigator couldn't find them and yet they'd only moved to another part of the city."

Her father sighed, a sound full of disappointment. "I never wanted to tell you this, but if you are going to insist."

"Tell me what?"

"Ah, well it was a messy business." He pursed his lips. "Mr. Barker came to me because his brother had significant gambling debts. He asked for a loan, which I was of course happy to do. When we got back from our week in Paris, they had both disappeared." He shook his head. "If they were indeed in Houston, it sounds like the investigator I hired was a charlatan as well."

It was a perfectly reasonable explanation but Imogen couldn't take what either of them said at face value. Mrs. Povey brought out the cooked breakfast and Imogen dropped the subject. It was too confusing. Someone was lying and she had to figure out the truth. She had to know who she could trust.

Instead she asked, "What have you got planned for today, Papa?"

***

It was close to midday when Christian headed to the kitchen to check if George was up yet. He'd been out like a light the moment his head hit the pillow the night before and obviously needed his sleep. He found his friend sitting at the kitchen island, nursing a cup of coffee.

"Morning. Coffee's over there," George said.

Chris made a cup and settled down next to George. His stomach rumbled but he remembered Imogen's promise to bring pizza. He could wait a little while.

"Great night," he said, really just to make conversation.

"Yeah, they deserve to be together."

Chris smiled. George was tough, authoritative and a regular guy, but about certain things he was a complete softie. It appeared seeing Adrian in love was one of those things.

"Kate will enjoy the week with her cousins."

"She's already got Adrian to promise to take her to Hawaii on the next school break, though."

Chris chuckled and sipped his coffee. He glanced out the window at all the decorations still hanging cheerfully in the garden. It wouldn't take them too long to pull them down and put the place back to normal.

The front doorbell chimed and then came the sound of a key turning in a lock. Piper called out, "Just me. Are you both up and decent?"

"Yes and no," George called back and Piper laughed, walking toward the kitchen.

"Is that coffee I smell?"

Chris was about to tell her to help herself when George got up and poured her a cup. He smiled.

"Thanks," Piper said as she put the box she was carrying on the counter, flopped onto a stool and cradled the coffee George handed her. "What a gorgeous night."

"Yep," Chris agreed. It was about all he was capable of saying. He yawned. His aim was to have the house cleaned up as soon as possible so he could go home and have a nap.

The doorbell rang again.

"That'll be Imogen," Piper said. "Can you get it, Chris? I'm not moving yet."

Chris was on his feet before she finished her sentence. He'd been waiting for Imogen to arrive. Unless she was a superb actress it had been real shock on her face when he'd confronted her about their summer. For years he'd painted her as a fickle princess and now it seemed she'd been as much a victim as he had.

He opened the door to find her balancing two pizza boxes, a bottle of soda and her bag. Quickly he took the bottle and pizza from her. "Morning."

"Good morning."

Unlike the rest of them, Imogen looked fresh and refreshed, as if she'd had ten hours' sleep followed by a massage. There was no hint she'd spent all yesterday rushing around helping out at a wedding and had had a late night.

But it was the first time he'd seen her dressed in jeans and a T-shirt. At the dinners they'd had she'd been dressed in work stuff – designer outfit after designer outfit. So this was the casual Imogen. He liked it.

The smile she gave him was a little cautious and when he just stood there, she slipped past him into the house. "Is Piper here yet?" She headed into the kitchen and Chris closed the front door and followed her.

"Just got here," Piper called.

"Hallelujah, she brought food," George said as Chris entered carrying the pizza boxes. He dumped them on the kitchen bench and George grabbed paper towel out of the cupboard to use as plates. "Fewer dishes," he explained as he passed it around.

"Do you want a coffee?" Chris asked Imogen.

"No, thanks. I've had my morning coffee already. I'll stick to water."

"You're disgustingly cheerful this morning," George commented. "What time did you get up?"

"She looks that way every morning," Piper said. "This girl does not do hungover or tired."

Imogen shrugged and smiled. "It helps when someone prepares you brunch," she said.

"You were up early enough to have Sunday brunch with

your father?" Piper asked, obviously incredulous.

"I can't miss it if we're both in town."

Chris watched Imogen. Had she asked her father about what had happened all those years ago? He handed her a glass of water and grabbed a slice of pizza. It was some kind of gourmet pizza with the lot. He bit into it and the flavors hit him. His eyes rolled back. So good.

"So what's the plan of action today?" Imogen asked.

"We clean up everything, inside and out. Dad's going to bring his truck around later and he'll return the hire furniture on Monday. Then we go home and sleep."

"I'll start outside while you guys eat," Imogen said. "Those clouds look like they could bring rain later." She walked outside and began packing up chairs.

She'd barely acknowledged him, even seemed reluctant to be near him.

Had her father said something? Or was Imogen regretting her enthusiasm the night before?

Annoyed, he grabbed the pizza box and headed out to survey the garden. Imogen was working about as far from the house as she could get. Right next to her were yards of fairy lights and decorations to take down. With a grin he headed straight toward her.

Someone inside turned the stereo on, and rock music blared into the backyard. Music to work to. He nodded in satisfaction as he deliberately squeezed between tables to where Imogen was folding up the chairs.

"Need a hand with that?" he asked, waiting for her reaction.

"No, I'm fine." She barely glanced at him.

This was definitely not the Imogen of the previous night. "Not feeling very chatty today," he commented.

"There's a lot of work to be done," she said as she lifted several chairs and carried them toward the garage. She looked tiny under them.

"Here, let me take them," Chris said.

"It's fine," Imogen said. "I'm stronger than I look." She smiled at him this time but it was a false smile. "Why don't you unhook the lights? I'm too short to reach them."

Chris watched her walk away. Something was bothering her

and he would get to the bottom of it later. The sooner this place was cleared, the quicker he could get Imogen alone.

He got to work unhooking the fairy lights and winding them up. As he worked, he kept an eye on what Imogen was doing. She'd moved all the chairs and together Piper and George had taken in all of the tables. Now she was stretching for one of the lanterns but she was inches too short. He wandered over and reached up over her to unclip it, standing close enough to her to feel the warmth of her body.

"Thanks," she said, reaching for the lantern. Her hand grasped the handle but he didn't let go.

She was so close to him, her fingers brushing his and he wanted to curl his hand around hers and hold on. The depth of his emotion stunned him, but at her tug he let go of the lantern. She gazed at him and it wasn't the steady, open look from their day together; it was more wary, more distrustful.

"What did your father say, Imogen?" he asked quietly.

Her lips parted in surprise and he had an urge to kiss her. He lowered his head and she stepped back quickly, clearing her throat.

"I'll clean up inside. I can't reach anything else." She fled inside and Chris let her. He'd hit a nerve and he knew who'd exposed it.

Remy Fontaine.

It wasn't anger that stirred within him: it was determination. Chris had let him get between them once. He wasn't going to let him do it again.

***

Imogen sighed as the door closed behind her, her heartbeat pattering overly fast in her chest. What had that all been about?

Christian had looked at her as if he wanted to kiss her, had held on to the lantern for longer as she'd been all but rubbed up against him.

And didn't her body like it?

She couldn't allow herself to feel anything for Christian. Not until she'd figured out who was telling the truth about what had happened all those years earlier. She would be devastated if she trusted him over her father only to discover he'd lied.

Imogen didn't know why she was even considering it. Her father never lied to her – the feedback he'd given her on her designs proved it. If ever there was a time to lie, it was then.

She walked down the corridor to the guest room where they'd got ready the day before. There was an overnight bag in there that wasn't hers or Piper's and a suit lying wrinkled on the floor. Christian had obviously spent the night in there.

The idea sent warmth through her but she ignored it. Instead she stripped off the sheets and went down the hall to throw them in the washing machine before going back and picking the suit up off the floor and folding it neatly back into the overnight bag. She tried to be impersonal about it but Christian's scent permeated the clothes and she caught herself inhaling deeply a couple of times. He smelled wonderful – all masculine and spicy.

Annoyed with herself she put his bag in the front hall and tidied up the rest of the room. She carried her and Piper's things to the front door too and left them there so they wouldn't forget them. Then she wandered through the house checking what else needed to be done.

In Kate's room she changed the sheets and tidied up the things strewn over her floor. Then she entered the male side of the house.

George had slept in the spare bedroom at this end and Libby and Adrian's room needed straightening up as well.

Imogen didn't mind housework. She'd not had to do a thing except keep her room tidy in all the years she'd lived at home, so she liked feeling useful, liked the mindlessness of tidying while she thought about other things.

The only problem was today her mind wanted to think about Christian and about her father's explanation.

She didn't know how to get to the truth.

If Christian was lying, then she didn't want to start any kind of relationship with him. She needed to be able to trust her friends fully and if she couldn't, then it wasn't worth it.

But if it was her father … She wasn't sure how she would deal with that betrayal.

They had always been close. When she was a child, he made a point of coming home from work not long after she finished school. He helped her with her homework, taught her how to draw and design clothing. She used to love sitting in the library, sketching dresses and having her father exclaim how beautiful they were. On wintry nights they would build a sheet fort and camp underneath or watch movies in the theater room. He'd been her best friend and constant companion.

She remade the beds, tidied the rooms and carried the sheets through to the laundry. Outside Christian and George had almost finished turning the yard back to normal and George's dad, Hank, had arrived with his truck. Piper was inside cleaning up the few dishes they'd used.

Imogen grabbed a dish towel and started drying.

"What's up with you today?" Piper asked.

Imogen looked at her in surprise. "What do you mean?"

"Honey, I know you're trying to be your usual cheerful self but you don't fool me. What's happened?"

She checked outside to see if the guys were still out there. They were heading back in. "Later," she said.

"We're done," George announced as he came through the door.

"Great. We're almost finished in here, just waiting on some washing. Why don't you guys head off and we'll lock up when we're through?" Piper said.

"Sounds good to me," George replied, yawning.

Christian hesitated. "You sure you don't need a hand?" he asked Imogen.

She shook her head. "No, it's fine. I left your bag by the door." Here's your hat, what's your hurry? The quicker he was gone, the faster she could talk to Piper about her troubles.

"You packed for me?" He sounded surprised, and frowned.

"You and George," she answered.

"Thanks," George said, and turned to Christian. "The Rockets are playing later. Want to watch the game at my place?"

"Sure." He turned to Imogen. "If you need a hand with your business plan, give me a call." He handed her a card.

Imogen took it automatically. "Thanks."

Piper waited until both men had left and then turned to Imogen. "So what gives?"

Imogen hesitated, wondering how crazy it was going to

sound that she'd been pining after a boy she'd met so long ago. "Do you remember that summer you went back to Australia when we were fifteen? I met a guy …"

Piper nodded. "The one you compared every boy to – Summer Boy."

Imogen smiled at the nickname Piper had given him. "Yeah, well, Christian is Summer Boy."

Piper's eyes bulged and her mouth dropped open. "Holy shit! You never mentioned he was the gardener's son."

Imogen laughed. It wasn't often she surprised her friend.

"Have you spoken to him about it? I can't believe you didn't tell me sooner!" She dragged Imogen to a chair. "Sit and tell me everything."

So Imogen did. It was such a relief to tell Piper about what Christian and his father had said and her father's response. She needed to get her confusion articulated.

As usual Piper got right to the crux of the problem. "Someone's lying."

Imogen nodded.

"How are you going to work out whom?"

She shrugged. That was the million-dollar question. Her father had already given her an answer and he wasn't likely to defend himself again, but she doubted Christian would react favorably if she asked for proof.

"Did Chris keep the letter your father gave him?"

"I can't ask him that," Imogen said. Not without implying he was lying.

"Sure you can. Tell him you want to get to the bottom of what happened and say you might recognize the handwriting on the letter if he still has it."

She made it sound so easy.

"That is, if you want to see him again," her friend added.

Did she? She barely needed to think about it. Of course she did. She'd had Christian as her happy thought for over half of her life; she wanted to discover if she'd imagined what was there between them or if there was more to it. "Yeah, I do."

"Then you should call him up during the week, get together for a drink. He offered to review your business plan. That was definitely a hint he wants to see you again."

Imogen loved how her friend was so confident about everything. It *wouldn't* be so easy: there were emotions involved, and long-held beliefs.

Was she brave enough to take the risk?

Chapter 6

"Chris, we need you to go back to Australia."

Chris glanced up from his computer to the doorway, where his manager, Samuel, was standing. He resisted the urge to groan. "What's happened?"

"A disagreement with our partners on the Glaucus Project. We need a representative from head office at the talks and John can't go."

He didn't bother arguing that he'd just returned from three months abroad and needed a break; he simply asked, "When do I leave?"

"Got you booked on a flight tomorrow morning. Finish what you're doing. There'll be a briefing in an hour." Samuel left.

Chris closed his eyes for a moment and then ran a hand through his hair. It was the closest he could get to the curse he really wanted to release. He was tired of racing all around the world in order to make his employer, the oil and gas company Dionysus, richer. For all their talk about their work for the environment or the communities they were enriching, he knew the truth. All they wanted to do was make more and more money. The community stuff they did was to keep people happy and comply with any minimum standards set in the country they were operating in.

And if they could pay to get their own way, they would.

Just like Remy Fontaine had.

Chris stopped that train of thought. Remy was the least of his concerns at the moment.

When he went into law he'd wanted three things: to make a difference, to climb to the top of his field and to have a secure income.

He was well on his way to achieving the last two goals. He'd bought an apartment, had money saved and was working his way up through the ranks at Dionysus. He could hold his head high and say to people he had made something of his life.

It hadn't been easy. He clearly remembered the days of eating canned soup while his father tried to find enough work to support them. It was why Chris needed more security, why he had to prove to his company that he was invaluable. There were always people who were happy to step up into his place if he failed.

But his first goal felt like it was a long way off. Pro bono and humanitarian work didn't pay well enough. Even if it did make him feel good.

The only difference he made at his company was making shareholders happy. Sure, he did pro bono work once a month, which his company sanctioned, but it wasn't enough. He wanted to really help people.

If only being a good person paid as well as being an asshole.

He didn't want to think about it now. He wrapped up what he was working on and got together the things he would need for his trip to Australia. As he was leaving for his meeting, the phone rang. He cursed and grabbed the receiver.

"Are you free for a drink tomorrow?" It was Imogen. Chris smiled and sat back down. The meeting could wait. The sound of her voice soothed his irritation at his company.

"Sure." Then he remembered he was flying out. "Shoot, no, I can't. I'm flying to Australia in the morning."

"Oh, never mind. We'll catch up when you get back. How long are you going for?"

Chris hoped it was disappointment he could hear in her tone. He wanted to see her. "I'm not sure yet. How about tonight? Are you free?"

"Should be by seven."

"Great. How about I meet you at Grechos? It's a wine bar

here in town."

"I know it. I'll see you then."

Chris hung up. He closed his eyes and smiled. This had to mean she was interested. Checking the time, he grabbed his laptop and notes and hurried to the meeting.

***

Chris wanted to swear, rant and rave. Again. From the discussions in the meeting, the project partners had a fair case against the company. Dionysus had not fulfilled the terms of the contract and were now trying to wiggle out of it. It wouldn't work, but Chris had to try. He hated this.

He checked the time and this time he did swear. Ten past seven. He was supposed to be at Grechos meeting Imogen. He dialed her number and when she answered he heard the noise of the bar in the background.

"I'm so sorry, I've been held up at work. I'll be there shortly."

"If it's not a good time we can meet up when you get back," she said.

"No, no, I'll be there soon." He could always come back later if there was anything else he needed. As he packed up, he checked all his notes, transferred everything he would need to the cloud storage his company used and sighed. He was ready as he'd ever be.

Grabbing his briefcase he locked his office door and hurried to the elevator. He was only twenty minutes late – what a way to make a good impression.

When he entered the wine bar five minutes later he scanned around for Imogen. She was sitting at the bar, chatting to one of the bartenders, who was ignoring customers in order to talk to her. Chris couldn't blame him.

He hustled over and slid onto the empty stool next to Imogen. "Sorry I'm late."

Imogen's smile was like a balm. "Rough day?"

"Yeah," he agreed. "Can I have a beer?" he asked the bartender.

The man scowled at him but poured his order.

"Do you want to grab something to eat as well?" he asked,

indicating an empty table in the corner.

"Sure."

They ordered food and went to sit at the table.

"Do you want to talk about it?" Imogen asked, continuing their conversation.

To his surprise, he found he did. He told her about how he had to go to Australia to sort out the mess his company had got themselves in to.

"Must be hard when you don't agree with them."

"It is. I'd much rather be doing something else."

"Like the labor rights work George spoke of?"

"Like that."

"So why don't you?"

"It doesn't pay." As soon as he said it he realized how materialistic and selfish he sounded.

Imogen didn't judge him though, she just said, "You need to earn a living."

Chris shifted in his seat and thanked the waiter delivering their salt and pepper squid. He was tired of talking about himself. "How's your business planning going?"

Imogen hesitated, taking some food. "I haven't had a lot of time for it lately. It's been busy at work with the next collection and making sure the spring sales are going well."

"Do you do all of that yourself?" It sounded like a lot.

"Not all of it, but I get called in for opinions a lot." She didn't seem very happy about it.

Intrigued, he asked, "Don't you like your job?"

She sighed. "Papa is really particular about the designs and clothing. I know what he likes and so if he isn't around everyone asks me."

Sounded rather controlling, but that was Chris's experience of Remy Fontaine. "Is that why you want to go out on your own?"

"No." She was silent for a long moment before she added, "Papa doesn't like my designs."

Chris sat back. That was a surprise. He would have expected Fontaine to say whatever his daughter wanted to hear. "Really?"

Imogen shrugged. "They're too mainstream, not quirky enough. It doesn't fit the Tour de Force brand."

"Yet he's not even supporting you to set up your own label?" Imogen had mentioned she had money saved.

"No." It was flat, didn't invite additional questions, but there was a sadness in her face. Chris wanted to take it away.

"When I get back I'm happy to help you with anything you need."

"How long will you be gone?"

"As long as it takes." At Imogen's look he added, "Probably a couple of weeks."

"Have you been to Australia before?" she asked.

"Yeah. Perth's a nice place, especially if there's time to get out of the CBD."

"That's where Libby's from," Imogen said.

"Kate told me all about the beach Libby took her to – all white sand, clear blue water and few people. I'm going to find it if I get a day spare."

"Sounds nice."

They fell silent as they ate some more food.

Imogen opened her mouth as if to say something and then closed it again.

He waited while she appeared to deliberate with herself. "What is it?"

She sighed. "I want to ask you something, but I don't know how to without offending you."

Was she going to tell him what had been bothering her yesterday? "I promise I won't get offended."

"You can't promise, but I'll say it anyway." She paused. "When you told me Papa sent you away, you said he gave you a letter from me. Have you still got it?"

He did. He had screwed it up into a ball but hadn't been able to bring himself to throw it out. He even knew exactly where it was. "Why?"

"I wanted to read what it said, check if I could recognize the handwriting."

"Did you ask your father about it?"

She hesitated and he knew the answer. "What did he say?"

"He said he loaned your father money to settle your uncle's gambling debts and you disappeared."

Always the good guy. It rankled but he understood the

position she was in, stuck between him and a father she loved.

"I've still got it. Do you want to come and see it?" They'd finished eating anyway.

"Now?"

"Sure. I live a couple of blocks down. We can walk there."

"Yes, please."

They got to their feet and left the bar. The evening was crisp and the tap, tap of Imogen's high heels against the pavement was loud.

"Do you have a car nearby?" he asked.

She pointed in the direction they were walking. "It's parked at work. I'll leave it there unless there's parking near your place."

He shook his head. "You going to be all right walking in those heels?"

She grinned. "I'm used to it."

They reached his apartment building and entered the elevator. He was ridiculously nervous about taking Imogen up to his place and he couldn't figure out why. He'd brought women up before, but it had never felt like such a big deal.

He opened the door to his apartment, hoping he'd remembered to clean up the dishes that morning. As he turned on the light he scanned the room, checking. It was tidy enough; there were a couple of magazines on the glass coffee table but that was it. Actually when he looked around his apartment, trying to view it through Imogen's eyes, he realized it was probably too neat. He spent most of his time in his home office working, or watching sport on television. Aside from one photo of him and his dad sitting on the breakfast bar, there was nothing showing his personality, unless you counted the sixty-inch television. He had no pictures on the walls, no throw cushions, no color. Everything was charcoal, black or glass.

It kind of depressed him.

"Do you want a drink?" he asked as he moved through the room to the kitchen.

"A glass of water would be great."

He poured the drink and put the coffee machine on for himself. Taking the glass into the lounge area he said, "I'll go find the letter."

He walked into his office and went to the wooden box he

kept it in. Though he'd read it a thousand times, he read it again, trying to figure out how she would interpret it. In the end he gave up. She would take it how she took it. Chris gave himself a minute more to brace himself and walked back into the living room. "Here."

She paused before taking it and stood holding it for a moment. He went to make himself a coffee and to give her some space to read.

***

Imogen held the letter in her hand, her heart beating rapidly. She'd recognized the paper it was written on instantly. It was the pink-monogramed stock her father had bought for her when she turned twelve. She had used it to write letters to Mrs. Povey and Mrs. Ashtead because she had no family or friends to write to.

There was no way Christian could have got hold of the paper, or had it copied.

Her father had lied to her.

Imogen squeezed her eyes shut as her heart pinched. Part of her didn't want to open the letter, didn't want to learn the extent of the betrayal.

But the other part had to know.

She opened her eyes, sat down on the couch and her hands shook as she unfolded the letter. The paper was wrinkled.

Delaying a little longer she traced her finger over her monogrammed initials as she'd done when her father first gave her the paper. Then she focused on the words.

She recognized the flowery letters immediately. Her father's writing. He did everything with a flowing, over-the-top grace, including his handwriting. A lump formed in her throat as she read.

Christian,

I have asked Papa to give you this letter because I do not want to see you again.

It was fun to see how the rest of the world lives for a while, but I much prefer the chateau. Don't come back to the garden, otherwise I will have to call the police.

69

Piper will be back next week. You are no longer required.
Imogen

Imogen closed her eyes. The last time she'd seen Christian was just before she flew to Paris with her father in a private jet. She remembered his awe when she'd told him about the plane and his offhand comment that she was slumming it with him. It was no wonder he'd believed the letter to be true.

She put herself in his shoes. They'd had a couple of weeks together having fun, with that underlying connection zinging between them. She knew he'd felt it too, even though neither of them voiced it aloud. Each sentence her father had written came with a solid punch to that connection.

Christian's reaction made perfect sense.

She wiped at the tears in her eyes.

"You all right?"

She glanced up; Christian was standing there, cradling his coffee, watching her. How long had he been there?

Imogen nodded, though she felt anything but all right, and handed him back the note. "Thank you."

"Did it help?"

She'd got her answer, but she wasn't sure if it actually helped her. She had no idea how to address Papa's lies. "It's my father's handwriting," she said. "He gave me the paper for my twelfth birthday."

Christian sat down beside her. Imogen wanted to turn to him, but if he hugged her she suspected she might give in to the tears building up inside. She had to *think*.

Remy had somehow learned her secret: that she'd found someone to spend her summer days with. But was he truly so concerned about who she fraternized with?

Even if he was, she couldn't understand why Christian hadn't made the grade. His father was a trusted employee; and he was polite and had done nothing untoward.

"Imogen, talk to me. There are a dozen different emotions crossing your face." Christian put down his coffee and shuffled closer.

"It doesn't make sense," she burst out.

"Which bit?"

"All of it. Why he would give you the letter, why he would send you away, why he would lie to me after I begged him to find you." Her voice was shaky and a tear slipped past her defenses and ran down her cheek. She brushed it away impatiently.

"I wasn't good enough for you," Christian said. "Maybe he decided the only way I'd stay away was if it appeared you didn't want me."

"He lied to me." Not only fourteen years earlier, but on Sunday, when she'd confronted him about it. That was what hurt the most. He'd always been particular about who she befriended – but to lie about it … it shattered the trust between them. They might not always see eye to eye but they were always honest with each other.

At least that was what she'd thought.

She stood, not wanting to break down and cry in front of Christian. She wasn't sure he'd understand; his feelings for her father were negative at best. "I should go."

Christian took her hand so she couldn't walk away. "Not like this." He tugged her hand so she sat back down next to him. "You're allowed to be upset." He put an arm around her.

That was all it took for her barriers to come crashing down. Tears flooded out of her eyes and she lowered her head, but Christian didn't freak out, he just pulled her close and held her while she sobbed her heart out.

***

Chris felt her sobs lessen, heard the little gasps for air, and his heart twisted. He'd not liked Remy before, but now he hated the man. How could he have done this to his own daughter? While Imogen had looked like an adult, there had been a sense of innocence and naivety to her as a teenager. He'd been two years older and two years wiser than her and he'd had the urge to protect her even then.

But he also knew how close she was to her father. She mentioned him on and off over their summer together and he'd got the impression he was her best friend.

More like her jailer.

When Imogen finally lifted her head, her eyes were red and

her cheeks were stained with mascara. He gently wiped the last tear from her cheek. Her lips parted slightly. Resisting the urge to kiss her, he got to his feet. This wasn't the time. "I'll get you some more water."

When he returned Imogen was twisting her hands together. She took the glass gratefully and sipped from it.

"What are you going to do now?" he asked, sitting back down.

She shrugged.

"Imi, it's in the past. Maybe the best thing is to let it go."

She smiled. "You were the only person ever to call me Imi."

He remembered. She'd said her father didn't like nicknames, which was why she had called him Christian. He liked the sound of his full name on her lips.

"It sounded more pixie-like and when I first saw you I thought you were a pixie in the garden."

Imogen laughed softly. "And I hoped you were a knight, come to rescue me from boredom." She sighed. "Thank you, Christian." She leaned forward and kissed his cheek.

It wasn't enough. He turned his head before she could pull back very far and she hesitated for a moment. Then she brought her lips to his, kissing him softly.

Her lips were sweet like honeysuckle, soft like rose petals, and he had to resist the urge to draw her closer, take more. She was still hurting.

He broke the kiss and leaned back.

"It's just like I remembered," she said. Her smile held more of a sparkle.

"Is that a good thing?" He wasn't sure he wanted to know the answer.

Imogen pursed her lips as if seriously considering the question. Then she grinned. "I think so," she said slowly. "But I need another sample to be sure."

Chris's heart leaped as she touched his cheek and then kissed him, taking the kiss deeper but with all the sweetness of the first one.

He could get drunk on her kisses.

When she pulled away, he wanted to pull her back but she was already on her feet. "I really should go. You need to get ready for your flight tomorrow."

Damn. He'd forgotten all about going to Australia. He'd never resented his job like he did right at that moment.

But she was right. Keeping things light, he took her hand. "I'll walk you to your car."

Imogen shook her head. "There's no need. It's not far and there are street lights the whole way."

He raised his eyebrows. "My father would be appalled if I didn't accompany you."

She didn't argue and they travelled down the elevator in silence. When they got out of the building, Christian said, "I'll call you when I get back?"

"I'd like that." She handed him a business card. "It's got all my details on it."

They arrived at the parking garage and her yellow sports car. It was the perfect size for her but he wasn't sure he'd fit in it.

"Get in. I'll drop you at your building."

"I can walk."

She gave him a look. "If I can't walk the streets alone, why can you?"

He didn't dare say because he was male. Instead he got in, tried to move the passenger seat further back to discover it was already as far back as it would go, and shuffled to make himself as comfortable as possible.

Imogen chuckled. "Maybe you would have been better walking." She fired up the engine and drove him the short distance back to his place.

Before he got out of the car, he kissed her again. "Call me if you want to talk," he said. "If I'm in a meeting, I'll call you back as soon as I can."

He really didn't want to leave her, especially now she knew her father had lied to her, but he had no choice.

He got out of the car and waited until her rear lights disappeared around the corner, then he trudged inside to get ready for his flight.

Chapter 7

Imogen had no time to think about her father's lie. Remy had flown to New York to examine some new fabrics for the line, which meant not only could she not confront him, but also she had to do everything around Tour de Force.

Part of her worried that if he'd lied about this, what else had he lied to her about? The other part of her argued it was in the past and there was no point confronting him. He'd done it because he thought he was doing the best for her: there was no doubt in her mind that he loved her. He was over-protective, but she'd known that her whole life – and she hated arguing with him. It was easier to acquiesce.

Work didn't allow her to dwell on it. Designs for the next year's catalogue were in full swing and although her father had put her in charge while he was away, she'd left it largely in Jacques's hands, knowing he would be able to run with it while she handled the day-to-day issues that only cropped up when her father wasn't in town. There were times Imogen wondered whether there was a conspiracy among Jacques's supporters in the firm to punish her for being Remy's right-hand woman. Processes that ran like clockwork when he was here suddenly had issues.

She didn't complain to her father, though, because she had no proof. Instead she worked longer hours to get her work done, along with all the extra work that came her way. By the time she got home she was exhausted.

Finally it was Saturday.

Imogen slept late and then made herself breakfast and

carried it and her laptop out to her little terrace.

It was a beautiful spring morning. The sun was shining, the sky was blue and there were chimney swifts darting around the garden. It was all very like a fairy tale. She took a deep breath of air as she sat down.

Imogen fired up her laptop and checked her emails. There was a short one from Christian to say negotiations were ongoing. She could read his frustration between the lines. In response she sent him a light email making fun of all the *major* issues people had brought to her attention during the week.

She missed him. It was silly really; they'd spent only a few days together and most of that time he'd been mad at her, but still she missed him. She didn't normally let her defenses down in front of anyone but he was different. He'd held her while she cried and then kissed her so sweetly afterward.

Imogen sighed.

Her laptop rang, signally she was getting a call via Skype. Checking who it was, she grinned, ran a hand through her hair and pressed answer.

Christian's face filled her screen and her heartbeat accelerated. "Hi," she said.

"Morning," he said. "Have you just got out of bed?"

Imogen's face went hot as she realized she was still wearing her pajamas. "I slept in," she said, desperately hoping she looked all right, and peeked at her picture at the bottom of the screen. Not great, but not horrible either. "What time is it over there?"

"After ten at night," he said.

"Are you still working?" She didn't envy him his job.

"Yeah, I'm finishing off some notes on today's discussions."

"You worked on Saturday?"

"Had to go over our plan with the managers here. I've got tomorrow free though."

"You can go and find that beach."

"After I've slept in."

Imogen leaned in to examine the screen. Christian had dark circles under his eyes and his skin was pale. "You should go to sleep now."

Christian smiled. "But I'm talking to you."

The way he said it, it was as if it was the best thing in the world. "I'll be here tomorrow too."

"Sounds like you had a rough week as well," he said changing the subject.

"Nothing I can't handle."

"You shouldn't let them treat you like that."

Imogen shrugged. "It doesn't happen very often." She didn't want to talk about it now. "So what's Perth like?"

"I haven't seen more than the hotel room, St George's Terrace and the office building," he answered. "I'm going to hire a car and drive down to Libby's beach and then back again via Fremantle, which she said I shouldn't miss. There're some markets there and good food."

"Sounds great." Imogen had traveled a lot but never to Western Australia: it had never been on the hot-spot list for fashion. She liked the idea of going places for fun rather than for work. She grinned as she remembered her Cancun vacation with Piper. That had been an experience in more ways than one.

Christian yawned, his jaw spreading so wide it almost looked like he was going to swallow the computer. Imogen laughed. "You need to go to bed now," she said.

"Will you be around tomorrow?"

"Sure, what time?"

They arranged a slightly earlier time and Imogen ended the call.

She grinned like an idiot.

Already her day seemed better. She finished her breakfast and rolling with her enthusiasm opened up her business plan and wrote down the companies she could use to manufacture the fabrics and clothing she wanted. Christian was right. She shouldn't let Jacques treat her like that. The only way she was going to get it to stop without getting him fired was going out on her own.

So that's exactly what she'd do.

***

Chris needed a vacation. He stood at the parking lot overlooking Libby's bay and breathed deeply. The fresh, salty air filled his lungs and soothed his soul. Libby had been right. This beach was peaceful. He couldn't believe how quiet it was. The sand was white, and the water a clear, aqua blue. A beach like this in other parts of the world would be packed so full of people, swimmers, sunbathers or people taking a walk, you wouldn't be able to see the sand. Here though there were only a dozen or so people spaced out along the wide shore, most of them walking dogs. A couple of people even splashed about in the waves, though Chris didn't think it was quite warm enough for a swim.

He had the urge to go down, take off his shoes and wander along the sand and so he gave in to it. There was a walkway parallel to the beach and from there paths ran down to the sand. He took the nearest one and walked down the limestone-and-sand slope. At the end of the path he took off his shoes and left them in the pile of flip-flops and other shoes nearby. He walked over the sand, feeling the grains slip under his feet and between his toes.

Again he breathed deeply to release some of the stress filling him. The negotiations were going where he'd guessed they would. Nowhere. The joint-venture partners had good lawyers who knew their stuff and, worse yet, they were in the right. It was his job to convince his employer there was no point fighting it. So far they wouldn't listen, certain that a particular point in the contract terms meant they had a loophole.

If it was, it was a minuscule hole.

Chris walked down to where the sand was firm and let the waves wash over his feet. The water was cool, but soothing.

He passed a walker going in the opposite direction and she said, "Morning!"

Surprised he said, "Morning, ma'am."

She grinned at him and kept walking.

Chris smiled. Australians were so friendly.

Most of the time.

He'd spent yesterday advising the Australian branch they needed to give in to the partners, that they had no case against them, but they were being stubbornly persistent. He debated calling head office and asking them to give the directive, but it would kill the relationships he'd built with the people here.

And they would listen to the senior lawyers in Australia over him. He hadn't proven himself yet.

He continued his way along the gently curving shoreline.

Chris sighed and kicked his feet through the water. He was tired of this. Tired of the business trips, tired of the politics, tired of working out ways to screw the people who signed contracts with his company in good faith. It wasn't what he'd imagined when he'd decided he wanted to be a corporate lawyer. What he'd wanted was the money and the prestige – to be able to show men like Remy Fontaine that he was worth something. He hadn't realized it would take up so much of his life, or make him so miserable.

The only things that made him feel good about himself were the pro bono work and Imogen.

Imogen. He smiled.

When her profile had popped up on Skype he hadn't been able to resist calling her, seeing her face and hearing her voice. He couldn't wait to speak with her again that afternoon.

He was worried about the way she was letting others take advantage of her. She had always been too nice.

Chris wanted her to keep planning her own clothing brand and he'd do what he could to help. There were quite a few organizations set up to ensure the ethical manufacture of clothing overseas if Imogen planned to do that. He could help her work through the options, make sure everything was legitimate, and set up the contracts to ensure the workers were treated fairly.

The thought of a worthwhile cause excited him.

Maybe it was time to change jobs, find something that was emotionally rather than financially rewarding.

A shiver ran down his spine. The very idea made him feel slightly nauseated. It didn't matter that he had his savings, he still had a mortgage and he remembered clearly those days after Imogen's father had kicked them out. They'd lived with his aunt and uncle before they could find somewhere to live and his father could find a job. It had been six months of uncertainty before his father managed to set up his own landscaping business with the help of a loan from the bank.

The first few years after the business started had been tough for both of them. It took his father a while to make a name for himself, and there had been some hard times when they'd been forced to eat canned soup for weeks while waiting for clients to pay their bills. That had been the hardest part: the debt collecting when his father had done the work required and people refused to pay. He remembered hearing his father on the telephone asking people to pay their bills. All the while he was struggling to pay his own bills because of it, but his father never got angry or mentioned the fact. It was something Christian had argued with him about, often.

But in the end it had all worked out. His father's business took off and more and more people wanted him to design their gardens. It got to the stage where he branched out and not only designed gardens but had a company that maintained them as well. Chris was proud of his father's success, but he never forgot the hard times.

Which was why he'd worked so hard to get where he was today. Sure, he didn't always enjoy it, but did that mean he should throw it all away? So many of his colleagues would kill for the opportunity Dionysus was giving him. He'd be foolish to give it up so soon. It would have to get better as he became a more senior member of the team.

The day was warming up and he would soon start to burn so Chris turned around and retraced his steps up to the parking lot, picking up his shoes on the way.

He had more thinking to do.

***

Imogen had spent the day planning her business and woke the next morning, eager to tell Christian about it. She set up her laptop on the kitchen table, making sure she was logged in to Skype, and then made herself a coffee. She still had another hour before brunch with her father at the chateau.

Settled at the table she checked whether Christian had logged in yet. The ring on her computer answered her question. Quickly she checked her reflection – she'd made sure she was dressed and presentable today – and pressed answer.

She grinned at Christian, who appeared a lot more relaxed today, dressed in a red T-shirt rather than a work shirt and tie. "Morning."

"Evening, Imi." He grinned.

"How was your day?"

"Great. Libby and Kate were right about the beach. It was beautiful. Hardly anyone on it at all."

"Did you go swimming?"

"Wasn't quite warm enough." He chuckled. "Then I went to the port of Fremantle and ate my way around the markets there. So much good food."

"Sounds like fun." She loved trying different types of food but was always conscious of the amount she ate. She had a certain reputation to uphold as Tour de Force's representative.

"What have you been up to?"

"I've been working on my business plan."

"How's it going? Have you come up with a name yet?"

"It's coming together. I've been brainstorming names but I'm not sure what to choose yet."

"Hit me with them."

Imogen wasn't sure whether they were a bit obvious. "Originally I was thinking *Tour* as a shortened form of Tour de Force but that was when I assumed Papa would support my idea."

Christian screwed up his face.

"You don't like it?"

"It's not different enough. It's not you."

Warmth filled Imogen's veins. He was right. She'd come to the same conclusion. "Then I considered *Fontaine* because Papa's name means something in this business and I could use it as a springboard."

Again Christian looked unimpressed. "What else?"

There was another name she was thinking about but she wasn't sure she was ready to tell Christian. It was possibly too soon for that.

"Come on, spill."

Imogen sighed. "I did think maybe *Imi*."

Christian's mouth gaped a little and he sat up straighter. "That's my name for you."

She nodded. "I know." She tried to gauge whether he was happy about it or not.

"How about if?"

She'd take that as a no. She frowned. "If?"

"Your initials, *IF*, capitalized. It makes me think of hope and possibilities."

"Maybe." She could visualize the label; a clean font – something modern but classy. "Hang on a second." She got up and grabbed a notebook and pen from the kitchen drawer and sketched her idea on the pad as she sat back down. Turning the notebook around so she was showing the screen she asked, "What do you think?"

"Wow, that's fantastic. You drew that just then?"

She nodded and fiddled with the design some more. She wasn't entirely sold: some people might think *IF* was conditional and view it as a negative.

"You're so talented." The admiration in his voice made her look up. He was so serious.

Imogen wished he wasn't half a world away so she could hug him. "Thank you."

"Who are you talking to, Imogen?"

Imogen's head shot up at her father's voice and saw him standing at the kitchen door. She glanced at the screen and from the expression on Christian's face she knew he'd heard him too.

"I'm talking with Christian via Skype. He's in Australia at the moment." She turned over her logo sketch so he couldn't see it and checked the time. "I'm not late for brunch, am I?"

"No, I thought we'd have it in the rose garden today, since it's so lovely outside."

Imogen didn't want to finish her conversation with Christian yet. "I'll meet you there."

"I'll wait for you in the salon," Remy answered and stepped inside, walking through to her sitting area.

He would hear her remaining conversation with Christian and she didn't want him to. She sighed and glanced at the screen. "I've got to go."

"Daddy's calling?"

The tone of his voice stung. She nodded. "Maybe we can talk tomorrow?"

"I'm not sure how busy I'll be with work. I'll let you know." His whole demeanor was now rigid. He wasn't happy.

She felt a twinge of guilt and tried to shrug it off. She wasn't going to apologize. She didn't want her father listening in to what she said with Christian. "Take care." She logged off.

Turning off her laptop, she got to her feet and walked into the living room. She froze. She'd forgotten she'd left all of her business planning things spread on the coffee table in there last night. Her father had her plan in his hand and he was reading it, his posture straight and his brows furrowed. She knew that posture, knew that look.

He was not happy.

She said, "Papa, I'm ready. Shall we go?"

For a moment he didn't respond and then slowly he turned to her. "What is this?"

Imogen waved a hand. "Oh, something I've been working on. Nothing, really. I'm starved and we don't want Mrs. Povey's breakfast to get cold."

"Nothing? So it would not matter if I threw it in the bin?" He made as if to screw it up.

Imogen took a couple of steps forward, one arm outstretched. "Don't." She'd scribbled a lot of notes down last night and hadn't transferred them to the computer yet.

"Then I suggest you tell me what it is."

Her father's face held a world full of disappointment and hurt. Imogen hated it.

Defeated, she slumped her shoulders. "It's my business plan."

"Stand up straight, Imogen. Posture is everything."

Imogen straightened automatically.

"Why do you need a business plan? You have Tour de Force. Is it not keeping you busy enough?"

"Papa, can we discuss this over breakfast?"

"No, we will discuss this now." He stood straight and proud, his signature defensive posture.

She took the business plan from his hand. "You know I've been playing with my own designs," she began.

"Playing? You think what I do is *playing*?"

"No, Papa." She had to be careful. Everything she said was going to cause him offense. "What I meant was doing some designs of my own. I showed some of them to you a couple of weeks ago and you said they would never suit Tour de Force."

"I remember. They were too common." He sniffed.

Imogen ignored the sting his words caused. "Well I like

them, and I was exploring whether I could produce my own label. Hence the business plan."

"Of course you *could*," her father said. "But why would you *want* to? Tour de Force is the pinnacle of fashion."

Imogen suppressed a sigh, knowing it would annoy her father. "Tour de Force is the pinnacle of couture fashion, Papa. I want to design clothes my friends can afford, clothes my friends will like."

"Your friends do not like Tour de Force?"

"They like it, but it's not the type of thing they would wear to work, or to the movies." She wasn't sure if she could get him to understand.

Her father harrumphed. "If you do this thing," he said waving toward the business plan, "you will not have time for Tour de Force."

She took hold of his hand. "I know, Papa."

"Tour de Force will be yours when I die. It is my legacy to you. You need to run it when I go."

He wasn't really listening to her. "Papa, Tour de Force is your baby, your style. It's not mine."

She might as well have stabbed him in the heart for the look of shock and outrage he gave her.

"*Non non non*! Everything I have done, I have done for you. You cannot refuse. Who else can it go to?"

Imogen didn't dare suggest he could make his workers shareholders. People like Abigail would carry on the Tour de Force brand gladly. "Once I'm established, and with the right team, there is no reason why I couldn't run both Tour de Force and my own label."

"*Non*. I will not have your commonplace designs associated with Tour de Force."

He clammed up and she was beginning to think he wasn't going to speak again when he said, "If you insist on doing this, you will break my heart. I have slaved for decades to provide for you, to be both mother and father to you, to ensure you never went without." His voice was tight with pain. "Tour de Force is yours. Why do you think I have made sure you learned every aspect of the business? It is not merely to give you something to do." His accent thickened. "Are you trying to kill me?"

"No, Papa!" Not even when she'd proposed moving out of home had her father been so upset.

"Then we shall have no more talk of this matter."

She couldn't let it go. She had to make him understand. "But Papa – "

"*Ça suffit!*" he said and he walked out of her house.

Chapter 8

Imogen sank into the couch and winced as the door slammed shut behind him. What had got into him? She understood why he wanted her to take over Tour de Force, but why was he so against her own designs? She was old enough to do her own thing. She didn't need his permission.

Tears welled in her eyes and she blinked them away. She'd cried too much of late. What she needed to do was go for a walk, clear her head.

She grabbed an apple out of the fruit bowl as she left her house and wandered down the path to her secret garden. She pushed through the doorway and found her tree house where it had always been, high in the branches of an ancient tree. The ladder still seemed sturdy enough, so she climbed up, squeezing through the trapdoor into the first story. The opening had definitely shrunk since the last time she made the climb.

Cautiously she checked the timbers of the tree house; they seemed to be in good condition. She opened the window and perched on the window seat that looked out between the branches and over the garden.

The tree house was a testament to her father's love and the things he'd done for her over the years. She might not have had many friends but her father had given her the tree house and her own secret area of the garden when she'd asked for it.

He was right: he had provided for her. She'd led a very

sheltered but affluent life. Was it selfish to want more? There would be hundreds of people in the fashion world who would jump at the chance to swap places with her, to have the opportunity to take over at Tour de Force, even if their own taste differed from Remy Fontaine's.

Was she just a spoiled, contrary child?

Imogen perched her forearms on the window frame and leaned out.

She hadn't thought her desire to have her own label was controversial. She loved Tour de Force, but it wasn't her; it would never be her. Her creativity was stifled there and she wanted to reach out, do something new, but now it seemed she'd never be able to do that while her father was alive.

What was she going to do?

Was his concern more about their different tastes as designers, or the fact that she was making new friends: first Libby and Adrian, then George and Christian? She'd spent more time away from the guesthouse than she usually did.

Was he worried he would lose her now that she was beginning to branch out and have her own ideas? Did he want to force her to stay? Imogen was all the family Remy had and he had no close friends. Imogen was pretty sure her mother's death all those years earlier had scarred him, though he rarely talked about her death, only her life; he'd loved his wife deeply and desperately. Her father reminded her often of how much she resembled her mother. Perhaps he felt his wife was still nearby when Imogen was around.

Imogen wished she'd known her mother, but she'd died only days after Imogen was born. Her father never told her the cause of death; he'd always just got upset and told her to leave it be when she'd asked about it.

Imogen couldn't stand to see her father upset. It was why she'd given in to him so often, let him talk her out of doing things she wanted to do.

Would she let him this time?

From her perch in the tree she saw his car go down the drive. That meant only Mrs. Povey would be in the house, probably cleaning up from brunch before having her afternoon off.

Mrs. Povey.

The cook had been around since Imogen could remember. Perhaps she would know a little more about what happened in the past. Imogen had never asked her because her father had always said Fontaine business was no one's business but the Fontaines'.

But this was too important.

She shut the windows and latched the trapdoor behind herself before shimmying down the ladder and hurrying across to the big house. She entered through the kitchen door to find Mrs. Povey finishing the dishes.

"Imogen, how lovely to see you. Your father said you were ill."

"I'm fine. We had a bit of an argument," Imogen said, picking up a dish towel and helping her dry the rest of the dishes.

Mrs. Povey turned to her. "You two never argue."

Imogen murmured in agreement. "Mrs. Povey, how long have you worked here?"

Mrs. Povey looked surprised. "Since just before you were born. Your dad hired me to help cook when your mother was too tired from the pregnancy."

Imogen felt hope lift inside her. "Was it a bad pregnancy for her?"

"I wouldn't say bad as such. She'd miscarried twice before and was being extra careful with you."

"She had trouble carrying to term?" Imogen asked.

"You should be asking your father, not me." The older woman hung up her dish towel and concentrated on wiping down the already clean bench.

"He won't talk to me about it. He never would."

Mrs. Povey shook her head sadly. "I can't tell you, Imogen. He said if I spoke about that time he would fire me and he meant it. I'm too old to find a new job and I like this one."

Imogen stared. *Fire* her? For telling her about her mother? She wasn't expecting that at all.

There was one place that might have answers: her father's study. "I might go upstairs for a while, wait until Papa comes home."

Mrs. Povey looked at her until Imogen dropped her gaze. "You could never lie, Imogen. Please don't do whatever you're thinking about doing. At least not while I'm here. I do still need this job."

Imogen couldn't defy her. "All right." She gave the cook a kiss on the cheek. "Thank you anyway."

She left the house and wandered back to her place. She was no good at investigative stuff; maybe she should get Piper's help.

The thought of Piper gave her an idea. When her mother died, her father was already a famous designer. The death of his wife would have surely made the news, if only in Houston. Hurrying inside she turned on her laptop, hoping some of the old editions had been digitized.

She searched for her mother's name and came up with articles just mentioning her as Remy's late wife.

She would have to go to the library or even the paper's archives. On a mission now, she rang Piper.

"Does your paper keep archives of their previous editions?" she asked when Piper answered.

"Of course."

"Can you get me access to them?"

"What are you searching for?"

Imogen told Piper about her argument with her father and her conversation with Mrs. Povey. "I need to find out more."

"Oh, honey. Of course you do." Her voice was sympathetic. "How about you meet me at the paper in an hour?"

Imogen's heart beat faster. "You can get in today?"

"There's always someone there," she said. "What date did your mom die?"

Imogen told her.

"All right. I'll meet you there soon."

Imogen hung up, excited and afraid. What if her father was hiding the information for a good reason? Did she really want to know the truth?

Of course she did. She had to figure out why he was so desperate to keep her by his side.

She grabbed a notebook and her bag and headed into town.

***

Piper let her into the *Houston Age* building when she arrived and gave her a big hug. "All the archives are on microfilm. I've found the one for that period. It shouldn't take long to find something."

They arrived at a room set up with several microfilm machines. "Do you know how to work these things?" asked Imogen.

Piper laughed. "Of course. I sometimes need to go back to the old information when I'm researching a story. They're slowly digitizing everything but there's a big backlog." While she talked she fed a roll of film into the machine and then fiddled with some knobs to get it to work. "We'll start with the day of her death and then go through the days afterward. It may have taken a while for the news to break." She indicated a chair. "Take a seat."

Imogen sat and as the screen in front of them lit up with the image of the front page the day her mother had died, she leaned forward to read. Piper slowly scrolled through the paper, but there was no mention of the Fontaines.

The next day was more fruitful. Only a few pages in was an article about how Imogen's mother had died suddenly. There was a picture of both her mother and father from happier days. Piper printed the page for Imogen.

The day after contained an obituary for Frances Fontaine.

Frances Margaret Fontaine (nee Ryder) died from complications with her pregnancy on Tuesday night. She was thirty-three. She is survived by her husband, owner of Tour de Force, fashion designer Remy Fontaine, and their infant daughter, Imogen Rae.

Frances grew up in Houston, daughter to Julie and Robert Ryder, sister to Allen and Peter. She enjoyed traveling and spent several years backpacking around Europe, where she met her future husband, Remy Fontaine.

Upon her marriage she became an active philanthropist, organizing various charity events and speaking publicly for the under-privileged. She was a much loved member of the community.

Imogen didn't read any further. She stared at the screen as the shocks hit one after another.

Her mother had died because of her.

What had happened? Why had her father never said anything?

It was a wonder he could *stand* Imogen, considering she'd caused the death of his one true love.

"You okay, Imogen?" Piper's cautious query brought her back to the room.

"No." She slumped down in the chair in response to the other shock.

She had a family.

Her mother had had parents and brothers – people Imogen had never known existed. Her father had always said she had no family on either side.

Were they still alive? She hoped so. She'd always longed for cousins to play with.

But why had he kept them a secret? Perhaps her mother hadn't got along with them.

The confusion was a whirlpool in her mind. It made no sense. What else was her father hiding from her?

"Do you want to keep looking?"

Did she? She wasn't sure she had the strength.

"You look." Imogen honestly didn't think she would take anything in.

"Sure."

It didn't take long for Piper to skim through a few more days of papers; there was only a small article about the funeral, which she printed. She turned off the machine and put the microfilm back in the cabinet. "Do you want to come to my place?"

Imogen nodded. The thought of returning to the chateau made her feel ill. She needed time away from Remy – time to figure out what the hell was going on.

They each drove to Piper's apartment but Imogen didn't remember the journey. She parked outside the building and joined her friend at the front door. Piper went straight through to the kitchen and put on the kettle. "Do you want something stronger?"

Imogen did, but she also wanted a clear head to think. "No."

Piper busied herself making the drinks. "I didn't know you had relatives on your mother's side."

"Neither did I." Her voice was flat.

Piper gaped at her. "What?"

"Papa always swore there was no family. None on his side, none on her side." So what had happened to them? Had they died as well?

"Wow. I always knew your father was controlling, but this is ridiculous."

"We don't know the reason yet." Ugh. She was still coming to his defense – it was her automatic reaction. He'd been the only one in her life for so long, the only one she could rely on, and now … She didn't know what he was.

"Do you want to find out?"

Imogen hesitated. It could get worse but she might as well keep going. "Yes."

"Are you going to confront your father?"

Imogen shuddered. He was already mad at her simply because she wanted her independence. How would he react when he found out she'd been digging up the past? Her head ached.

"Not yet." She took the mug Piper handed her and sank down on her sofa. She blew into it, but her hands were shaking. Carefully she put the tea down on the coffee table, took a deep shuddery breath and calmed herself.

"I'm here for you, honey." Piper's voice was full of sympathy and strength. "I can do some investigation if you like."

"Yes, please." She didn't want to do it on her own. She curled her feet up underneath herself on the couch. Christian's face flashed across her mind. She'd love a hug from him right now.

"I'll let you know what I find."

They sat quietly while they sipped their drinks. Imogen's thoughts kept going around in a loop: about her father lying to her again and again; about her mother, about her family, about Christian. Was he even the man she believed him to be?

"So," Piper said with a cautious smile, "I've been dying to ask you something."

Her eyes twinkled and Imogen knew she was trying to lighten the mood. "Yes?"

"Have you seen Chris lately?" She waggled her eyebrows in a suggestive way.

"As a matter of fact, we Skyped this morning."

"Skyped? Sounds kinky. Tell me more." She leaned forward, eyes eager.

Imogen laughed and let herself be distracted for a while. Her issues weren't going to go away any time soon, but she needed some relief.

"Well, it's like this …"

***

Imogen wanted to call in sick on Monday; she didn't want to see her father and pretend everything was all right, but her sense of loyalty was too strong. She shut herself in her office and spent the morning on the phone, calling their stockists and confirming they would take this year's winter collection, and getting numbers.

She didn't mind this kind of work. She'd formed good relationships with the retailers she dealt with and the phone calls were as much about networking and catching up with news as about selling. Many of the people she spoke with knew what would sell and what wouldn't; they'd tell her which were their most popular items and what people were looking for. It often gave her ideas for the next season's collection.

Then she confirmed the Tour de Force table numbers for a big charity fashion event being held on Friday. In a fit of defiance she added an extra ticket. If Christian wasn't back by then, she was sure Piper would jump at the chance. And that way Imogen wouldn't have to spend the night on her father's arm.

At lunch she noticed Christian's email. He'd managed to convince everyone involved to settle the matter and was flying home; he would arrive Wednesday night. Imogen grinned.

After lunch she collected samples of fabrics that had been sent for their approval. There were a couple of gorgeous ones that Imogen would love to use, but she knew it wouldn't suit Tour de Force. She took down the details for her own label before attending a meeting with her father, Abigail, Jacques and Derek. Jacques was doing a fabulous job with the collection. It was fresh and interesting, and entirely on brand. When he talked about the designs, enthusiasm lit up his face. As much as she disliked the man, Jacques *was* Tour de Force.

He'd be the perfect person to take over from Remy.

Derek showed off a couple of the toiles he'd made up from Jacques's designs. Remy tweaked them here and there, raising a hem and widening a collar. Jacques nodded in agreement.

"What fabrics have you got for us, Imogen?" her father asked.

Surprised he was talking to her, she opened the samples and took out a couple of woolens she thought would suit the coat. "How about these?"

Her father picked up the fabric, rubbed it between his fingers, pulled it to check if it would stretch and then held it up against the outfit. "It needs to be ocean-in-storm blue."

Imogen made a note, used to her father's way of describing colors.

"How are the rest of the patterns coming?" Remy asked Derek.

"Quite well. There are a couple of issues, but Jacques is going to come down and go through it with me later this afternoon."

"Good."

The meeting ended and Imogen gave the sample fabrics to her father so he could review them. He took them without a word.

Imogen caught the assessing look on Jacques's face but she ignored him. She walked out of the room and went back to her office to phone the fabric supplier and ask them if they could do the wool in ocean-in-storm blue.

***

Chris was exhausted. He'd just disembarked from his long-haul flight home after finally convincing his company it would cost them more to fight the issue than to do what they said they would. It was close to midnight and all he wanted was to find a cab, get home and go to sleep.

He walked out of the passenger area pushing his luggage cart and headed toward the cab rank.

"Christian!"

At the sound of his name, Chris glanced over ... and saw Imogen rushing toward him. The sight of her washed away some of his fatigue. Without thinking he opened his arms for a hug. As she dove into them he wondered what she was doing there. But then his thoughts disappeared as her warm, soft body pressed into his and he inhaled her sweet scent. He didn't want to let go when she stepped back, but he loosened his hold and she kissed him on the lips.

It felt so natural, so right, as if they'd been together for years rather than just meeting again.

"Surprise!" she said when she broke the kiss.

"What are you doing here?"

"I came to pick you up. You said you were getting in today so I checked the flights and worked out which one you were on." She turned and pushed his luggage toward the exit. "Come on."

It took a second for Chris's brain to catch up but he hurried after her and took over pushing the cart. "Let me get that."

"The car's this way."

Chris followed her, a smile on his face as she strutted through the parking lot. It was a model's walk but she did it unconsciously. She'd walked that way when they met. It had mesmerized him then, like it mesmerized him now. As she popped the trunk he came back to his senses.

He hadn't ever had someone pick him up from the airport: it was too much of a hassle and he could claim the cab fare as a work expense. But having Imogen there was a thrill.

She squinted at the size of his suitcase. "It should fit."

He laughed. "Have you ever considered getting a bigger car?"

She nodded in all seriousness. "Yeah, I might need to upsize soon."

Chris put his luggage in the trunk and shut it. Imogen had already grabbed the cart and was returning it to the collection point. It was good to see her. He'd been cross when she'd ended their Skype call so suddenly, even though his anger had been of

Remy's making. When she got back to the car he wrapped her up in another hug, eager to touch her, and then lowered his mouth to hers.

Her lips parted on a sigh and Chris's heart tightened. He explored her lips, touching, tasting, needing her. As his body stirred he forced himself to let go. "Thank you for picking me up."

She looked flustered and swept her bangs out of her face. "Any time." Her voice was breathless. Blinking, she came back to herself and said, "Hop in." She went around to the driver's side and climbed into the car.

On the journey to his apartment she kept up a light conversation, asking about his flight, and wanting more details about Australia. By the time they arrived, he realized he hadn't asked her anything about what she'd been up to.

"So what's been happening with you?"

She didn't look at him. "We'll chat about me later. You get upstairs and to bed."

The image of Imogen in bed with him was instant and erotic. It wasn't until she'd bundled him into the elevator and said goodbye that he came to his senses and realized she'd avoided his question, which meant there was something definitely happening with her.

He would have to talk to her about it tomorrow when his brain was more alert.

***

The next day he arrived at work jet-lagged and short-tempered. Samuel called him into his office straight away to be debriefed. He was not happy with the resolution but Chris didn't care. It had been the right thing to do.

He reviewed the report he'd written on the flight home and checked what new work was waiting for him. There was an email from Imogen. He smiled and clicked on it.

Christian,

I didn't want to call and wake you, so I'm sending you this instead. If you're free Friday night, do you want to come to a fashion event with me? Dress is formal.

Imogen

Chris didn't really care what the event was, as long as he had a chance to spend time with Imogen. He responded quickly.

Sure. Does that mean I need to get a penguin suit?

He grinned and clicked send, before concentrating on the other emails in his inbox.

Moments later the reply came.

Yes. It will look good on you.

Chris immediately searched for suit shops nearby. He had plenty of business suits, but no tuxedo. He browsed through an online catalogue and found one he liked; it was close enough to check out on his lunch break. Setting himself a reminder so he didn't lose track of time, he focused on work.

When the reminder went off several hours later, Chris saved his document and grabbed his jacket before heading toward the elevator.

"Chris! Where are you off to?" someone called.

He turned to see a colleague hailing him from across the room. "Just grabbing some lunch. Won't be long." He stepped into the elevator and closed the doors before the guy could respond.

He sighed. There was definitely a problem when he'd rather go try on suits than stay and listen to what his workmate had to say.

On entering the shop he noticed the finely crafted wooden desk which served as the cash register counter, the thick plush carpet and the quiet, clean room where assistants hovered to serve. It screamed money.

Chris walked up to one of the attendants and told him what he wanted. The attendant showed a hint of surprise but hurried to retrieve the suit and showed Chris to the change room. It was a good fit and he had to admit it looked good. He let the attendant fuss around him for a moment.

"The trousers need to be taken up a touch," the man told him.

Chris peered at the bottom of the pants. It was just touching the ground near the heel. "I need it for tomorrow night."

The attendant was stricken. "We cannot do it for tomorrow. It's the Homeless Foundation's annual Fashion Auction tomorrow and everyone is preparing for it."

Chris didn't tell him he was attending as well. He also didn't want to attend such an event with his pants too long. The people who went to these things lived and breathed fashion and would definitely notice a bad fit. And he wanted to make a good impression on Remy Fontaine.

"Can you recommend someone else?"

"No, no. Any common seamstress would butcher the job."

Chris's temper began to build. He was too tired for this. He just wanted to be with Imogen.

Imogen.

He whipped out his cell phone and dialed her number, walking away from the attendant as he did so. When she answered he said, "You know this thing you want me to go to tomorrow?"

"Yes."

"I need you to do me a favor so I can come."

She wasn't the least bit cautious when she replied, "Sure, what is it?"

"Can you take up the bottom of the pants I'm about to buy for it?"

She laughed. "It's the least I can do. Why don't you come to my place this evening about seven?"

Chris hesitated. He'd not been back to Chateau Fontaine since they'd been thrown out. "All right." He couldn't very well ask her to bring her sewing machine to his place.

"Great. Buzz the guesthouse when you get to the gate and I'll let you in."

Chris hung up and turned to the attendant. "I'll take it."

***

That night Chris pressed the button for the guesthouse and looked through the wrought-iron gate to where the roof of the chateau rose over the trees. He'd loved living there, even if they'd only had a small section of the garden away from the main house. He used to pretend it was all theirs and that they had chosen to live in the small gardener's house rather than the French mansion.

Imogen's face appeared on the intercom. "Come in. Take

the driveway to the left."

The gates swung inward and Chris drove his car through, slowly making his way up the drive as memories of his childhood assaulted him. He shook them away when Imogen's guesthouse came into view.

It was extraordinary. A tiny replica of the chateau, but still probably bigger than the average suburban house. Imogen came out the front as he parked his car.

He retrieved the suit out of the passenger's side and moved up the stairs, pulling her close for a kiss. "Hi."

Imogen grinned at him. "Hi. Come in. Do you want something to eat first or do you want to do the pants?"

There was a tomato-pasta smell coming from somewhere in the house and he inhaled it deeply. "You didn't need to cook."

"I was making it for myself so I did a little extra."

He breathed in again and said, "We should do the pants first. I might not fit into them after I've eaten."

She smiled and beckoned him with a wave. "Come into my workshop then."

He followed her down a hallway into a room probably meant as a dining room. It was large and rectangular and had a huge table in the center, covered in machines and fabrics. Every piece of wall space was covered in storage and there were materials and threads all over the place, but everything was neatly ordered. "Wow."

"I have a bit of an obsession with fabrics," she admitted with a guilty grin. "If I find something I like I buy it, even if I don't know what I'm going to do with it yet." She turned to him. "Show me the pants."

He laid the garment bag on the table and unzipped it, a little bit nervous about how she was going to react to his purchase.

She stroked the fabric and breathed out. "Lovely," she said. "This is a Chantelle Vision, isn't it?"

He shrugged and Imogen checked the discreet label with a nod. "I thought so. She does fabulous men's clothes."

Imogen grabbed a few reels of thread from her massive wheel. They all looked the same color black to Chris but when she held them up against the tuxedo he could see the difference. When she'd chosen the thread, she said, "Put on the whole suit while I thread the machine." She pointed to a doorway he hadn't noticed.

"Don't you just need the pants?"

She shook her head. "I want to see the whole thing."

With a shrug he went into the next room and changed into the suit and the dress shirt he'd bought to wear with it.

When he came out, Imogen turned toward him and stopped. Her eyes slowly panned up and down.

He waited for her verdict as she came closer, her steps almost stalking. He glanced down to check if there was something wrong with the way the suit was fitting and her arms came around his neck, bringing his head down so her lips met his.

Chapter 9

The kiss was scalding. Taken completely by surprise, Chris desperately tried to keep up. Her tongue danced with his, sending heat straight to his groin, and he groaned.

Then she stopped and gazed at him. "The suit works," she said, her voice husky.

He resisted the urge to pull her back into his arms, just. "I'll say." He ran a hand through his hair, trying to get his breath back.

She took his hand and led him over to the table. "We should get this done before I forget why you came over."

"Why did I come over?" Chris asked and earned a laugh from her.

She cleared her throat and examined him, straightening up his bow tie, running her hand slowly over the lapels to make sure they sat right.

Chris coughed. "If you want to make sure the pants fit, you need to stop doing that."

Imogen glanced down and grinned. "Do you want a drink?"

"Please."

She left the room and Chris used the opportunity to get himself under control. The problem was every time he thought of her reaction to him in the suit he hardened again. She returned and handed him a glass of red wine, which he sipped from before putting it carefully on the table. The last thing he needed to do was spill it.

Imogen grabbed a container of pins from the table and knelt on the floor at his feet. Chris desperately thought of his seventeen times table to distract himself.

"It's a good fit," Imogen said as she pinned the hem. "It might have been made just for you."

"Thanks." He didn't know what else to say. He was too busy concentrating on a spot on the wall and not on the fact Imogen's head was very close to his groin.

It had been too long since he'd had sex.

"You can take them off now."

It took Chris a second to realize Imogen hadn't read where his mind was going and had actually finished pinning the hem. He stepped back and headed for the room.

"Keep the jacket and shirt on," she called. "You'll need to try it all back on when I'm finished."

Chris did as she asked, putting his work pants back on and coming back out of the room to hand her the tuxedo pants.

As she got to work, he sat on one of the nearby chairs and watched her. Her focus was absolute and her fingers moved quickly over the pants, checking it was all lying correctly before starting the sewing machine. The machine zipped through the work and it wasn't long before she was cutting a thread and holding the pants back out to Chris.

"Put them on."

Inside the room he checked her work and couldn't tell it had been done. It looked like the original.

When she was satisfied it was right, had pressed the suit and repacked it she turned back to Chris. "Hungry?"

He was hungry for more than food but he simply picked up his wine glass and said, "Yes."

She took him through to the kitchen, which had a small round table in it, set with two places. The room was bright and cheery with yellow walls and accents all around.

Turning the stove off, she dished up two plates of the pasta and gestured for him to sit. "Are you jet-lagged?" she asked him before taking a mouthful of the pasta. Her lips closed over the food and he quickly looked away. He was ridiculously worked up. Maybe it had something to do with the fatigue.

"Tired mostly."

"I won't keep you late then," she said.

He had no objection to staying late, none to spending the night even, but he didn't mention it. Instead he asked, "How are things going with your business plan?"

She examined her food and then she sighed. "Not great. Papa freaked out when he saw it; he told me if I went into business it would kill him."

Chris stopped with the fork halfway to his mouth. "What?"

She shrugged but her eyes were sad. "He has an issue with mass-market clothing and he wants me to take over at Tour de Force."

He reached out and covered her hand, giving it a squeeze. "What did you say?"

"I haven't had the chance to say anything. He walked out and we haven't spoken all week."

"He's being rather melodramatic, don't you think?" Chris knew Remy was controlling but wasn't that because he loved his daughter?

"Yes, but he was really upset," she said, her voice quiet.

"There's something else, right?"

She glanced at him in surprise and then nodded.

"Tell me."

He listened while she told him what she'd discovered about her mother's death and how she possibly had relatives she'd never met.

Chris leaned back, stunned. What a jackass! To keep Imogen away from family who might love her.

"Do you know how she died?"

"No. The obituary said it was related to the pregnancy."

"You haven't asked your father?"

She shook her head. "How can I? He's barely talking to me because I want to leave Tour de Force; to find out I've gone behind his back about Mama will infuriate him even more."

"What about your mother's family?"

"Piper's doing some research for me. There are *sixty* Ryders in the Houston area," she said. "I checked the telephone directory. And that's if they haven't moved away or died."

"I'll help if you need it."

She smiled at him. "I could really do with a hug."

He pushed aside his empty plate and stood up. He wrapped his arms around her and she became part of him. He kissed the top of her head and held her, wanting to take away the pain her father was causing her.

There was a loud bang at the kitchen door and Chris moved, shifting Imogen behind him as he turned toward the sound.

Remy was standing there. Imogen pushed past Chris and stepped over to the door. "Hello, Papa."

"I need to speak with you."

Imogen looked to Chris and back at her father. "I'll come over to the house after Christian leaves."

Remy bristled. "This is important."

"I have a guest." Imogen's voice was even, but there was an edge to it Chris had never heard before. "Papa, this is Christian Barker."

Chris saw the recognition in the old man's eyes before he masked it. Anger stirred but he kept a lid on it. Imogen didn't need him to rehash old battles now.

"I asked you to let me know when you have guests," Remy said to Imogen.

"No, you said to tell you if I'm having a gathering."

Remy's expression was getting darker and darker. As much as Chris disliked the man, he didn't want to make things more difficult for Imogen.

"I should go, Imi," he said. "If I'm going to look my best in that tuxedo tomorrow night, I need to get my beauty sleep." He kept his voice light and friendly.

Imogen glanced over at him and was immediately concerned. "Of course." She turned to her father. "Come in. I'll walk Christian to his car."

It annoyed Chris that her immediate concern was for him and his stupid jet lag, rather than for herself. She was too kind. He grabbed the tuxedo bag from where he'd left it and followed Imogen out of the house to his car. He laid the suit on the back seat and then turned to embrace her. "Call me after your father leaves," he said. "I want to know you're all right. In fact call me at any time, day or night, if you need me."

He kissed her deeply, hoping to make her understand he was

there for her.

She sighed. "Thank you. Drive safely."

He got in his car and drove away, wishing he didn't have to.

***

Imogen waited for the tail lights of the car to disappear before she turned and went back inside.

In the kitchen her father was pacing.

Not a good sign.

"Would you like a drink, Papa?"

He stopped moving at the sound of her voice. "I'll have some of your wine," he said, gesturing at the bottle on the table.

As she got out another glass she asked, "What did you want to talk to me about?"

"You're not taking that man to the auction tomorrow night." It was a statement not a question.

"Yes, I am. Christian is my date for the evening." She handed her father the glass of wine.

"*Non*. We always go together."

It was true but this year she didn't want to be seen on her father's arm. This year she didn't want to be with her father at all. "I figured you wouldn't want to go with me after our argument," she said instead.

"Words said in the heat of the moment. You must go with me."

Imogen gaped at him. How could he brush their argument off so quickly when it had been haunting her for days? "I've already asked Christian."

Her father frowned. "His type are not welcome there."

Imogen stared at her father. "What type is that: males, lawyers, friends of mine?"

"The event is very prestigious – only the wealthy and notable will be there."

"Oh, so he's not rich enough?" Imogen's temper rose.

"*Exactement!* You will have to tell him he cannot attend."

"No," Imogen said.

Her father's eyes widened.

"Papa, I'm tired so you need to tell me what you came here for so I can go to bed."

"I came here because I was concerned for you. A strange car enters our property and goes to your house. It could have been anyone."

He'd been spying on her.

Imogen shook her head in disbelief. "The property is surrounded by security. The only way the *strange car* could get through the gates is if one of us let it. That means I knew who it was."

Her father stepped back, put up his hands. "Don't be mad, *ma bichette*. It is only because I love you that I do these things."

It was as though his words flicked a switch in Imogen's brain, because suddenly anger came rising from nowhere and the words came pouring out. "Did *love* stop you telling me Mama died giving birth to me? Is *love* why you kept my grandparents and uncles away from me? Is it why you won't let me form my own business? Is it why you won't let me move out of home?"

Remy held a hand over his heart and sank into one of the chairs.

Imogen ignored his theatrics.

"Who has been telling you these things?" he demanded.

"I read them in the newspaper," she said. "When you wouldn't tell me, I decided to find out for myself what happened to Mama."

"You didn't trust me?"

"It's not about trust. I needed to know the truth."

"I told you, you *didn't* need to know the truth."

"Well you were wrong!" she shouted.

Remy closed his eyes for a moment, then got to his feet. His expression was calm but his eyes were hard. "You think you know best? You think you are ready to hear what those monsters who called your mother family said about you?" He waved a hand. "Fine. Go. Talk to your mother's brothers and her parents if they still live. But when they call you a murderer do not come crying to me. In fact, if you go to them, don't come back at all." He walked out the door.

Imogen stared after him. It was the second time he had entirely withdrawn from her for trying to live her own life.

She sank down on a chair. He couldn't really mean it, could

he? He loved her. He wouldn't disown her for wanting to connect with other family.

She rubbed the sides of her head. She honestly wasn't sure. She didn't know her father any more, didn't know how he would react or why he was doing this. The only thing she did know was she couldn't live like this. Couldn't continue under his emotional blackmail. She'd had enough.

She was twenty-nine years old. Definitely old enough to make her own decisions, and to choose where her life was going.

Her heart clenched at the thought of spending the rest of her life without her father but she pushed it aside. He couldn't really mean it. He'd only just said their last fight had been words said in the heat of the moment. Surely it was the same tonight?

Whatever the case, it was time she found her own place so at least he couldn't throw her out on her ear and make her homeless as well as fatherless.

Her heart panged, but she pushed through the hurt.

She fired up her laptop and searched for places to rent.

An hour later her cell phone beeped. She checked the message. *R U Ok?* Christian. She'd forgotten to call him. She picked up the phone and rang him.

"You're supposed to be asleep," she said, hoping for a bit of levity.

"And you were supposed to call me after your father left. I've been lying here worrying about you since I got home."

His voice was warm and the image of him lying naked in bed popped into Imogen's head, dissolving some of her pain and confusion. She smiled and focused on the conversation. "I'm sorry."

"So what happened?"

He didn't need to know her father didn't want him at the charity event the next night. "We argued and I got angry." She sighed. That in itself rarely happened. "I told him I knew about mother's family and how she died. He told me if I met with them, I wasn't to come home." She squeezed her eyes shut.

"What?"

Imogen swallowed past the lump in her throat. "It's past time I moved out anyway. I'm searching for somewhere to rent now."

"Imi, he can't mean it." He sounded uncertain.

"I think he does." Her voice wavered and she cleared her throat. "Anyway I don't have any privacy here." Her father had interrupted conversations with Christian twice now. She couldn't have a serious relationship if he kept turning up, and she wanted one with Christian.

"You're upset. Do you want me to come back tonight?"

She did. She really did, but it would be selfish of her to ask. He had jet lag and he was coming to the auction, which would run late. Plus she needed to learn to make it on her own, not to lean on someone so much. She'd done that enough with her father.

"No, it's all right."

"I'll help you look for a place on the weekend if you like," Christian offered.

She'd love the company. She had little idea about real estate. "That would be great. I've found about a dozen options."

She heard him yawn. "Go to sleep. I'll pick you up tomorrow at seven."

"Sweet dreams," he said.

"Same to you." She hung up the phone and smiled. At least one thing in her life was going right.

***

The next evening Imogen picked Chris up at seven o'clock, and when he opened the door he stared. Imogen looked different – amazing, yes – but different. It was Imogen, but not. He ran his eyes over her spiked-up hairstyle, the colorful and quirky dress, and down to the black, four-inch stiletto heels on her feet. It had to be a Tour de Force dress, but Imogen didn't suit the Tour de Force style. She was more elegant, more beautiful than the outrageous styles of Tour de Force.

Before he could say anything, she stepped forward, ran her hands up the lapels of his suit and kissed him.

Thoughts vanished from his head and he closed his eyes, enjoying the dance of their lips and the feel of Imogen in his arms.

When they parted, Chris's heart was racing and he was firmly in favor of staying here and discovering what Imogen had on *under* the dress. He tried to keep things light. "I think you have a tuxedo fetish."

Imogen laughed. "When you're wearing them I do." She tugged on his hand. "Come on, we're going to be late."

"Wait, I've got something for you." He walked back into his apartment and picked up a small wrapped package from the coffee table. He'd been debating whether he would give it to her since he'd bought it in Australia.

Imogen took the package and frowned at him. "What's this for?"

He shifted his stance, feeling like he was a teenager again and asking a girl to a dance. "I found it at the Fremantle markets and thought you might like it."

She beamed at him and the nerves racked up.

What had he been thinking buying her a cheap, handmade bauble from a market stall? This was someone who was used to draping herself in the latest and most expensive fashions. She wasn't going to like the necklace.

She unwrapped it. "It's gorgeous," she said, examining the craftsmanship carefully. "So intricately designed." It was the dark brown gemstone that had caught his attention first. Imogen walked over to the mirror by the door. She held the necklace up against her throat and sighed with pleasure. "It will go perfectly with a summer dress I just made." Turning back to Christian, she said, "Thank you so much."

"It's nothing special." He shrugged. "The brown reminded me of your eyes." It sounded so cheesy.

She brought the necklace up to her chest. "Of course it's special." She walked over to him and put her arms around his neck. "No one's ever bought me a necklace before."

She kissed him and he forgot his nerves and his doubts.

"In that case – " he pulled her closer, molding his body to hers " – we could stay here and you can thank me some more."

She chuckled. "It's a charity event. I can't be late."

He let her pull him into the elevator and then captured her in his arms to kiss her again.

Chris's blood heated and his breath was coming fast when the elevator doors opened. He needed to get himself under control. No more kisses or he'd never make it through the event without dragging her into a dark corner somewhere. Though the idea had a lot of merit, he was pretty sure it wouldn't be acceptable behavior for a Tour de Force representative. As they walked through the lobby, Imogen said, "Wait a second. Let me check my lipstick."

She stopped by one of the mirrors and sighed, quickly taking something out of her little clutch bag and painting it onto her sexy mouth.

Chris stood behind, grinning at her in the mirror. She looked like she'd been kissed and he'd put that look in her eyes. He couldn't help but feel smug about it.

She rolled her eyes at him and then avoided his gaze while she redid her lips.

***

Imogen had parked in a temporary parking zone outside Christian's apartment building. She opened the car door for him and waited until he squeezed inside before shutting the door. It was a tight fit and he vowed the next time they went on a date they would take his way more comfortable car.

The charity auction was being held across town in a large, high-end hotel, but he didn't know much about the event.

"So what's the big deal about this fashion show?" he asked.

"It's a fundraiser. All proceeds from the ticket sales and the auction are being donated to the homeless and destitute."

"So how much do I owe you for the ticket?"

"Nothing. You're my guest, and besides, work is paying for them."

"Are you sure?"

She nodded.

"What are they auctioning?"

"Top fashion designers each donate an item to be auctioned. Tour de Force has put together an amazing outfit this year. We always raise a lot of money from the auction as they're all one-off pieces."

Chris was beginning to get a sense this event was a big deal and not just a fashion show as he'd thought. He should have guessed it was something more by the fact he had to wear a tuxedo, but now he was beginning to get nervous. He knew nothing about fashion and he didn't want to embarrass Imi with some kind of faux pas.

Imogen pulled into the valet parking of the hotel and handed over her car keys. Chris joined her at the hood and put his arm out so she could take hold of it. His heart was beating a million miles an hour as they walked up the steps of the most elegant hotel in Houston.

He was way out of his comfort zone.

The event was being held in the ballroom. At the entrance Imogen handed over her tickets and together they entered.

Chris wanted to stop and stare but he kept moving with her. The room was done out in a beautiful summer theme with sun-shaped chandeliers and ice sculptures of waves. Everything was tastefully decorated in blue and gold: it had been transformed into a vacation paradise.

"This place looks amazing," he said.

Imogen nodded, scanning the room. "They outdo themselves each year." She waved to someone and turned to Chris. "Are you ready?"

"As I'll ever be."

With a deep breath to calm his nerves, he walked into the fray.

***

Within an hour he'd rubbed shoulders with politicians, CEOs, movie stars and musicians, as well as far too many fashion designers to count. Imogen knew them all, or else they knew her and she stood and chatted to them quite happily. He held his own too. Making small talk was something he was good at – he needed to be for his job.

"When I designed that suit I only dreamed it would be worn by someone as handsome as you." The voice came from his left and at the same time a hand with meticulous nails manicured in tiger stripes clamped down on his arm. Chris turned to the speaker, who was a woman a good twenty years older than him wearing a long slinky black dress that promised seduction.

Imogen had told him the designer's name ... what was it again? "Chantelle, I presume?" he said, holding out a hand to shake hers.

She took his hand and stepped in to kiss him slowly on both cheeks. "Darling, what is your name?"

Chris was rather bemused by her show. "Chris Barker, ma'am."

She stood back and examined him, brushing at non-existent fluff on the base of his jacket. "Divine."

He grinned. "I must thank you. My girlfriend is rather appreciative of the tuxedo as well." The moment he said the word he wondered if it was the right one. Could he say he and Imogen were dating, were an item, were … whatever the latest word was for being in a relationship? Or did a couple of Skype conversations and a few kisses not amount to that?

"Girlfriend?" Chantelle pouted. "Where is she?"

Imogen had finished speaking to another designer and turned to stand next to him. "Chantelle, how are you?"

The two of them kissed each other's cheeks.

"Imogen, are you responsible for this hunk wearing my clothes?"

Imogen smiled and shook her head. "He chose it himself."

Chantelle sighed dramatically. "Fabulous taste and gorgeous to boot. You're so lucky."

"I know." Imogen slipped her hand into Chris's and everything was right in the world.

"What has Tour de Force got for us tonight?" Chantelle asked.

"You know I can't tell you. You'll have to wait and see like everyone else."

"What is Chantelle Vision showing?" Chris asked.

"Touché. *You* can wait," Chantelle said and smiled. She glanced around. "Where is that incorrigible father of yours?" she asked. "I haven't seen him this evening."

Chris had been wondering the same thing.

"He was talking to Jacques over there," Imogen said, pointing to a section of the ballroom.

"I will hunt him down then. Have a wonderful night." She waved and then was off, slinking across the ballroom. More than one male watched her go past.

Chris grinned. "That's some lady."

"Chantelle's a delight. One of the hardest-working women I

know and yet she always looks fabulous – and as if she doesn't have a care in the world. I don't know how she does it."

Chris was intrigued. "Doesn't she just design suits?" It didn't sound like hard work to him.

Imogen raised her eyebrows, which warned him he was about to get a lecture. "Chantelle Vision isn't as big as Tour de Force. Chantelle does almost all the work herself; she designs the line, makes up the patterns and toiles, sources the fabrics, finds markets. She has a business partner to deal with contracts and finances but everything else is on her."

Chris never realized there was so much to designing a clothing line. He looked over at Chantelle with new respect.

Then he noticed Remy Fontaine, or rather he saw the hostile look Remy gave him before turning and greeting Chantelle.

"Your father doesn't appear to be very happy to see me," he said. Imogen hadn't mentioned the reason for her father's surprise visit the night before and it was obvious that even after all these years Remy didn't approve of his daughter dating the gardener's son.

"It doesn't matter." Imogen turned away, her voice quiet. "I can bring a date if I want to."

Something in her words made him stop, face her. "Am I not meant to be here?"

"Yes, of course you are." She shuffled her feet and looked around the room.

There was something more. "Who do you normally come with?"

"Papa and I usually come together," she admitted.

Well it was one reason for Remy to be mad at him. It made Chris uneasy. As much as he disliked the man, he didn't want to come between him and his only child. He glanced around the room at the tables that were set for dinner. "Where are we sitting?"

"At the Tour de Force table."

Great. He would have to sit right next to the man. Maybe it would give him a chance to win him over for Imogen's sake.

A bell chimed and people made their way to the tables.

"Good, I'm starving," Imogen said and took his hand to lead him across the dance floor to their table.

At their table was Abigail, the business manager, and her partner Doug; Jacques, one of the designers, and his partner, Stacey, as well as Derek, the pattern and toile maker and Remy. The only friendly greetings came from Derek and Abigail. Chris pulled out the chair for Imogen and waited for her to sit before taking his own. He felt a little as though he was sitting down for an interrogation.

At least he knew how to deal with hostile situations.

It was what being a lawyer was all about.

Chapter 10

Chris sat next to Jacques and immediately he didn't like the man. He was one of those overly enthused people who gushed about everything and meant nothing. The word *insincere* had been invented for people like him.

"What is it you do, Chris?" Jacques asked.

"I'm a lawyer."

"Oh, criminal law?"

"No, corporate and business law."

"Is that how you met Imogen?" The question was innocent but Chris knew the sound of digging when he heard it.

"No, we met through friends."

"You must know Imogen well for her to invite you to this event," Jacques said.

He was not going to discuss the status of his relationship with this rat. "Well enough."

"Oh, you're being modest. No one invites just a friend to an event where tickets are five hundred dollars each."

Chris was glad he'd had years of practicing his game face, making sure no surprise ever showed, because otherwise that bombshell would have lit him up. Five hundred dollars each! He had to respond. "Maybe Imogen does."

"I'm sure it didn't even occur to her, since Tour de Force was paying."

"Is that why you brought your wife along?" Chris asked, not

letting his temper show.

Jacques smiled as if he were pleased by the verbal tussle. Before he could respond, the master of ceremonies took to the microphone to welcome everyone to the event. The man explained how the evening was going to run: the auction would continue between each of the meal's seven courses.

It was a good way of organizing things, Chris decided as the evening began. It gave the guests enough time between courses to digest their food and the excitement of the bidding kept everyone entertained.

The bidding for the first garment, a hat, gloves and shoes combination from a well-known designer, started at one thousand dollars. Chris knew right then the evening would be a success. People were determined to purchase something, if only so they could say they had.

He leaned over to whisper to Imogen, "How much is it worth?"

"If it was part of the retail collection it would cost around thirteen hundred dollars, so that first bidder was being a little cheeky."

Chris bit his tongue. He had no idea when it came to the high end of the fashion industry.

To spend over one thousand dollars on accessories was beyond his comprehension. A normal person could put together a whole year's wardrobe for that amount of money.

He knew Imogen was wealthy, but he'd never really realized just how wealthy. She never would have had to scrimp and save for anything she'd wanted. Did she even understand the value of money, understand how important it was to have someone pay a hundred-dollar invoice on time because it meant the difference between being able to go on a school excursion or being left behind?

Imogen passed him the auction pamphlet, a glossy high-resolution bound brochure of all the items available during the night.

"Is there anything you like?" he asked her as he passed the brochure back.

"These earrings are gorgeous," she said, pointing them out. "But I'll see how the bidding goes."

He doubted he'd be able to afford to buy them for her. But she'd be able to buy them for herself.

What would life be like with Imogen if she earned more than he did?

He didn't like the thought, though not because he cared whether women earned more than men. He had promised himself as a teenager that he would never rely on anyone for money. They could too easily turn on you, as Remy had shown.

"You okay?" Imogen asked, squeezing his hand.

He was frowning; he smoothed it into a smile. "Of course." He pushed his concerns aside.

He distracted himself by watching the bidders, some coolly disinterested as if they were only bidding because it was for charity, and others wildly waving their bidding cards in their excitement.

When the earrings came up, Imogen sat straighter and took hold of her card.

Starting bid was five hundred dollars. Imogen waited while the bids went back and forth in one-hundred-dollar increments.

Chris wanted to bid for her but it had already gone past the price he was happy to pay for a pair of earrings.

The bidding slowed, and Imogen was about to raise her card when Remy did. "Two thousand," he said.

Imogen stared at him across the table and Remy winked at her. "A gift, *ma bichette.*"

Chris wasn't sure what to make of the gesture, considering how Remy had threatened his daughter, but then Remy directed a look full of triumph at him, which explained it all. Remy was showing Chris he had more money and could buy his daughter whatever she wanted.

Unlike Chris.

It was a chest-beating exercise.

Chris glanced at Imogen and it appeared as if she understood that too. Her lips were parted and there was a slight furrow in her forehead. The round ended and Remy won the earrings.

"Thank you, Papa," Imogen said, and although she smiled, Chris could tell she wasn't happy. Did her father not notice her unhappiness or did he not care?

When the auction and dinner ended, a jazz band started playing. Couples moved to the dance floor and a hum filled the air as people mingled again.

"Would you like to dance?" he asked Imogen. He wasn't the best dancer in the world but he wanted to get Imi away from her father, see a smile on her face.

"Love to," she replied and he helped her out of her chair and on to the dance floor. As he pulled her into his arms he blessed the person who invented dancing. The opportunity to hold someone so close in public while still being socially acceptable was a pure stroke of genius.

"Are you having a nice evening?" he murmured to her.

"I am now." Imogen's eyes were sad. "Papa bought those earrings to show he could still control me."

Is that what she thought? "No, Imi. He was directing that at me. The look he gave me after his bid was to show me I can't afford you."

Her eyes widened. "Don't be silly. It's got nothing to do with money."

He wished it were true. "To your father it does. It's got everything to do with me not being good enough for you." Remy didn't even know him but he wasn't willing to give Chris a chance.

"But he doesn't know you." Imogen echoed his thoughts.

"Doesn't matter." He spun her in a twirl. "Let's not let him ruin the night. I've enjoyed being with you, enjoyed learning about your world."

"Really?"

"Of course. There's more to the fashion industry than I realized. It's great that all the money is going to a good cause too. A lot of people have hit hard times over the past few years."

"It sounds as if you know."

"I do pro bono work once a month. The people who come to the office are people who can't afford to pay a lawyer's bill but want to get their life back on track. Most of them are good people who are doing their best." He debated confiding in her and then realized he wanted her to know. "Dad got advice from a pro bono lawyer when he was setting up his gardening business. It highlighted a few issues he hadn't been aware of."

"Wow." She beamed at him, her eyes bright. "And now you're returning the favor. It must be great to be able to help them."

Some needed more than legal advice, they needed someone to give them a chance. "You're helping here. The funds raised from the Tour de Force dress alone would help feed and clothe people for a month."

"It's just money. I'd like to do something hands on, something that actually allows me to help, but Papa always said it was too dangerous. He said desperate people did desperate things and if they found out who I was I could be held for ransom."

Chris stopped dancing. "Seriously? Your father has some strange ideas."

"I know. It was always easier to give in. I hate hurting him."

So she gave up on her own hopes and dreams? He hoped not. "Are we searching for apartments tomorrow?"

"Yes, if you still want to come."

"I like spending time with you." It was true. He couldn't get enough of her.

The song ended and Imogen stepped back. "I really should do some more networking."

Chris didn't want to let her go but it was a work function for her. "Do you want to do it alone, or do you mind if I tag along?"

She seemed surprised. "Come along if you don't think it will bore you."

"Great." He followed her off the dance floor to where a man stood watching the other dancers.

"Wasn't Hans able to come today, Simon?" Imogen asked as she greeted him and kissed his cheeks.

"Ah, the lovely Imogen. Unfortunately Hans was not well this evening."

"That's a shame. Your accessories set was divine."

"Thank you, dear. As was Tour de Force's creation. When are we going to see some of *your* designs in the range?"

Chris examined the man. He obviously knew Imogen well if he knew her designs were not the same as Tour de Force's.

Imogen ignored the question and instead introduced the two of them. "Simon did an internship with us many years ago."

"Yes, and it was back then I told you you had the talent to have your own label. Why are you wasting your time there where you're not needed?"

Imogen stiffened next to him. "I'm needed there. I have to make all the decisions when Papa isn't there."

"Of course. What I meant was they have other designers." Simon was quick to soothe.

"I imagine it's quite difficult to set up your own label," Chris said.

"It is," Simon replied and focused some attention on Chris, pleased he understood. "I still work out of my home and it's a constant struggle to make sure I keep costs as low as possible."

Chris blinked. How could it be that bad? This man's clothing sold in the hundreds of dollars. That set of hat, gloves and shoes had gone for close to two thousand dollars in the end. And he still worked from home.

Chris considered Imogen's business plan. He now wanted to have a closer read of it. To figure out what her numbers were so he could help her work out what the start-up costs were going to be. If it was as difficult as that, maybe she was sensible not to go out on her own just yet.

"If you'll excuse me, Imogen and Chris. I've spotted Chantelle and I must catch up with her." Simon turned to Imogen. "Remember my offer still stands. If you want help setting up your label, I'm here for you. My time at Tour de Force was life-changing and I would like to pay it back if possible." He directed the last sentence at Chris before walking off.

"He seemed nice," Chris said. Imogen had been quiet since the comment about her not being needed.

"He is." She was distracted.

"Would he be a useful resource when setting up your own label?"

She nodded.

"We can go over your business plan tomorrow as well if you like," Chris said, eager for her to make a move against her father.

Her eyes were sad. "I'm not ready for that."

She'd gone from really keen to uninterested in the space of a couple of weeks and it was her father's fault.

"The plan might need a little bit more work, but it won't take long," Chris said pretending to misunderstand.

"No, Christian." She turned away from him and then said, "Ah. There's Michelle." She walked away without waiting for him.

Chris paused a moment to swallow his annoyance. Now was not the time to fight about it. He would talk to her tomorrow, make her realize she couldn't put her life on hold for her father.

She deserved more than that.

***

Imogen pushed down her irritation at Christian's comments. Things were rocky enough with her father as it was. She wasn't willing to test him further. It didn't mean she wouldn't do her own label eventually, just not right now.

She smiled as she walked up to Michelle and kissed both of her cheeks. "You look gorgeous," she said. Michelle was the owner of a chain of high-end boutique shops in Texas.

"So do you, babe. Who's that gorgeous guy you're with?"

Imogen glanced back at Christian, who was talking with Abigail. "That's Christian." She didn't want to talk about her relationship, at least not with Michelle. "Are you enjoying the evening?"

"Always do. It's the best event on the calendar. Ah, it looks as though your father wants a word." She gestured to Remy who was walking over with a guy about Imogen's age. The guy's blond hair was messily styled with gel and he wore a dark grey tuxedo. The color was a brave choice considering the event, but he carried it off well.

Imogen pasted a smile on her face.

"Imogen, you must meet David Randall. His father is the CEO of Dionysus Oil and Gas."

Imogen shook David's hand. He had a firm grip and his blue eyes twinkled at her.

"It's a pleasure to meet you. Your father has told me so much about you and I see he hasn't exaggerated."

Alarm washed over her. What had her father been saying to

this man? "Well now, he hasn't told me anything about you."

"How about we have a dance and we can get to know each other?"

Too polite to refuse, she took the hand he held out and said goodbye to Michelle and her father, who was beaming. What was he planning?

The music was slow and David drew her close, his hand on her waist. She put her hand on his shoulder to keep a decent distance and hoped the song would be short. "I like your suit. The grey really works."

David laughed. "My father nearly had a conniption when he saw it. Said it wasn't appropriate." There was defiance in his tone, which Imogen warmed to.

"Well you can tell him I approve," she said. "What is it you do?"

"I'm the finance manager at Dionysus. If you need help with your finances, I'm your man." He said it in a lighthearted way and Imogen found herself smiling at him.

"Oh, my boyfriend Christian works there."

"Ah. Your father gave me the impression you were single. He insisted I meet his beautiful daughter." David shrugged self-consciously.

Imogen stopped dancing. Her father was playing matchmaker? He knew about Christian.

Which explained the setup.

Anger stirred in her stomach, but it wasn't David's fault. She started moving again. "I'm sorry if he gave you the wrong impression."

"I knew it was too good to be true. Can't blame a guy for trying though." He spun her around, making her laugh. "So in which section of Dionysus does your guy work?"

"He's a lawyer – Chris Barker."

"I know Chris. He works hard." David glanced down at her. "So if you're not single, do you have any single friends?"

She grinned. He was a nice guy, and if she'd met him a few weeks earlier she would have gone on a date. "You know, I believe Michelle is still single." She gestured toward where Michelle and her father were talking. "Why don't I introduce you?"

"Sounds good to me."

The song ended and they left the dance floor together. After making the introductions, she excused herself, ignoring her father's protestations to stay, and went to find Christian.

It was the best show of defiance she could have here.

***

It was close to three in the morning before the event started to wind down. Imogen was struggling to stay focused, struggling to keep her posture straight and her smile bright and dying to pry her feet out of the heels she was wearing.

She'd managed to catch up with a number of designers who she considered friends as well as those people who had worked at Tour de Force over the years. Her father always insisted on running a paid intern program and chose the candidates based not only on their talent but also their financial situations. He always tried to give those people who were doing it tough a chance. It was one thing Imogen admired about him. Even when there wasn't a permanent job available at Tour de Force, her father helped them find work either through recommendations or by helping them set up their own business.

She wished he'd do the same for her.

Christian appeared next to her with a glass of water. "I thought you could do with this."

She took it gratefully and sipped. She'd stopped drinking wine after dinner and was parched from all the talking and smiling. It had to be time for her to be allowed to leave.

Christian had dark circles under his eyes, which he was obviously struggling to keep open. Guilt punched her in the gut. "You must be exhausted," she said. He'd had a long working week, was still recovering from jet lag and here she was dragging him out to an event into the early hours of the morning. She was so inconsiderate.

But he had been fantastic during the night. He'd chatted to people, asked intelligent questions and been genuinely interested in the answers. At no stage had she felt he was bored.

"I can keep going as long as you can," he said and winked.

It surprised a laugh out of her and she took his hand. "I definitely think it's time to go. Let me say goodbye to Papa."

Scanning the ballroom Imogen found her father chatting to Simon. Together they walked over and nerves built in her stomach. She hated this. Hated the hesitation she felt now talking to her father, hated not knowing what his response was going to be, hated feeling she had something to apologize for.

"Imogen, have you said hello to Simon yet?" her father asked. He completely ignored Christian.

"Yes, Simon and I caught up earlier. I think I've spoken to almost everyone here." She laughed lightly and added, "We're going to leave now."

Her father frowned. "But the night is still young. There are bound to be people who want to speak with you."

Imogen reminded herself to stay strong. She was tired and Christian even more so. "If there are, they know where I work." She kept her tone upbeat. "I'll see you at work on Monday."

"What about our Sunday brunch?"

She didn't have the energy to sit across from him and pretend everything was going to be all right, but they always did Sunday brunch. How could she avoid it?

"I'm afraid I've stolen her away on Sunday," Christian spoke up. "My apologies, sir."

Imogen turned to him so her father wouldn't see the surprise on her face. "Yes, I forgot to tell you, Papa. I'm sorry."

"Ah, young love makes us all forget," Simon said before Remy could say a word. Imogen smiled at him.

Her father frowned and pursed his lips together. "Monday it is."

Imogen kissed him on the cheek and then said goodbye to Simon, and together she and Christian left the ballroom.

When they got outside she turned to him. "You didn't need to lie for me," she said.

"Who said I was lying? I'm sure I can come up with something to keep us amused on Sunday." He grinned at her and blood rushed to Imogen's cheeks.

She turned to the valet and gave him her ticket in order to give herself time to recover.

It didn't take long for her car to arrive and she gratefully slid into the driver's seat. "Thank you for coming tonight," she said to Christian.

"I enjoyed myself."

She glanced at him to check if he was kidding but he seemed sincere. She appreciated his engagement with her world, because she'd had dates at other events who had been so obviously bored and derisive of the fashion industry that she couldn't wait to get rid of them. Those evenings were usually followed by her begging Piper not to set her up any more.

Imogen pulled up in front of Christian's apartment building.

Her hands were clammy on the steering wheel and she hoped he didn't notice. Would he ask her up? Would she accept? She didn't quite know what she wanted at the moment and was too tired to really think clearly.

He leaned over and kissed her. It was pleasant but simple. "What time do you want me to pick you up in the morning?"

Imogen blinked. She'd forgotten about the house hunting. "I'll pick you up about one."

Christian shook his head. "I'm not riding in this thing if I can help it." He laughed. "My car is big enough to fit two. I'll pick you up."

Her car was rather small. "All right."

He got out of the car, waved and she waited until he was safely inside his apartment building before she drove off.

She ignored the disappointment that he hadn't asked her to stay.

***

Imogen woke earlier than she'd expected to the next morning. She made herself coffee and sat at her kitchen table, thinking about the night and about Christian. There was one thing he'd said to her which had stuck with her all night. She was able to do more than just attend charity events to help people.

She wandered upstairs to her walk-in robe and gazed at the mass of clothes in there. She loved clothes – loved making them, loved buying them – but there were some things in there that hadn't seen the light of day in years. There were others who could benefit from them more than her and it was as good a place to start as any.

Putting down her coffee mug, she got to work.

***

When Christian buzzed the guesthouse a couple of hours later, Imogen was surrounded by bags of clothes. She opened the gates remotely and hoped they would all fit in his car.

Her wardrobe was significantly clearer, though there was still plenty in there. Imogen held up a blue skirt suit that was the final piece she was deliberating about. She loved the style, loved the cut, but she had never worn it. It had been slightly too big for her when she'd bought it and she'd never got around to altering it. When Christian knocked on her door, she put it into the last bag and hurried downstairs to let him in. He looked slightly tired when she opened the door and she felt a twinge of guilt. He'd had a long week and now he was going to spend the afternoon house hunting with her.

Kissing him quickly she said, "You look tired. You don't have to come with me today."

He smiled at her and pulled her back toward him to kiss her slowly.

Imogen's body warmed all the way down to her toes and tingled all the way back up.

"I'm already feeling rejuvenated," Christian said as he stepped back.

After a kiss like that she wasn't going to argue. Feeling a little flustered she glanced over his shoulder and noticed his car definitely had a bigger trunk than hers.

"Do you mind if we stop off at the charity thrift shop on our way out?" she asked. "I've been going through my wardrobe this morning."

"Sure. Where are the bags?"

Imogen led him upstairs to her bedroom and laughed at his exclamation when he saw the ten trash bags full of clothes.

"You sure have been busy."

It took a few trips until they managed to fit all the bags into his car—some on the back seat—and then drove to a thrift shop she'd found whose proceeds helped women in need.

As they were carrying the bags inside, a tall woman with long, lank brown hair came outside holding the hand of a crying boy about five years old.

"I want the cowboy," the boy cried.

The woman looked stressed. "I know, Toby-boy, but I can't afford it," she said.

"Elle?" Christian asked, stopping the woman.

The woman looked at Christian in surprise and then seemed to deflate even further. "Hi, Chris."

"How's the business going? Have you been to the bank yet?" he asked.

She shook her head. "My meeting is on Monday and I was looking for something to wear, but Toby's tired."

"Can we help?" Imogen asked impulsively. "I could help you find something to wear and Chris could keep Toby amused."

The woman glanced at her and Chris quickly made the introductions. "Elle is one of my clients."

She must have been one of his pro bono clients.

"I don't want to interrupt your day," Elle said.

"Nonsense. We'd love to help," Imogen said, hoping she wasn't going to offend the woman with what she was about to do. She took out her purse and handed Toby a twenty-dollar bill. "I'm looking for a small vase to put flowers in. Do you think you could find me one while I'm helping your mom? You can keep whatever change there is and buy a toy." She didn't think a vase would cost more than five dollars. "Maybe Christian can help you look." Toby wiped his eyes and glanced up at his mother. She looked horrified.

"No, I couldn't."

Imogen touched Elle's arm. "Please?"

The woman closed her eyes and then opened them, more determination in them than before. "Thank you." She bent down to her son. "You're so good at finding things. Why don't you go with Chris and maybe you'll have enough left over for the cowboy."

He nodded, face serious, and then took hold of Chris's hand. Chris pointed to the homewares section.

Imogen and Elle watched them go.

"What do you need to find?" Imogen asked her.

Elle turned and let out a sigh. "A business suit. I have a meeting next week to see if I can get a loan to start my business."

"What kind?"

"A bookshop café."

"Sounds wonderful. Let me know when it opens; I'd love to come." Imogen handed her a business card and then examined the woman, trying to think what would suit her. "You know, I think I have the perfect thing for you." She hurried over to Chris's car and dug through the bags still in the trunk before finding the blue suit. She pulled it out and held it up against Elle.

Elle took the jacket and slipped it on. "It's gorgeous."

Imogen sighed in satisfaction. It fit her perfectly. "It's yours." She dug a bit further to find a couple of shirts she knew were there somewhere.

"I can't accept this. It must be worth a fortune."

Imogen turned back. "I was going to give it away anyway. This way I know which good home it's going to." She handed her the shirts. "Let's see if they'll let us use their change rooms."

After a brief discussion with the shopkeeper, Elle tried on the suit while Imogen found some shoes to match: a gorgeous pair of black pumps.

The whole outfit made Elle look professional and in charge. Imogen could see the change in the woman from the way she stood straighter, shoulders back and head held high. The only thing that was missing was a decent haircut.

Imogen hesitated but when Elle brushed back her hair and sighed, she had to speak up.

"Can I do something else for you?" she asked, and when Elle looked at her she continued: "I have a great hair stylist and I'd love you to have your hair done by him. Just to finish off the outfit and give you a boost. It would be my treat, of course."

Elle had already begun to shake her head. "I can't. You've done too much."

"I know how a good haircut makes me feel so much better. Please. How about I give him a call and see if he can squeeze you in? If he can't, I'll drop it."

The woman hesitated and then nodded. "All right."

Imogen dialed her stylist's number and walked away so Elle could get changed. "Joseph, I need a favor," she said when he answered. She explained the situation. "Can you squeeze her in?"

"For you, Imogen, I will."

She sighed in relief. "Do whatever you and Elle want and call me with the bill. I'll pay for whatever you think is needed."

Joseph chuckled. "I think I'm going to have fun."

Imogen smiled. "I'll send her around when we're finished here." She hung up. Toby and Christian had returned from the homewares. Toby was holding the vase and Christian was holding a cowboy, horse and other toys.

"Is this all right?" Toby asked, handing her the little crystal vase, only big enough to hold a single bloom.

"It's perfect!"

Toby grinned and turned to take the cowboy and horse from Christian. Elle came out of the change room.

"Look, Mom. Look at all of this!" The delight on the little boy's face was beautiful.

"You're very lucky. Have you thanked Imogen and Chris for the gifts?"

Toby turned to Imogen. "Thank you, Imogen. Thank you, Chris."

"You're most welcome."

She walked next to Elle and scribbled down Joseph's address. "He can squeeze you in," she told Elle. "Do you have a car to get there?"

Elle glanced at the address and her eyes widened. "I can't go there!"

"Of course you can. My treat. Joseph is under instructions to do whatever you want but I need to warn you, he is pushy. Whatever he suggests will be fabulous, so trust him." She handed Elle the paper and she took it with reluctance.

"Are you sure?"

"Positive." She held her breath. She really wanted Elle to accept but knew some people found taking charity difficult.

"Thank you." Elle hugged Imogen, who exhaled in a rush, her heart giddy.

Imogen waited while Elle paid for her shoes and Toby paid for the vase and his toys and then walked them out to Elle's white, slightly rusty car. "Don't forget to let me know when your café opens," she said and watched as they drove out of the parking lot.

"That was a lovely thing to do, Imogen," Christian said as he put his arm around her.

"It felt so good. Is this how your pro bono work makes you feel?"

"Yeah," he said. "Come on, we need to lug the rest of these bags inside and then get to your house appointments."

That's right. She'd completely forgotten about looking for a place to live.

She smiled.

"Let's go."

Chapter 11

"So you're thinking of renting, rather than buying?" Christian asked.

They were on their way to the first property and his question brought Imogen up short. She'd not considered buying anything, though she wasn't sure why. It made perfect sense. Most people rented because they couldn't afford to buy, but that wasn't a problem for her.

If she did buy, it would mean she was definitely not going back to Chateau Fontaine. The chateau was the only home she'd ever known. To leave it behind would be like leaving a part of her behind.

"I'm not sure," she said slowly.

"I can recommend buying," he said. "Owning your own place means no one can take it away from you and you've got security. Plus if you're going to pay rent, you might as well use the money to pay off your own mortgage instead."

She didn't want to tell him that even if she bought she'd probably not have a mortgage. Her mother had bequeathed her life insurance to Imogen and it had been accruing interest ever since. "I'll think about it."

Christian pulled up in front of an apartment complex where there was a sign declaring two apartments available for rent.

They got up and walked into the first.

It was tiny.

The kitchen, living and dining area would fit into her kitchen in the guesthouse and when they'd seen the two bedrooms she realized she'd be lucky to fit a decent-sized bed in either. There definitely wasn't enough room for her clothes, as her walk-in robe was about the size of the smaller bedroom.

Imogen held a polite conversation with the realtor and then got out of there as fast as possible. She headed for the car.

"Don't you want to look at the other one?" Christian asked.

She shook her head. "That was the bigger of the two and it's way too small."

Christian looked at her as he started the engine. "What size do you want?"

"The living area was fine but I need two bedrooms double the size. I want to set up my sewing room in one of them."

"Then yes, you definitely need a bigger apartment. What have you got on your list?"

She passed it over to him.

"That one's the biggest," he said pointing to one a bit further out of the city than she would have liked. "Maybe we should check if it's big enough."

She checked the time. It would be open by the time they arrived. "All right."

"Have you considered a house?" he asked. "It's possibly the best option if it's space you need. You've got one hell of a sewing room."

She did and she wasn't willing to give it up. If she did start making samples and designs, she'd need all the space she could get. "It seemed a bit pointless if it's just me, but you might be right."

They arrived at the next apartment complex. It was quite pretty from the outside, with nicely tended gardens full of roses. They walked upstairs to the first-floor apartment.

This time the living area was much bigger, perhaps the size of her sewing room for the kitchen, dining and living room. The bedrooms were also marginally bigger. She'd be able to get a bed and a bedside table in one of the rooms. Wandering to the other bedroom she pursed her lips. There was no reason she had to use the front rooms as the living room. She could fit a couch and television in the second bedroom and she rarely had people over for dinner so she could get a stool for the kitchen bench and eat her meals there. That would leave the whole front room free to be her sewing room.

She headed out to have a closer look. As she studied the room Christian asked, "What are you thinking?"

She explained her vision to him while the realtor listened in.

"It'll still be a tight squeeze. You'll have to leave a lot of your furniture behind," Christian said.

She waved a hand. "None of the furniture is mine. It came with the house. I'll have to buy my own anyway."

Christian's mouth dropped open.

The realtor, who'd introduced herself as Nancy, spoke up. "You might be better searching for a house," she said. "You won't get a bigger apartment than this in this price range and it's only cheap because of the location so far out of the city. I've got some houses for rent that will give you more space."

Imogen considered it. A house would mean she would have a garden to maintain and as much as she loved the garden at the chateau, she wasn't sure she had the time to maintain it. But it may also mean she could have the space she needed.

"Can you give me some details?"

"Sure." She went to her briefcase and took out a few brochures. "This is my last open house today so if you're interested, I can take you to them afterward."

"Thank you." Imogen sat on the couch while Christian asked, "Do you have any houses for sale in the area?" He didn't look at her, just took the other brochures the woman handed him. He came and sat next to her. At her look, he said, "It's worth checking it out. There might be a bargain."

She flicked through the houses for rent and found a couple in a location she'd like to live. They were relatively close to work and also to Piper and Libby's places. She put them to one side.

"Check out this one." Christian handed her a brochure and she was amazed by the price. It was so incredibly cheap for a very sought-after neighborhood, again not far from her friends' places. It was listed as a renovator's delight, whatever that meant.

"Probably needs a lot of work done to it but if the structure is solid, it could be perfect," Christian said.

Nancy wandered over. "That one's just been signed up. I haven't had a chance to put it on the internet yet."

"What's it like?" Imogen asked.

"It's the quaintest place. A really old two-story house with high ceilings and big rooms, but it's been left to run down. The old woman who lived there didn't have any family to help her and didn't have the finances to fix it herself. From what I was told, she ended up living in about three rooms by the time she died."

Imogen's heart went out to the woman. To not have anyone to care for you when you got old and to watch your house go to pieces would have been awful. Is that why her father was so reluctant to let her go?

"Can we view these two?" Imogen asked holding up one rental and one to purchase. She'd be foolish not to consider buying at the price.

"Absolutely. I'll make some calls now."

Within ten minutes Nancy had everything organized and was closing up the apartment.

Imogen fidgeted in her seat on the drive over to the first house, the one which was available to rent.

"Just because you're looking at it, doesn't mean you have to take it," Christian said. He reached out to still her hands. "There's nothing to be nervous about."

Little did he know. The last time she'd talked about moving out was after high school and she and Piper were going to share an apartment together. Piper was heading off to study journalism and Imogen was starting full-time work at Tour de Force. They'd been incredibly excited about the adventure ahead of them.

When her father had found out about their plans he'd been devastated. He'd given her the mother of all guilt trips about her not loving him, and abandoning him at the first possible opportunity. It was hard to be excited about houses when her father was already upset with her. Would this be the last straw?

Christian parked outside the first house and Imogen examined it. There was nothing special about the outside. The garden bed was sparse and the brick-and-tile house looked like any 1980s project build. She got out and followed Nancy up the path to the front door. Imogen listened as the realtor gave her spiel about the house, describing the features and the nearby amenities. Then she left them to look around.

It was much bigger than the apartment. It had three bedrooms, though none of them overly large, a family bathroom and a separate dining room and living room. There was more than enough room here for her sewing things and for her wardrobe and bedroom.

So why wasn't she enthusiastic?

She walked out the back to find an unmown lawn and a few plants in dire need of TLC.

"Thoughts?" Christian asked.

"It's big enough," she said.

"But?"

She shrugged. "I don't really feel anything for it. Should I?"

Christian took her hand. "You're going to be coming back to this place every night. You want it to be a place you feel comfortable and happy."

It made sense. She loved coming home to her guesthouse and not because it was still part of Chateau Fontaine. It was beautiful and it felt like it was hers.

This was neither.

Imogen walked inside and smiled at Nancy. "May we view the other house now?"

"Sure, honey. Why don't you wait outside while I lock up?"

It didn't take long for them to arrive at the 'renovator's delight'. As Christian pulled up, Imogen got her first look at the house and gasped. The paint was peeling on the porch and the wood siding and garden clearly hadn't been touched in decades but the house itself had character. It was two-story and eerily like one of those houses Hollywood always depicted as the witch's house in children's movies: wooden structure, small porch, big windows, pointy roof, almost falling apart.

She loved it.

Christian chuckled. "That's more like it."

She grinned at him and hurried up the driveway to the house. Nancy stopped them before they went inside. "The inside hasn't been cleaned yet. The estate has only cleared out the furniture so it's a bit of a mess. Look beyond the dust and the mold."

Imogen nodded, eager to get inside.

There was a long hallway running down the center of the house and a staircase leading up to the next level. The white paint was yellowed with age and flaking in some places, but everything looked to be solid underneath the grime.

Trying to calm her excitement, she grabbed hold of Christian's hand and made her way through the house.

There was both a formal dining room and a formal living room. The kitchen was large and light, though it had appliances from the 1950s.

On the second level there were watermarks on the ceiling where there must have been a leak at some stage. In all, it had five bedrooms and two decent-sized bathrooms, even if one was covered in mold.

Outside there was a huge magnolia tree and Imogen inhaled the sweet scent of the flowers. She could picture a swing underneath the tree, could see herself pottering in the garden, bringing it back to its original glory.

She walked out on to what had been the lawn and turned to Christian. "What do you think?" She needed a second opinion from someone who wasn't as caught up in love with it as she was.

"It needs a lot of work," he said. "Some of it might be cosmetic but you'd want to get it checked by a builder to make sure there's nothing structurally wrong."

He was right. No matter how much she loved it, there was no point buying a house that might need more work than it was worth.

Even if she could afford it.

She had enough money to purchase it and do the renovations without having to delay her own label – if she ever decided to go ahead with that plan.

Damn, she wanted it. For the first time in her life she *really* wanted something. Something she could call her own. Something her father had no control over. Something just for her.

"I love it," she confessed.

"I know." He chuckled. "You really need to work on your

poker face, Imi. Nancy's probably ringing up the sale as we speak."

"I need to be sensible about it," she said, more talking to herself than Christian. "I need to get a builder to check like you said."

"I'll give George's dad, Hank, a call. He's a builder."

Imogen spun around to him. Was it too much to ask for him to come out on a weekend? "Do you think he'd come now?"

Christian smiled. "I'll ask." He got out his cell phone and made the call. Too nervous and excited to stand still she walked deeper into the garden and discovered a lemon tree and an orange tree laden with fruit. She could make iced lemon tea and sit out on her porch and survey her garden. She could *see* herself here.

"He's on his way," Christian called. "I caught him on his way home from the shops. Should be here in about fifteen minutes."

Imogen flung her arms around him and squeezed tightly. "Thank you." She kissed him quickly, but he held on, taking it deeper.

Breathless, she stepped back when he let her go.

"You're beautiful, Imi. I love the way your face lights up when you're excited about something."

Imogen's heart thudded louder in her chest. She gazed up at him, saw the honesty in his blue eyes. She could stay in this moment, looking at him, and she could be happy.

The depth of her emotion worried her.

The back screen door banged shut and Imogen blinked, breaking the moment. It was Nancy. "What do you think?" she asked.

Before Imogen could respond, Christian said, "It needs quite a lot of work. I've rung a builder friend who's going to come around and check if it's still structurally sound."

The realtor frowned and asked Imogen, "What about you?"

Christian squeezed her hand and she remembered she was supposed to put on a poker face. "It's very quaint. I'm a little worried about the mold. That can be difficult to get rid of, can't it?" She had no idea but it sounded like a good thing to say.

They walked inside to wait for Hank and it didn't take him

long to arrive. Imogen followed him from room to room as he checked the house, prodding here and there, getting down on his hands and knees to check something and then getting up. At one stage Imogen almost tripped over him in her eagerness to watch what he was doing.

Hank laughed. "Imogen, a little space, please."

"Sorry." She backed off, glad Christian was keeping Nancy busy while they went through the house again.

"Where's the laundry?" Hank asked.

Imogen glanced around. She hadn't noticed a laundry in the house.

"The laundry is in the outside building," Nancy said and pointed to a shed to the right of the back door.

Imogen hadn't realized the building was part of the property. She wandered over to go through it.

It was bigger than it appeared on the outside and had obviously been used as a shed at some stage recently because it smelled of oil and manure. In one corner was a trough and power points for a washing machine and dryer.

It was the perfect size for her sewing room.

Hank examined the structure. "Needs more weatherproofing," he said and then they walked outside again to talk. Imogen clenched her hands together while she waited for a verdict.

"I'd say she's structurally sound," Hank said and he smiled at Imogen's squeal of delight. "But you'll probably need another sixty thousand to modernize her. I'm guessing you'll want a new kitchen and bathrooms, plus the floors need a good sanding and the walls need painting. Then if you want to do the garden as well, there'll be work and cost in that."

She added the cost to the selling price. She could afford it. "If I did some of the work myself it would reduce the cost, wouldn't it?"

Christian looked surprised.

"It's not too hard to paint, is it?" She directed the question at Hank.

"Nope. Not hard at all: you just need to get the equipment. And if you can rope in a few volunteers," he nudged Christian, "then you'll be done in no time."

"How long do you think it would take?" It was the downside of buying versus renting. If she rented she could move out next weekend but buying was a much longer lead time.

"If you got all the tradesmen lined up, maybe a month. I can help if you like. We don't often do renovations but I'll make an exception for you. I know all the good tradesmen in Houston."

"That would be wonderful." It didn't matter how much he charged, she trusted he would do the right thing by her.

"So does that mean it's a yes?" Christian asked.

"Give me a minute," she said and wandered toward the magnolia tree. This was a big decision. The one thing she knew for certain was she had to move away from Chateau Fontaine. Her father's increasingly erratic behavior meant she no longer felt she had a safe, secure place to live.

Renting would give her a secure place for as long as her lease lasted but might also mean she would have to move regularly, and if she *did* set up her own label, the disruption would be annoying at best.

She ran her hand over the bark of the magnolia tree and surveyed the backyard, not looking at Christian or Hank. The place sang to her. It needed work, a *lot* of work, but she could see the potential, see herself living there, and see children playing in the yard. She could bring it back to life.

Then there was the financial aspect. She'd never been a big spender. Her one guilty pleasure was buying clothes and half the time she made her own anyway. That meant she had enough capital to pay for the house and the repairs outright. But it reduced the amount she would have for her own label.

She wanted that: she wanted to design the clothes she wanted to design; she wanted control over the fabrics she bought, the shops she supplied, the whole process from idea to sale.

But her father had said it would kill him. Would he threaten to disown her like he had if she met with her mother's family?

A month earlier she wouldn't have considered it a possibility but now she wasn't sure. He'd been so angry and upset. Part of her thought he *couldn't* mean what he said but that was before she'd discovered he'd kept the existence of her mother's family away from her. Now, she didn't have a clue what he would do.

Imogen got out her phone and logged in to her bank accounts.

There was enough. Enough for the house, the renovations and to start her label, if she wanted to start small.

If she wanted to start it at all.

Imogen sent a thank you to her mother and pocketed her phone.

She could do this. She could have the house and not forgo her dream of her own business.

Walking back to the others, she smiled at them.

"Well?" Christian asked.

She nodded, elation building up like a wave forming. "Yes, I'll take it."

She was buying a house.

Chapter 12

Chris drove Imogen to Nancy's office, where it took another hour to get the paperwork sorted.

"I'd like to close the sale as quickly as possible," Imogen said.

"The sooner you can get finance, the faster it will be," Nancy said.

"I don't need finance. I've got cash. I can arrange a cashier's check on Monday."

Chris didn't hear the woman's response; he was still reeling from Imogen's statement. She could pay cash for a house? He couldn't quite fathom it.

They operated in such different social circles, in such different financial circles. Was her father right, was he kidding himself if he thought he could keep someone like Imogen interested in him?

She couldn't possibly comprehend where he'd come from, how hard it was not knowing where your next pay check was coming from. Did that mean she wouldn't be able to understand him?

He wasn't sure. But he needed to find out.

By the time they walked out of the office it was getting late.

"Want to go for dinner?" Chris asked Imogen.

"Yes, I'm starving."

He laughed as he held the door of his car open so she could

get in. Climbing in the other side, he said, "Do you have any preference where we go?"

"None at all."

Chris started the car and headed for one of his favorite restaurants. It would be interesting to find out how Imogen liked it. It wasn't a gourmet place but it had the best steaks in town.

He found a parking place and they went into the restaurant. It was bright and cheerful with mounted bull's horns and rifles crossed on the wall. It was still early enough for it not to be too full.

Imogen scanned the room and she positively beamed. "This place looks fantastic."

The part of him that was uptight, waiting for her to reject his favorite restaurant for not being classy enough, relaxed.

They settled at the table and took the menus.

"What's good?" Imogen asked.

"Everything," Chris said honestly. "The steaks practically melt in your mouth."

When it came time to order, she chose steak with chips and salad and a bottle of wine for them to share.

Another part of him relaxed. He liked a woman with an appetite.

Imogen's cell rang and she excused herself to answer it. "Hello, Nancy."

He waited, holding his breath.

Imogen's face broke out in a huge grin. "That's wonderful news. Do you think I could go in again to measure up in the next few days?" A pause. "Lovely. Thank you so much. I'll be in touch."

She hung up. "They accepted the offer!"

Chris heart warmed at her delight. He raised his glass of wine. "Congratulations, Miss Fontaine. You are now a home owner."

They clinked glasses and Chris took a sip, but Imogen's face fell.

"What's the matter?"

"How am I going to tell Papa?"

Chris wanted to curse the man for spoiling Imogen's

excitement. Instead he said, "How about, 'Papa, I bought a house'?"

She grimaced at him but smiled.

"It's going to take a while before it's livable so if you tell him now it will give him a month or so to get used to the idea. It's not as if you're abandoning him. He'll see you at work every day."

She nodded. "You're right. I shouldn't worry."

But she was worrying. He could tell by the slow, absent way she sipped her wine. Wanting to distract her, he asked, "What work do you want done on the house?"

His question had the desired effect. Imogen brightened and said, "The kitchen and bathrooms definitely need replacing and the roof will need to be checked for leaks." She ticked off items on her fingers. "The outside needs painting and the floorboards inside need sanding." She paused. "I was considering knocking down the wall between the formal dining and living to make one big room. Hank should be able to give me an idea of what is possible."

"When can you close the sale?" Chris asked.

"Nancy said within two weeks, because I've got cash. Hank said he'd help me with the plans next week. That way we can have something drawn up and ready to go when I get the keys." She was positively bubbling with excitement.

"Will you do much work yourself?" he asked, curious. He couldn't picture Imogen with a hammer in her hand.

"I'd really like to, but the only DIY I've done is watching renovation shows on television."

"Might be worth buying a book and taking some time off work when you're ready to start. It can be draining."

"You've done it before?"

"Yeah, I helped George with his house and Adrian with the place he had before Daniel died."

"Maybe you could tell me what I need to do."

"Hank's the best person to do that." At her disappointed look he added, "I did what I was told, but I can provide some muscle."

"That would be great."

The food arrived and Imogen got stuck in with the gusto of

someone who hadn't eaten for days. They held an easy conversation about her house renovations as they ate. It was comfortable, relaxing, and Chris could be himself around her. Why had he been worried about her money? She was still the Imogen he'd met as a teen, enthusiastic about life and wanting to experience it.

He remembered their date the next day. "If you could do one thing in Houston, what would it be?" he asked.

Imogen stopped eating. "Why?"

"We're spending Sunday together, remember? So you don't have to have brunch with your father."

"You don't have to – "

"I want to. Unless you've got other plans."

"No. No plans." She pursed her lips together. "There is one thing I've always wanted to do." She hunched her shoulders.

"What is it?"

"I've never been to Kemah Boardwalk."

Chris leaned back. Kemah Boardwalk was on the Texas Gulf and full of arcades, amusement rides and restaurants.

She shrugged. "It could be fun. I've never been on a rollercoaster before."

It amazed Chris how sheltered Imi had been. He grinned. He hadn't been to the boardwalk in years but he was more than happy to take her. Especially on the rollercoaster.

"Great. The boardwalk it is."

They finished the meal and Chris insisted on paying. It was still relatively early in the evening and though he was tired from the late night the night before, he wasn't ready to say goodbye. "Do you want to grab a coffee?" he asked as they walked to the car.

Imogen turned to him. "Why don't we go to my house for coffee?"

There was something in the way she said it that put Chris's mind and body on alert. "Sure."

Chris wasn't sure whether it was simply an invitation for coffee or something more and it made him a little nervous.

This was Imogen. Someone he cared for. This wasn't some fling; it wasn't just a fun way to spend an evening, followed by goodbye in the morning.

Imogen buzzed him through the gates and he drove up to her guesthouse, ignoring the itchy nerves on his skin. They got out and Imogen led the way through to the kitchen, where she put the coffee on.

Chris sat at the table while she prepared the coffee. She motioned him to follow her as she carried the mugs into the living area and sat on the sofa, placing one mug in front of Chris.

"Do you think I made the right decision about the house?" she asked.

Surprised, Chris looked at her. "Do you doubt it?"

She nodded. "I probably should have viewed more places, done more research, rather than buying the first place I fell in love with."

She was right to a certain extent, but Chris had seen the expression on her face when she'd gone through the house – which had frankly looked like it was about to fall down. He would have expected her to take one glance and run, but she'd seen past the scratched floors, peeling paint and 1950s-style kitchen and bathroom and recognized what she could do with it. In the neighborhood it was situated in, it was the worst house on a good street, and it wouldn't have lasted on the market for long.

"It's a great investment. With the work you do it will be worth so much more when you're finished."

"You're not just saying that?" she asked, her voice uncertain.

"No. Why are you doubting yourself?"

She took a sip of her coffee. "I've never made such a big decision," she said. "I've always had Papa telling me what I should do and even at Tour de Force I'm just confirming decisions someone else has made."

Chris was astounded. She'd let her father have that much control over her life? No wonder she was worried now.

"Buying a house is one of the biggest decisions you'll make in your life. But that place has great bones and you'll dress it up perfectly."

She smiled at him. "Dress it up." She nodded, pleased at the way he'd phrased it. "If there's one thing I can do, it's dress things up."

"Exactly." He shuffled closer and put his arm around her. "You don't need to worry. I'll be here for you, helping when you need it." It was true. He wanted to spend as much time as he could with her.

She put a hand on his cheek. "Thank you. That means a lot to me."

He leaned in and kissed her. There was something about her lips that soothed and aroused him at the same time. He wanted more. So much more.

Her hand came up to his chest, fingers splayed. Would she push him away?

***

Imogen grabbed his shirt and pulled Christian closer. She wanted to be reckless and stop thinking – she wanted to just feel. He deepened the kiss, teased her mouth open and ran his hand up to her breast sending heat down to her toes.

She pressed in to him, arching her neck as he trailed kisses down her neck, nibbling at her earlobe. Her whole body was hot. She needed more.

Unzipping her jacket, she pushed him away. She shrugged out of her jacket, peeled off her T-shirt and pulled him to his feet. "This way." She wanted him in her bed, she wanted to claim what they had nearly had so many years ago – she just wanted him.

He caught up with her halfway up the stairs and unclipped her bra as they entered her bedroom. She turned to him, sliding her bra off, and stood there, suddenly unsure. She'd had other lovers before, but this was Christian. It meant so much more.

"You are so beautiful, Imi," Chris said, moving forward to crush her against him.

Any doubt disappeared as she kissed him again. She tugged at his T-shirt, slipping her hands underneath it and forcing him to step away so she could take it off. She didn't want to wait, didn't want to go slow, she wanted him now. Her hands explored his exposed chest, ran over his back and down to his buttock. He groaned and picked her up, carrying her to the bed and dropping her on to it.

***

Imogen sighed as Christian rolled over and cleaned up before sliding back onto the bed with her. He gathered her close to him and cuddled her. She didn't want to let him go, didn't want him to leave.

"That was amazing," Imogen said, kissing him and snuggling closer. "Can you stay?"

"Of course."

Imogen grinned. "Mmm, then let's get under these covers." Rather than getting up, she wriggled until the sheets had been pushed down and then pulled them up again. She turned to him and wrapped an arm around his waist. "I'm so tired. Is it rude if I go to sleep?" She was pretty sure he had to be exhausted.

"Be my guest."

She smiled, closed her eyes and in minutes her breathing was even.

***

"What the hell is going on here?" The outraged yell of her father had Imogen sitting bolt upright in bed, clutching the sheet to her chest.

She blinked and someone moved next to her.

Christian.

Her vision cleared and she saw her outraged father at her bedroom door, staring at them. What was he doing there?

Blood rushed to her head and she said, "Papa, go to the kitchen. I'll meet you there."

For a moment she thought he was going to stay, demand an explanation, but then he straightened, turned on his heel and walked away.

How mortifying.

Imogen waited until the footsteps faded down the hall before she dared turn to Christian. There was an inferno under her skin.

"Ah," she said, having no idea what to say, no idea why her father had walked into her house, into her *bedroom*, without invitation.

"I think your wake-up call could do with improvement. It

was a little too abrupt for me." His face was serious but there was a twinkle in his eye.

Imogen burst out laughing. It was too weird.

The first time she'd ever had a man stay over at her place and her father sprang them in bed together. It had obviously been a good decision to have her other liaisons away from the chateau. She groaned and put her hands to her hot cheeks. "This is awful."

"You want me to come and help explain the birds and the bees to your father?" Christian joked.

She chuckled, amazed she could find any humor in the situation. "I'm going to take a quick shower and go and talk to him. It might be best for you to wait a little while before coming out."

"Can I shower with you?"

The look he gave her had her considering it for a nanosecond before she remembered Papa in the kitchen. No. It would have to wait.

She washed quickly, terrified Christian might go and talk to her father, and then threw on three-quarter-length pants and a green top. Giving Christian a towel and a kiss, she took a breath and went to face her father.

He was pacing the kitchen.

"Good morning, Papa," she said and turned the coffee machine on.

"What was that man doing in your bed?"

Imogen had considered what she was going to say while she was in the shower. "I think the more pertinent question is what were you doing coming into my house uninvited?"

"It is *my* house," her father said. "I thought you might have changed your mind about brunch since you hadn't left this morning."

Imogen stared at him. *His* house. Of course it was. If she'd needed more reassurance that purchasing her own home was a good idea, this was it. She had no privacy here. He'd been keeping an eye on the gate again.

Imogen checked the time. It was already ten o'clock. Obviously they had both needed to catch up on some sleep. "No, I haven't changed my mind. We're having a late start."

Her father scowled when she said 'we'. "I told you that man was no good for you."

Imogen didn't want this conversation now, particularly not while Christian was in the house. "Papa, I would appreciate it if you wouldn't come into the guesthouse without my permission. I have the right to a little bit of privacy, don't I?"

"I was only concerned for you." The French in his accent was more defined.

"I appreciate your concern but it could have been a lot more awkward than it was."

Her father had the grace to look away.

Until she moved out she would have to remember to lock the doors before she went to sleep at night.

"That man only wants you for your money," he said.

Imogen stared at him. Did her father really think the only thing she had going for her was money? Did he think no one could desire her? Urged on by the hurt, she said, "If last night was anything to go by, it's not all he wants." She very nearly ruined the comment by slapping a hand over her mouth in shock that she could say something so audacious to her father but she resisted.

Her father gaped at her, his mouth opening and closing but no words came out.

Good. She'd shocked him. Maybe he would recognize she was a grown woman who could make her own decisions.

Imogen took him by the arm and led him to the door. "I'll see you tomorrow at work."

Without a word, he left.

***

Christian stepped in to the room and opened his arms. He'd been waiting like she'd asked him to. She rushed in to his arms, needing the comfort he could provide.

"I never thought you'd say something like that to your father," he said.

Imogen felt the blood rush to her face. "I wanted to shock him."

"Oh, I'm pretty sure you did that. You shocked me too." He chuckled and then he gently pushed her back. "You know it's not true, don't you?"

Imogen frowned at him, not sure where he was going.

"I'm not after you for your money."

Imogen laughed. "Of course." It had never occurred to her that he would be. He was Christian, the guy she knew before money was even a consideration. "Let me get us some coffee and then I believe you promised me a date."

He tugged her closer and kissed her. "I believe you may be right."

***

Imogen was ridiculously excited by the time they arrived at the boardwalk. She had to laugh. Her father would be absolutely horrified. The boardwalk represented everything he hated: crowds, cheesy souvenirs and mass-produced food.

Christian took hold of her hand. "Where do you want to begin?"

"The rollercoaster." She'd seen it from a distance as they drove in and was worried she'd chicken out if she didn't do it right away.

Christian laughed. "All right. Let's get some tickets."

They wandered along a path. There was a mixture of families with small children, teenagers on their own and young adults. Imogen glanced up at a ride proclaiming itself the Iron Eagle Zipline as the chair at the top of the line came rushing back to earth. Her heart thumped at the screams issuing from the chair. "We need to do that as well," she said.

"Whatever you want," Christian said. "Come on, the ticket booth is over there."

While Christian bought the tickets she scanned the park, deciding what else she wanted to do.

"Here." He handed her a ticket. "It's a day pass."

Imogen hadn't offered to pay. "How much do I owe you?"

He gave her a look. "You're my date; I'm paying today."

She opened her mouth to protest, but he interrupted, "Unless you want me to pay for my ticket from Friday night."

She closed her mouth again. He was right. If he wanted to pay for her she should let him. It was weird because she usually paid when she went on dates. "All right," she said. "But I should warn you that I'm expecting both donuts and cotton candy."

He grinned. "I can manage that."

They lined up for the rollercoaster, the Boardwalk Bullet. It was huge, and as Imogen watched a carriage plummet down the first drop, she squeezed Christian's hand. She was going to do this. She was going to ride this wooden rollercoaster. She was going to take this risk.

It wasn't long before it was their turn. The front seat was free and Christian pulled her in.

"It's the best spot."

Imogen wasn't so sure she wanted to be right at the front, but she went with him and waited for the safety bar to lock in to place. She glanced at it dubiously. It wasn't a whole lot to keep her from falling out.

The carriage moved and Imogen clutched Christian's hand. This was it! Nerves and excitement clattered queasily around in her stomach. The carriage was dragged up an incline and Imogen could see across the parking lot and marina to one side and the Texas Gulf on the other. Then, before she could catch her breath, the ride was going around a bend and dropping straight down.

"Hands up," Christian shouted, putting his hands up in the air and hers went with him. Her stomach dropped along with the ride and she shrieked as they twisted and turned. It was insane. Her body was thrown violently around and she had no control over what she was doing, where she was going.

It was terrifying and it was thrilling.

She didn't breathe properly until they came to a slow stop.

"Oh my gosh," she said, her skin tingling.

"What did you think?" Christian asked as they exited the ride.

She couldn't think straight. Adrenalin was racing around her body and she couldn't stand still. What a buzz. "That was so much fun." She tapped her hands on her thighs. "Can we go again?"

"Sure thing."

She flung her arms around his neck and kissed him. "Thanks." She grabbed his hand before he could kiss her again. "Come on." She dragged him back to the line.

***

They rode the rollercoaster another three times before Imogen declared she'd had enough and they tried some of the other amusement rides.

Chris followed wherever she wanted to go, caught up in her exuberance. True to her word she made her way through cotton candy, donuts and whatever other snack foods caught her interest. All the sugar probably helped fuel her energy.

This was the Imogen he remembered from his childhood. So full of life, passion and excitement. She'd been missing her spark for several weeks. Her father had almost snuffed it out.

Determined not to let thoughts of Remy ruin his day, he noted Imogen's energy was waning.

"Do you want to walk along the boardwalk and visit Stingray Reef?" he asked.

"Yes, please. I'm feeling a little queasy."

He chuckled, not in the least bit surprised. They'd spun and swirled and dropped and swung. He barely knew which way was up. But he felt like a kid again.

Stopping at a food vendor he bought a bottle of water for them each and then took her hand and together they wandered along the boardwalk. The gulf was calm today and lapped against the pilings, producing a soothing sound. There were a lot of people out and about and Chris was happy to mosey between them.

"There are a lot of great restaurants here," Imogen commented.

Chris stared at her. "You can't possibly be hungry." He couldn't believe how much sugar she'd consumed.

She grinned. "Not at the moment, but dinner isn't far off."

He shook his head. She was incredible.

They wandered the length of the boardwalk to the Aquarium Restaurant where the stingray reef was. There were a lot of families in there with small children but that didn't stop Imogen. Before he could protest, she'd bought them tickets and handed him his share of stingray food.

He followed her around the tank to where there was a clear spot. The stingrays were all on the other side being fed by other visitors; Imogen didn't seem to mind though.

"Look at the way they're coming right up out of the water," she said, pointing. She perched herself on the edge of the tank and dangled one of the fish in the water.

Several of the stingrays broke away from the main pack and glided over toward them. Imogen stayed seated and kept still, watching their approach. She was calm, and not at all squeamish like some of the other tourists. When the stingray rose to the surface, she let go of the fish and stroked a hand down its back.

"It's so soft," she said.

Another stingray rose to the surface and splashed with its body. Water washed over the edge of the tank, wetting Imogen's pants.

"Oh," she said, twisting to see the wet spot now covering her butt.

Christian waited for her reaction.

"We may need to go shopping after this," Imogen said and turned her attention back to the stingrays.

She was wonderful. Little things didn't faze her. Chris moved closer and dangled one of his fish into the tank. Two stingrays dove for it and the wave of water splashed up over his front.

"I think you might be right," he said, glancing at his wet T-shirt. He laughed.

***

When they were done feeding the stingrays, Imogen dragged him into the kitschiest souvenir shop he'd seen. It was full of boardwalk gear and novelty items. Imogen was like a kid in a candy shop as she went through the T-shirts and chose ones for them both.

"Papa never let me have kitsch stuff when I was little."

Then she purchased a skirt to replace her soaked pants and used the change room to get changed.

Pleased with her purchases she dragged Chris into the other shops in the area. There was a ladies fashion shop where Imogen spent a lot of time, browsing through the clothes and examining the labels. She wasn't interested in purchasing as much as checking what was available. It was fascinating to watch her. She held out garments, checking the seams and testing the fabric by stretching or scrunching it. She had a long conversation with the shop assistant and took a card from her.

Chris was content being with her, watching the joy she got from talking about clothes and examining the outfits. Clothing wasn't just something to wear to her: it was an extension of personality.

She should be designing her own label. She shouldn't be locked up at Tour de Force, made to follow her father's whims.

He needed to convince her of that.

When she was finished shopping he took hold of the bags she'd collected. She'd bought something in each shop, not able to help herself. "Hungry yet?" he asked.

"Surprisingly I am," she said. "Where do you want to go?"

"Lady's choice," Chris said. "This is your day."

"There." Imogen pointed without delay to the nearby movie-themed restaurant with shrimp and fried food.

She never stopped amazing him. He'd expected her to choose the Aquarium with its aquarium tanks or the Sushi restaurant.

"This is fantastic," Imogen said as they walked through the door and the waitress explained to them how the restaurant worked. Her smile got wider as she read the menu and pointed out the names and what they were. "I'm never going to be able to decide," she pronounced.

"The shrimp's good," Chris said with a grin.

She scowled at him and then said, "Have you been here before?"

He nodded. He'd been there several times over the years but never before had he enjoyed it so much as now, experiencing it with her.

She hesitated. "We can go somewhere else if you want." She closed the menu.

"No way. I'm having way too much fun." He kept it light but it annoyed him that she'd put him before her own enjoyment. She was too selfless.

She watched him for a moment and then said, "All right."

In the end Imogen ordered a ridiculously large cocktail and a smallish entree. "I need room for dessert later," she explained.

Chris waited until the drinks were served before he broached the subject he'd wanted to talk to Imogen about. "How are things going with your label?"

Some of the happiness left her eyes and Chris cursed himself for bringing it up, but she'd wanted to do it so badly, and he didn't want others, namely her father, to stop her.

"I've put it on hold for now," she said.

"Imi, you'd be great at this. Your business plan was good – it just needed a bit more work."

Imogen took a sip of her drink. "Christian, there's too much happening in my life right now. I've bought a house which needs renovating and there's potential I have family I don't know. Papa's upset enough about those two things. I don't have the energy for anything else at the moment."

She had a point but he didn't want her to give in. "You could still work on your business plan. You don't have to actually set up the business straight away." From what he'd read, there was a lot to it. "You could even talk to Simon."

Imogen hesitated. "I don't know."

"Imi, your designs are fantastic." He didn't know much about fashion but if his friends liked them and Simon thought she was good enough then he was sure they were right.

Her smile was small. "It's not all about the design," she said.

The food arrived and Imogen changed the subject. "So what's new at your work?"

Chris was tempted to continue the conversation but he didn't want to upset her further. "Same old, same old."

"Could you do more pro bono work?" Imogen asked. "It sounds as if you enjoy it and I'm sure people like Elle appreciate it."

"Not all my clients are like Elle."

"You're still lucky," she said. "As much as I love designing clothes, I don't think it has any impact on anyone."

"You helped Elle immensely yesterday," Chris said.

She smiled. "That was easy. She needed a boost and it was just a few dollars."

Chris suspected it was more than a few dollars. He'd seen the name of the high-end salon Imogen had sent Elle to. "You could call up a charity and volunteer your time. I'm sure they'll accept any hours you offer. I can give you a name or two."

"I might do that," Imogen said.

He hoped she did. He could see how much joy she'd received helping Elle.

The waitress came and cleared the plates and Imogen ordered the chocolate-chip-cookie sundae. It came out in a cast-iron pan with a warm chocolate-chip-cookie base and ice cream, cream, toppings and nuts poured over it. She took one bite and her eyes rolled back. "So good." She licked the cream off her top lip and Chris forgot what they'd been talking about.

All he could focus on was her lips.

Imogen caught him staring at her. "You want to taste it?"

The *it* he was thinking of was not the cookie. "Sure."

She fed him a spoonful and she was right: it was good. But as she savored every mouthful, his attention was not on the food.

When she was finished he said, "You ready to go?"

She seemed surprised by his rush.

"We can go back to my place," he said, and she realized what he meant.

She grinned. "Shall we?"

He hoped so.

***

It was after dark when Christian dropped Imogen off at the chateau. There was no sense in staying at his place because she didn't have a car to get her home in the morning.

He didn't come in. "If I come in, I'll stay and I need to be at work early for a brief," he said after he'd kissed her until she was breathless.

She wanted him to stay but he was right. It wasn't fair of her to ask him to fight the morning traffic to get to his apartment and then to the office.

"I'll call you tomorrow." He kissed her again and then got into his car and drove off.

Imogen walked up the steps and into her house.

Apart from the surprise start, it had been a perfect day. She put on the kettle and while waiting for it to boil she had a shower. She slipped into some flannelette pajama bottoms and a singlet. Then she headed for the kitchen to make her coffee.

As she sat down with her mug there was a knock on the kitchen door. She knew who it would be. It was very late for him to be coming around.

"Come in, Papa."

"I am glad you are alone."

He meant he was glad Christian wasn't there but part of Imogen couldn't help asking whether he didn't want her to have anyone ever.

"Papa, who I choose to spend my time with is none of your business." She really didn't want to go into this, not after the wonderful day she'd had, but it needed to be said.

"While you live under my roof, you need to respect my wishes."

Perhaps he was right. Perhaps in some small way she was being disrespectful. She debated for a minute whether she should tell him. Now was as good a time as any.

"Then it's just as well I've bought a house."

"What? When?" Her father took a step back.

"Yesterday. It is time I got my own place and I found a wonderful 1920s house."

"You did not think to ask my opinion?"

No, she hadn't. And she was pretty sure if she had, he wouldn't have seen past all the work that needed to be done. "I fell in love with it," she said honestly.

"Then you have probably wasted your money. You must show it to me tomorrow so I can check it."

"No, Papa. It's too late. I've signed the paperwork. But I did have a builder look it over for me to make sure it was structurally sound."

"Who is this builder?"

"He's George's father. I met him at Adrian and Libby's wedding."

Her father frowned and then said, "George was the groomsman?"

"Yes."

"How do you know he is trustworthy?"

Imogen sighed. "Papa, he owns one of the biggest private building companies in Houston. He knows his stuff."

"I still wish to view it."

"It needs a lot of work. I don't want you to see it until I've had a chance to do it up."

"And so when it is ready, you will leave me?"

Imogen was hoping he wouldn't ask about that. "It will still be a few months before it will be ready," she said and then took a deep breath. "And then I will move out of your guesthouse."

"But this is your house, your home."

"That's not what you said this morning." The words snapped out before she could stop them. She didn't deserve these manipulations.

He glanced away. "I was shocked this morning."

She was certain he had been, but that didn't excuse it. "Then I suggest you don't enter the guesthouse without permission in future."

Her father looked down at the ground but she refused to feel sorry for him. "Chateau Fontaine will always be home, Papa." She took his hand, ready to lead him to the door. "But I'm twenty-nine years old. It's time I became independent."

"You are already very independent. You come and go as you please."

And you track every visitor I have.

"Papa, this is important to me. Please be happy for me." It was a simple request. She didn't cajole, she wouldn't stoop to his level.

He scowled at her but there was no heat in it. "I could never say no to you."

There was no point refuting his statement.

"But," he added, "I insist you show me your house tomorrow."

Imogen squeezed his hand. "I'll show you my house when I get the keys for it. That way you can see inside as well as outside."

"You win!" He threw his hands up in the air. "Now it is late and I must get to sleep. Good night, *ma bichette.*"

"Good night, Papa."

She waited until he was out of sight before she let out a breath and slumped over the table. She felt as queasy as she had on the rollercoaster, without all the fun. It was exhausting talking to her father, but at least she'd won the first battle. She would worry about the next one when it came.

Right now she agreed with her father. It was late and she wanted sleep.

Chapter 13

The first thing Imogen did the next morning was ring her bank and arrange for a cashier's check. Then she rang Hank and sorted out a time he could meet her at her house to review what she wanted to do. Nancy had told her she was available at any time so Imogen arranged the meeting on Thursday afternoon and cleared a place in her diary.

With that done, she collected her notes and went to the morning meeting.

She was the first one there so she turned on the computer and got the room set up. Her father, Jacques, Abigail and Derek filed in about five minutes later.

"What are we all doing this week?" Remy asked.

They each went around the room discussing the high-priority items for the coming week.

"I have decided this year we should attend a few of the smaller fashion weeks around the world," Remy said when they were done.

Imogen frowned. Her father had never been interested in any of the fashion shows aside from Paris, Milan, London and New York.

"There is an opportunity to expand to more markets and meet more people."

Did it mean Tour de Force was not doing as well financially as they used to? The one area of the business she didn't have much to do with was the final yearly figures.

"An excellent idea, Remy," Jacques said. "Will you send us each to a different city?"

"No. I believe Imogen is capable of this task. There are a number of shows in May and if I send one person, she can spend the month going to all of them."

Imogen ignored the dirty look Jacques gave her. The idea of going to a range of shows was exciting, but she didn't want to be away for a whole month. She'd just bought a house, and she wanted to spend more time with Christian. Her thoughts stopped. Maybe that was it. Maybe her father was trying to get her away from Christian.

"Papa, perhaps it would be better if we all went. Each person will view things from a different perspective. It would give us a wider range of ideas, maybe even for the next season's line."

"Pah," her father spat. "We do not get inspiration from other people's designs. We are our own inspiration."

"Then Abigail – "

"*Ça suffit*," her father said, holding up a hand. "I will give you the list of shows you will attend and you can arrange your airfares and accommodation."

Remy adjourned the meeting and left the room, with Abigail and Derek quickly following.

Imogen sighed and gathered up her notes. She would try again later. As much as she relished the opportunity, she had to be here to oversee her home renovations and she wanted the others at Tour de Force to share in the experience.

"It's always Papa's little doe who gets everything."

Imogen glanced up. Jacques was still in the room and the look he directed at her was vicious.

"Jacques, I tried to change his mind."

"It doesn't matter. You will always get everything. The best opportunities, the highest pay, the least amount of work. You do realize you're not needed here, don't you? You don't add anything to the production of Tour de Force; in fact you slow it down. All because Papa's little doe needs a job and is too lazy to go out and find her own."

Imogen gaped at him, the words piercing her head.

"You'd better find a way to share the trip because it was my idea and I deserve to go." Jacques turned to go.

"Wait a darn minute." Imogen grabbed his arm to stop him leaving, anger bubbling up inside her. She was tired of his attitude. "I work my butt off for this company doing the jobs *you* don't want to do. Someone has to check the orders, arrange shows, order fabrics, and if I didn't do it, you'd have to." He had no idea how frustrated she was at not having the freedom to do what she wanted. It was like being trapped in a cage that everyone mistook for a palace.

Jacques was staring at her as if she'd grown two heads.

"Yes, Papa gives me opportunities – he wants me to take over when he retires. So if you have a problem with that, you go talk to him." She clenched her shaking hands together. "It's past time you knocked that chip off your shoulder." She walked out the door.

With frustration still humming in her veins she strode to her office, shutting and locking the door behind her. Then she sank into her chair.

She shouldn't have let Jacques's words get to her. She knew he didn't like her, but his comments came at a time when she'd had enough of everything.

His words echoed something Simon had said to her at the charity event. *"You're not needed."*

It was true.

She wasn't really contributing anything special to the business. Sure her job was important – she did a myriad of things that others didn't want to do, things that needed to be done – but it didn't necessarily need to be done by her. None of her designs were suitable and they were the only thing she could offer that no one else could.

The only reason she was still there was her father. He always insisted she was vital to the company and she'd never really stopped to question it.

Opening her calendar, she checked her schedule for the day. She had to order fabric, check on the samples, call and confirm Tour de Force's attendance at a few events and look after the new intern who was starting that week.

But really any administrative assistant could do that.

She checked her calendar for Tuesday and then Wednesday and then the rest of the week.

Jacques was right. What she really was was an over-paid administrative assistant.

But how could she leave? Papa was determined for her to take over one day.

The thought of having to ignore her own dreams just added to her frustration.

How could she explain it to Remy? How could she tell him she didn't want the business he'd built up? It would devastate him.

She shook her head and sighed. She couldn't keep putting her life on hold for him. The house was the first step, and this would be the next.

She just needed to figure out how to tell him.

***

Imogen still hadn't decided what to do by Wednesday when Piper rang. "I'm in the neighborhood and hope you might be free for lunch."

Imogen desperately wanted to talk to someone. Christian hadn't called on Monday as he'd promised, so she had called him and left a message on his cell phone. He'd not returned it. She hadn't wanted to appear needy so after that she'd just sent him a breezy email – again, no response.

He'd had a busy week scheduled but surely he could have managed to reply to an email or send a text.

That was if he was still interested in her.

Her words to her father echoed in her head. *That's not all he's interested in.* But perhaps it had been just sex for Christian. Perhaps spending a day at the Kemah Boardwalk had been too immature for him. Perhaps he'd got what he wanted and moved on.

"I'll meet you downstairs in five." She hung up the phone, grabbed her coat and went to meet her friend.

"What's new?" Piper asked as they sat at their usual restaurant. Piper had been away for a week with her family so Imogen hadn't seen her.

Imogen grimaced. "I bought a house, slept with Christian,

my father found us in bed together and on Monday I realized I don't like my job." Despite her turmoil, she couldn't help but smile. It wasn't often she surprised Piper.

Finally Piper shook her head and said, "Okay. Let's take this one thing at a time, in order. You bought a house."

"Yes. A real renovator's delight."

"You're going to be renovating? Honey, I don't mean to be negative, but I've never seen you even pick up a screwdriver."

Imogen laughed. "I can learn, and Hank and Christian have both agreed to help."

"Hank as in George's father?"

Imogen nodded. "He checked the house before I bought it."

"Okay. That's good. Next point. You slept with Christian. Good for you. But your father walked in on you? I'm not sure which one of you would be more scarred from that."

"Well, he woke us up." She explained what happened.

Piper laughed. "If Christian didn't run from that experience, you know he's a keeper."

Imogen said nothing. Maybe that was the issue. Her father.

"He didn't run, did he?" Piper looked incredulous.

"I haven't heard from him all week, and yes, I have tried to call him."

Piper frowned. "Maybe he's been busy." She was trying to be hopeful but it looked bad.

Maybe they'd both misread him.

Piper changed the subject, putting her journalist face on. "What's this about you not liking your job?"

"I realized on Monday I'm sick of the Tour de Force brand. I don't have any freedom to do my designs or choose the fabrics I like. As it stands, I'm a well-paid administrative assistant."

"Honey, we all have days when we think all we do is administration."

"No, I mean there is actually nothing I do that an assistant couldn't. The only reason I get paid so well is because my father owns the company."

Piper watched her. "Take me through it."

It was the way Piper worked: she needed to go through each step logically, examining it before moving to the next step. It was one of the reasons she was such a great journalist – because she was so thorough, she noticed things other people missed.

When Imogen was finished Piper's expression was sad. "I'm sorry, honey. I have to agree with you."

Part of Imogen was relieved that someone else could see what she'd only now realized, and part of her was just plain sad. "Have I wasted the last ten years of my life?"

"No way." Piper's answer was instantaneous. "Think of everything you've learned being with Tour de Force. You know the business inside and out. Why do you think you wrote such a damn good business plan? Think of the time as training for your own label."

Was Piper right? Imogen thought about all of the interns they had through Tour de Force, thought about people like Simon who had told her again and again what value they'd gained from their time with the company.

Perhaps she'd had the best internship of anyone, ever.

"Then why did Papa make such a big fuss about me creating my own label?"

Piper hesitated. "I might have an answer for you."

"What is it?"

"I've been doing some digging into your mother's side of the family," she said.

Imogen closed her eyes. She wasn't sure she was ready to hear this yet. Not with everything else that had happened lately.

"Is it bad?"

"It depends on how you look at it."

Imogen made her decision. "Don't tell me now. I have to go back to work this afternoon." Her father had to be involved, and she was having enough difficulty keeping her thoughts to herself at work. She did not want to make a scene.

Piper nodded in understanding. "How about dinner tomorrow night?"

"I'm meeting Hank at my house at four to go over plans but I'll be free after that."

"This is your new house?" Piper asked.

"Yes."

Piper grinned. "Give me the address. I'll meet you there."

Imogen blinked.

"What? You didn't think I would jump at the first opportunity to check out your new digs, did you?"

Imogen laughed. "No, I guess not."

Feeling a lot better about the whole situation, she went back to work.

***

On Thursday Imogen left work early and arrived at her new house at the same time as Nancy, who opened it up.

She stood at the front verge, feeling the same warm tug of emotion she had when she'd first seen it. She got out the notebook she'd brought with her and started writing.

The picket fence had a dozen or so palings missing and some were hanging on by a nail. The whole thing needed a decent coat of paint. There were some shrubs in the front yard which might be pruned back into life, but what was left of the lawn had mostly turned to weeds. She'd give Mr. Barker a call and get him in to do an evaluation of both the front and back yards. It would be great to watch him work again.

Examining the front of the house she decided the whole thing needed a new coat of paint. Some of the porch also needed to be repaired. As she was writing it down a car pulled up in the driveway.

"Holy hell, Imogen. You bought this place?"

Imogen laughed at the disbelief in Piper's voice.

"You should have said demolition delight not renovation delight."

Knowing her friend was mostly kidding, Imogen said, "It's got good bones."

Hank pulled up behind Piper and got out.

"Sorry I'm late. Got held up at the last job of the day."

Imogen smiled at him. "That's no problem. I was making notes about what needs to be done."

Piper muttered something about nothing a wrecking ball wouldn't fix, but Imogen ignored her. She introduced her to Nancy who was waiting on the front porch.

"The cleaning crew is due tomorrow," Nancy said.

Imogen didn't care how it looked. She entered her house.

Her heart beat a little faster. This was hers. Every square

inch of it was for her to do exactly as she pleased. Walking through it again slowly, she sketched the floor plan out on her notebook. Hank showed her the things she would need to do in order to make it livable again.

"These rooms here don't need more than sanding and painting," he said of four of the five bedrooms.

"Could we knock out that wall and make those two into a big bedroom?" she asked him, pointing at the wall she meant.

He went over and examined it, checked the ceiling. "Doesn't appear to be load bearing. I'll have to get up in the roof to check, but if it isn't, it wouldn't be a problem."

They discussed the upstairs bathroom and Hank measured its dimensions, marking up where the plumbing and electrical points were. Imogen wanted to keep the huge bathtub but the rest of it needed gutting. She drew a quick sketch at how she wanted the layout.

Hank nodded. "If you change that to there," he pointed, "you'll have more space and you won't need to move the pipes."

Imogen grinned. Hank was a gem.

Downstairs she checked about knocking out the wall between the formal dining and living area and then explained her vision for the kitchen, which included enlarging the windows so there was a better view of the garden.

"Yep, that should be easy done."

"Hey, Imogen, if you put up a wall here, you could make this room your study and have space for a laundry," Piper said.

Hank nodded in agreement. "It backs on to the kitchen so it wouldn't be hard to move the pipes a bit further."

Imogen made a few adjustments to her floor plan while Hank took the measurements.

Her body vibrated with excitement. This was her house and she was going to bring it back to life.

She walked out the back and made notes of what she wanted to do with the sewing room and garden. When Hank had finished his measurements he said, "I'll get this drawn up into proper plans. Then I'll cost up all the work. I'll give you rough estimates on the bathrooms and kitchen because it will depend on what quality you want to have. I should have something to you by early next week."

Imogen gave him a hug. "Thank you, Hank."

Hank blushed but hugged her back. "It's a pleasure."

Imogen thanked Nancy for showing them through and then she followed Piper back to her apartment for dinner.

****

"So what did you think of the house?" Imogen asked her when they sat down to eat.

"You're right. It's got good bones."

It was a relief to hear someone else say it. Piper wouldn't lie to her.

"I'll help out where I can. I've painted a wall or two in my life."

"Thanks." She took a mouthful of the tomato soup Piper had retrieved from the freezer and heated up for them.

"So do you want to know what I found out?" Piper asked.

Her maternal family. The idea she might have extended family was so tenuous, so hopeful, it could break with whatever Piper said.

Either way she needed to know. "Yes."

Piper opened the notebook she had next to her. "Your grandmother, Julie Ryder, is still alive."

Hope sprung to life. Imogen smiled. A grandmother. She'd dreamed of having a grandmother for years, particularly when she was younger.

Piper's expression sobered. "Your grandfather died ten years ago."

Imogen's smile faded. She'd never have the opportunity to meet her grandfather but she needed to focus on the positive. She'd gained a grandmother.

"Both your uncles, Allen and Peter, are alive – one is married and the other divorced. You have five cousins, ranging from twenty-five to thirty-one." Piper watched her.

Cousins. She'd only ever dreamed of having cousins before and now she actually had *five*.

But why had they never come to visit her? She glanced at Piper. "There's more."

She nodded.

Imogen breathed in a deep breath and let it out, preparing

herself. "Hit me with it."

"Your grandparents weren't happy when your mom married your father. He was closer to their age than your mother's and they didn't approve. She gave up her studies to move in with him and start a family." Piper paused. "Your father was desperate for children and your mother had two miscarriages before she fell pregnant with you."

Imogen bought a hand up to her chest. It must have been difficult for her parents.

"Frances did everything the doctors said to reduce the chance of a miscarriage with you. Two days after you were born, she died from a deep vein thrombosis. Apparently it's a common risk in pregnancy, but it was sudden and unexpected."

Imogen closed her eyes. It explained why her father was so protective of her, explained why he wanted to keep her at Tour de Force. Her mother had died bringing her to life.

Tears welled up in her eyes. "My grandparents blamed me for her death?" Imogen asked.

Piper shook her head. "Not so much. They lashed out at your father. From what I was told, they each said nasty, hurtful things and when they tried to make amends your father wouldn't listen to them."

Proud and stubborn Remy, who'd probably felt all of the guilt her grandparents had piled on top of him.

"How did you find this all out?"

"I spoke to your uncle, Peter."

Piper had spoken to her family. It was too much. "He was willing to talk about it?"

"I explained who I was and we met for coffee." Piper paused. "He'd really like to meet you."

The tears spilled over her cheeks. "Really?" Her voice was a whisper.

"Of course, honey." Piper got up and gave her a hug. "He said they're all really sorry about what happened and want to make up for lost time."

Imogen's heart swelled so large she thought it might burst through her chest. She had family who wanted to meet her.

But her father would not be happy.

The thought gave her only a moment's pause.

It didn't matter. She needed to see them and she didn't have to tell her father until afterward. "When can we meet?"

"How about on the weekend? That will give you time to get used to the idea and you won't have to rush off anywhere."

Imogen nodded. "Saturday. Can you set it up?"

"Sure. Do you want me to come with you?"

Imogen thought of Christian briefly, but pushed it away. He'd sent her a text message that day but it simply said, *Work's a madhouse. Call you soon.* Vague enough to have no meaning. Soon could be tomorrow or three months from now. He must have had second thoughts about the relationship. She couldn't blame him especially with the way her father was acting. Or perhaps he'd lost interest now she'd slept with him. The idea stung more than she wanted to admit it but she had to admit the possibility.

She turned her attention back to Piper. The idea of facing her uncle on her own was too daunting. "Yes, please."

"All right. I'll give Peter a call tomorrow and set something up."

"Thank you, Piper." Imogen hugged her friend.

"It's my pleasure." Piper took the empty plates to the dishwasher and turned back to Imogen. "Now, I want to know more about your plans for that wreck of a house."

Imogen laughed and they settled down on the couch to chat.

***

Christian had never been so relieved the week was done. His whole schedule had been so out of whack that he had barely been at his desk all week. His company had decided to put in a takeover bid for a smaller company. He'd been involved in discussions, reviewing legal documents of the new company and arguing about the best way to go forward. Plus he'd had to do it according to the United Kingdom's time zone because that's where the company was. He'd barely had any sleep and no time to himself. Listening to Imogen's voicemail message when he'd received it had soothed him, but he hadn't had a chance to call her back. It had been too late at night when he'd heard it and then there hadn't been time during the day. He had managed a text message, but every time he went to pick up the phone, someone came in. It wasn't until Friday afternoon when things quieted down that he noticed the email he'd written her was still sitting in his draft folder, unsent. He'd been interrupted halfway through writing it. He swore. What must she think of him? He debated calling her and realized he'd be seeing her at Adrian's place in an hour. He could explain then.

He'd missed her.

Through the whole week of endless talks about money and power, she was his one ray of light.

He packed up and left work at six pm for the first time all week and turned off his cell phone. He was fairly sure work would call him about some minor point so he was determined not to be available. They'd sucked him dry. In the morning he'd check his messages and determine if any needed answering.

He ducked home to change and on his way out to Adrian's he stopped to buy Libby some flowers. Taking a bottle of wine would be pointless since Adrian didn't drink. Then as he examined the flowers he decided to buy Kate a small bunch as well; she'd get a real kick out of it.

As he went to pay for the two bunches he hesitated. He hadn't bought Imogen flowers yet. Was it considered bad form to buy another woman flowers before he'd bought his girlfriend some?

But they were a 'thanks for dinner' gift rather than a gesture of feelings. And if he bought Imogen a bunch now, he'd have to buy Piper some too because otherwise she'd be left out.

He should have sent Imogen some flowers during the week, to show her he'd been thinking of her.

He shook his head. He was over-thinking things. Imogen would think the gesture of the flowers for Libby and Kate was sweet.

He hoped.

He paid for the flowers and drove the rest of the way to his friend's house.

***

For once he was the first person there. Kate answered the door.

Chris flourished the flowers toward her. "These are for you."

Kate stared at him, speechless for a moment, before she squeaked, "For me?"

He grinned, pleased he'd bought them for her. "For you."

She took the bright yellow flowers and held them up to her nose and smelled them. "Thank you."

She led him through to the kitchen where Adrian was preparing food. "Chris bought me flowers," she said.

Adrian smiled. "They're nice."

Libby walked in and Chris handed her the other bouquet. "These are for you," he said.

"Oh, you didn't need to do that," Libby said but took them and admired them. "They're gorgeous."

She turned to Kate. "Let's find vases to put them in and you can put yours in your room if you like."

While they did that Chris sat down on one of the stools.

"You trying to win over my girls?" Adrian asked with a grin.

"No need," Chris said with a shrug. "They already love me." He winked.

Adrian laughed and pushed over a cutting board and a cucumber. "Make yourself useful and cut that up."

Chris took a knife from the knife block and did as he was asked.

The others started trickling in shortly after; Imogen was the last to arrive.

She walked in and greeted everyone, smiling but it didn't reach her eyes. It looked as though she'd had as rough a week as he had.

Damn it, he should have made more of an effort to speak to her. He didn't like the idea she'd been struggling without anyone to talk to.

He got to his feet and walked to her. "Hi, how was your week?" He went to hug her and she hesitated before wrapping her arms around him.

It stung.

He kissed her cheek and she smiled at him but it was her fake smile, the one she did to make it appear as if she was happy when really she wasn't.

Unease skittered down his spine.

She was upset with him.

She stepped past him. "Sorry I'm late."

He was a little alarmed at how he wanted to take her into another room, find out what was wrong and make everything right again. He resisted the urge. Now wasn't the time to go into it. Not in front of all of their friends.

He sat down at the dinner table and Piper shot him a dirty look. He'd definitely done something wrong.

They settled in to dinner and shared their news. Libby and Adrian had had a great time in Hawaii, Piper had got a scoop on her latest story and George was considering signing a new Native American artist.

"I hear you bought a house," George said when he finished talking about the new talent.

Imogen nodded. "It's needs a bit of fixing."

"A bit?" Piper said. "It's amazing it's still standing."

Chris felt a twinge of jealousy that Piper had visited the house as well.

"When you get the keys we can have a demolition party," George said.

"Demolition party?" Imogen asked, her tone concerned.

"It's when you get a whole group of people together and rip out what you don't want," George explained. "It's one of my favorite parts of renovating because I get to bring my sledgehammer."

Imogen laughed. "Sounds like fun. You'll have to show me how to do it."

"I reckon I can rustle up a few people to help," George continued. "My sister Isla loves to demolish stuff; she's just not keen on the rebuilding."

"Thank you." Imogen seemed amazed.

"Dad would take a look at your garden, if you want him to," Chris told her.

Imogen smiled. "I was going to call him when I got the keys."

Chris realized then that she hadn't mentioned her father. He didn't know whether she'd told him about her purchase yet. He'd been so busy with work that he'd forgotten about the things Imogen was going through.

It was inexcusable.

Piper's cell rang and she excused herself. "Sorry, it's work." She got up and left the table and the others gathered up the dishes and took them to the kitchen. When Piper returned she made a beeline for Imogen. Chris wandered closer so he could listen to the conversation.

"Work wants me on a story tomorrow morning. One of the other reporters has called in sick."

Imogen clasped her hands together, then touched Piper's arm. "It's all right. I'll go on my own." She didn't sound thrilled about the idea.

"Go where on your own?" he asked stepping up to them.

Imogen widened her eyes and hesitated. Finally she said, "Piper found my uncles on my mother's side. I'm going to meet one of them tomorrow."

This was a big deal. Why hadn't she told him?

He answered the question himself. Because he'd not called her all week. Not given her the opportunity. Work had been crazy busy.

Anger threaded its way into his thoughts.

What must she think of him?

"I can come if you like," he offered.

"I ... well ..." she stuttered.

"I'm sorry for not calling this week. Work was a madhouse."

"I'm not sure. Let me think about it."

"Of course." He took hold of her hand. "I'm here if you need me."

Her eyes filled with confusion and she took her hand back. "I'd better help with the dishes."

Chris absently rubbed at the pain in his chest as he pushed down a sliver of panic. Had he blown things with Imogen? He had to fix it. And when he did, he would be more attentive no matter what work was like.

***

At the end of the evening Chris walked Imogen to her car. Piper and George left with a wave and Libby and Adrian went inside to give them some privacy.

Chris wasn't ready to say good night yet. He hadn't had Imogen to himself all evening, but she was already unlocking her car.

"Imogen, wait."

She turned slowly.

"Do you want me to go with you tomorrow to meet your uncle?"

Imogen looked up at him. "Christian, what's going on? We spent a great weekend together, we had sex and then I didn't hear from you. You didn't call me back or answer my emails. The text you sent was vague at best. I thought maybe you wanted a fling but now you offer to go and meet my uncle with me." She sighed. "It doesn't add up. I don't know where I stand."

Chris cursed. "I'm so sorry, Imi. You're right. I thought I'd sent you an email, but I found it in my drafts folder just before I left work today." He ran a hand through his hair. "I've been thinking about you a lot but there was never a good time to call."

She held her head high and met his gaze. "I don't want you to feel obligated in any way. If you're not interested just say so. I can meet my uncle on my own."

He shook his head and drew her closer. "Of course I'm interested. Work was hell this week and it was late before I finished. I didn't want to call and wake you up. Your message brightened my day." He wanted to take away her hurt. "I missed you this week and I was an idiot not to make the time to contact you."

She didn't look like she believed him.

"I can only imagine how hard it will be meeting your uncle after all of this time. I want to be there for you."

"Are you sure?" she asked, her voice uncertain.

He hated that he'd put any doubt in her mind. Hated that he had taken her for granted. "Yes. Come home with me, Imi." He kissed her and she responded. "Please. I want to be with you."

Her smile was a little more certain this time. "All right."

Relief flooded him. He couldn't mess this up. She was the best thing in his life.

***

Imogen parked her car in one of the guest parking spots and

got an overnight bag out of the trunk. "I was going to stay at Piper's," she explained.

She should have been planning on staying at his place. He should have known Piper had found her family. He took her bag from her and carried it up to his apartment. They were silent the whole way and nerves began to settle over Chris's skin. He couldn't allow work to get in the way of this. If he'd blown it with Imogen he didn't know what he'd do.

No, he couldn't have. She wouldn't be here if he had.

He hoped.

Imogen sat down on the couch. "So how was your week?" she asked.

He didn't want to talk about his week, didn't want to talk about work, but he needed to explain to her why he hadn't called. "The business wants to buy a UK company. We've had a lot of overnight meetings I've had to attend which means being awake at two in the morning."

"Sounds important."

He shrugged. "It is for them. There was a lot of documentation to go through and I had to do it in UK business hours."

"You don't sound like you're enjoying your work."

"Not at the moment." He couldn't remember the last time he enjoyed it.

"So why don't you find a different job? I'm sure someone with your experience would be in high demand."

He'd have to prove himself at another company, start at the bottom and work his way up again. He really didn't want to do that, not when he was so close to the top. And there were no guarantees it would be any different. "Better the devil you know," he said.

Imogen frowned at him but he didn't want to go into that right now.

"Tell me about your week."

The sigh that came out of Imogen was full of sadness, confusion and exhaustion. He pulled her close to him, needing to hold her and she relaxed back into his arms.

"On Monday it really hit me how unfulfilling my job at Tour de Force was."

Chris frowned. "What do you mean?"

She explained what Jacques had said and how she'd critically examined her role.

"So what are you going to do?"

"I've been working on the business plan again," she said. "But before I do anything I need to figure out how to deal with Papa."

"He's still threatening to disown you?"

"I haven't spoken to him about it. He believes I've dropped it. But Piper thinks she knows why he's acting that way." She told him what she'd discovered about her past and her maternal family.

Chris hugged her closer. "I'm sorry I wasn't there for you, Imi." She'd been in a world of hurt and confusion and his only excuse for not being available was work.

"Piper was there."

And didn't that make him feel like a failure? "So tomorrow you're meeting your uncle, Peter?"

She nodded and tensed.

He rubbed her arms. "Where?"

"We agreed to meet at a coffee shop not far from where he lives. I'm still not sure of the reaction I'm going to get so I didn't want to go to their house."

It was a good idea. Piper could have got the wrong impression or the man might be hiding a grudge. At least he'd be by her side to protect her.

"I'm nervous," she admitted in a quiet voice.

"Of course you are." He turned her so she was facing him. "But he can't possibly not like you."

She gave a small smile. "It's been almost thirty years. It's a long time to be stewing over the past."

"Whatever happens, we'll deal with it." It was getting late, so he pulled her to her feet and wrapped his arms around her, trying to convey his positive thoughts to her. When he pulled away he said, "Let's get some sleep."

He led her into his bedroom and kissed her deeply before undressing her and helping her into bed. He wanted to take care of her. He wanted to protect her. Show it wasn't about the sex. Getting in the other side he pulled her close to him and they fell asleep.

Chapter 14

Imogen woke to strange surroundings but the warm body beside her was familiar. This was a much nicer way to wake up than having her father yell at her. She smiled as she turned over to face Christian.

He opened his eyes. "Good morning."

"Morning." She ran a hand down his arm, to his hip. She was pleased they'd cleared up their issues the night before.

"Have we got time for that this morning?" he asked with a grin.

All at once she remembered what she was doing today. Meeting her uncle. She caught sight of the clock against the wall. It was almost eight. She sighed. "No."

Christian got out of bed and walked around to her side. He held out a hand. "Let's have a shower instead."

She admired his body as she followed him to the bathroom. His shoulders were well defined and his butt was rounded in a way that made her want to squeeze it.

Chris turned on the shower and pulled her in. The water washed over the two of them and he pulled her close, pressing his body against hers and making her aware he was wide awake in all areas.

Mindful of the time, she washed, stepped out of the shower and grabbed one of the towels. She dried herself quickly so she wouldn't get distracted by Christian and wandered naked back to his room to get dressed. As she pulled on her pants she called, "We need to leave in five minutes."

"Right behind you," Christian said and stood there in his naked glory. She looked him up and down and smiled.

"Keep looking at me like that and we might not make your appointment," he said with a smile.

He was right. She didn't want to give her uncle a bad first impression.

"I'll be in the kitchen," she said.

As she peered into his fridge to find something to eat, her stomach did a flip-flop with nerves and she closed the door. She could get something at the coffee shop if her stomach decided to behave.

"Ready to go?" Christian asked as he walked into the room.

She nodded and grabbed her bag from where she'd left it on the couch the night before.

***

The trip to the coffee shop took about twenty minutes. Imogen didn't talk. She kept her mind busy running through all the possible ways this meeting could go. Her legs wouldn't stay still and she tapped her foot against the floor of the car.

"Do you know what he looks like?" Christian asked as he pulled up.

"Piper took a photo when she met him." Imogen showed him a picture of a man in his fifties whose hair was the same shade as Imogen's with the addition of a whole heap of gray.

Getting out of the car, she took hold of Christian's hand and checked the time. Five to nine. She wasn't late. When she walked into the coffee shop she scanned the people sitting and saw the man stand up from a booth on the side and raise a hand, his whole body language hesitant. She recognized him from the photo. Her uncle.

"Over there," she said to Christian. She took a deep breath before smiling at the man and walking over to him, ignoring her rapidly beating heart. She hesitated. What did she call him?

"Uncle Peter?" It felt right as she said it and the huge smile he gave her was worth it. His eyes welled with tears.

"Yes, Imogen. How are you?"

"I'm well." They stood awkwardly for a second and then Imogen slid into the booth. "This is my friend, Christian."

Peter shook Christian's hand. "Pleasure to meet you." He was enthusiastic.

There was silence while they got settled and Imogen wondered what to say.

"You look so much like your mother." There was a little sorrow in his tone.

She smiled; she liked that she had something of her mother in her, since she couldn't remember the woman.

"I don't know where to start," Peter admitted, holding up his hands.

"Neither do I. Perhaps you could tell me about your children." It was too early to go into what had happened to make the family split like it did.

He grinned and pulled over a book she hadn't noticed on the table. He flipped it open and she saw photos. Family photos.

Her heart tugged.

"I'm married – thirty-five years now! My wife is Ingrid and we have three great kids, all grown up. Cecily is thirty, Sadie is twenty-eight and Connor is twenty-five." He showed her pictures of her cousins.

She stared at the photos. Ingrid had blond hair and both Sadie and Connor had inherited it. Cecily had the same dark coloring as Imogen. These were her family.

A waitress came to take their order and she had a moment of respite. When she was gone, Imogen asked, "What do they do?" It was hard to talk through the lump in her throat.

Christian squeezed her hand.

"Cece is an architect, works for Jones Construction. Sadie is a teacher at the local primary school and Connor's still working out what he wants to do." There was a lot of pride in the man's voice.

"Jones Construction is Hank's company," Christian said.

"You know Hank Jones? He's a great guy," Peter said.

Christian nodded. "He's my friend George's father."

Imogen was amazed. How long would it have been before she would have run into Cece at some social function or other? "Do they know about me?"

"Yeah. We kept tabs on you, whenever you were mentioned in the news. We told them what happened. None of us realized you didn't know about us, though, until your friend Piper contacted me."

What must they have thought of her? "No, I didn't." She wanted to know more. "What about my other uncle?"

"Allen's the good-looking one." Peter laughed as if it were a running joke. "He's got two kids and is divorced now. His boys are Blake and Trent; they're thirty-one and twenty-nine respectively. Blake's a scientist and Trent is a stay-at-home dad. He's got baby, Kristy, who's going to be one in a couple of weeks."

Cousins – and second cousins.

"Do they all know you're meeting with me?" How did they feel about her now? Did they think she was some stuck-up snob who didn't want to be seen with them because they weren't wealthy?

He nodded. "We had a bit of an argument because they all wanted to come but I thought it might be a bit overwhelming for you. It can be a bit boisterous when we all get together."

They all wanted to come? They were all excited to meet her? It was unbelievable. She'd gone from having only a father to having a whole family who wanted to meet her. Imogen sniffed, to keep the tears in. "And my grandmother?"

Peter sobered and Imogen braced herself. "Well, we haven't told her about you yet. We wanted to make sure you wanted to meet her before we told her the news. She's getting on, you see, and we didn't want to disappoint her."

She understood. They were protecting her. She couldn't blame them. She took a sip of the coffee. "I would like to meet her. I'd like to meet all of my family."

Peter beamed at her. "They'll be mighty happy to hear that."

Imogen hesitated and then asked, "Uncle Peter, can you tell me what happened when my mother died?"

He frowned. "It was a long time ago."

"Yes, but whatever happened stopped me from knowing you all existed until a couple of weeks ago."

He sighed. "I was about your age when it all happened. Frances and Remy were besotted with each other. They were desperate for children, before Remy got much older." He sipped his drink. "Franny had a couple of miscarriages so she was real careful with you. Your father hired a cook and a housekeeper to look after the house."

"Were you friends with Papa?"

He shook his head. "I wouldn't say friends. We only saw each other on social occasions and he was much older than I was. I would say we had a common interest in loving your mother, but I did like him."

"So what happened?"

"After you were born everything seemed fine. She was recovering well and you were a healthy baby. Then a day later she was struggling to breathe and died within minutes. They found out later it was a deep vein thrombosis. Apparently it can be common with pregnancies." He sighed and slumped his shoulders. "Mom and Dad were distraught. She was their little girl. Everyone was upset and people said things in the heat of the moment, things that shouldn't have been said."

Imogen waited for him to elaborate and when he didn't, she asked, "Like what?"

He paused for a long moment. "They blamed the pregnancy and your father. Said she was dead because of you."

Imogen sat back and Christian put his arm around her.

"They didn't mean it. They were so upset and they both regretted it ever since," Peter said. "Your father was of course furious and swore we would never have to see either of you again. Allen and I tried to smooth things over but your father wouldn't speak with us. We had no idea what you were told. Over the years we tried contacting you, but could never get through your father. Then when you got older we figured you'd contact us if you wanted to see us."

Imogen could understand a bit more now. Her father thought he was protecting her from people who hated her.

It made sense.

Peter watched her anxiously. "Do you understand?"

She reached out and covered his hand with her own. "Yes, I do." It was a case of two families grieving over the death of one person. She couldn't be held responsible for her mother's death. She hadn't chosen to be born, but, oh, how sad she was that words said in grief all those years ago were still resonating today. It was time to heal those hurts.

"When do you think I can meet the family?"

Peter's shoulders rounded and a light flush lit his cheeks. "We're having a family lunch today," he said. "Everyone wanted to hear about meeting you and so we arranged to get together. You're both welcome to come."

Today. Was she ready for that?

She glanced at Christian.

"Whatever you want to do," he said, hearing her unasked question.

What the hell. "We'd love to."

Peter beamed at her. "I'll give them all a call."

***

A couple of hours later Imogen was questioning what she'd got herself into. They'd left the coffee shop after agreeing to go to lunch so Peter could tell the family and visit his mother to break the news. She and Christian had taken a walk along the bayou to kill some time and walk off some of the nerves skating around her body.

"We'll stay for as long as you're comfortable," Christian said. "Just give me the word when you're ready to leave and I'll come up with an excuse."

"Thank you."

They pulled up in front of a modern, cream brick house that had a well-manicured lawn and pretty roses in the garden bed.

There were already cars in the driveway and all up and down the street. She was meeting a grandmother, two uncles, an aunt, five cousins and any associated partners and children they had.

"Ready?" Christian asked.

She huffed out a breath. "As I'll ever be."

They walked up the path and knocked on the front door. From inside there were voices calling and the sound of laughter. She was debating whether she should knock again when a voice behind her said, "They'll never hear you knock over that racket."

Imogen turned to the dark-haired woman behind her, who she recognized from one of Peter's photographs.

"I'm Cece, and you must be Imogen."

"Yes."

Before she could decide what to do, Cece hugged her. "Nice to finally meet you." She smiled and walked to the front door. "Come in and I'll introduce you to the clan."

She was so matter-of-fact, so welcoming. Imogen hadn't quite expected that. She shot a look at Christian, who nodded at her, and she followed Cece into the house. Peter was coming down the hallway with his arm around an older woman who had to be Imogen's grandmother.

Imogen froze as she waited for the woman to notice her, taking in her still dark, permed hair, her neatly pressed gray slacks with a bright pink shirt, and the laughter lines at the corners of her eyes. This was her grandmother.

"Hi, Dad; hey, Grandma. Look who I found on the doorstep." Cece stepped back.

Imogen's grandmother put a hand to her mouth. Tears pricked her eyes. "Imogen?"

Imogen moved forward, drawn to the woman. "Hello, Grandma." She went with her instinct and hugged her.

The old woman's arms shook as they circled Imogen and hugged her fiercely. "I never thought I'd live to see the day," she whispered.

Tears welled up in Imogen's eyes.

"How about we go into the living room for a moment before you meet the others?" Peter suggested. "Cece, tell your mother we'll be in shortly."

Cece nodded, smiled and left the room.

Imogen helped her grandmother down onto the sofa and then sat next to her. Christian and Peter remained standing at the door.

Her grandmother clung to her as if she was afraid Imogen would disappear. "I can't believe you're here," she said. "Tell me about yourself."

Where did she start? "I work with Papa at Tour de Force," she said. "I oversee a whole range of things there." None of which excited her. "My best friend Piper is the woman Uncle Peter met. She's a journalist."

"What do you do for fun?"

It was a good question. "I go to the movies, design clothing, meet with my friends." She paused.

"Don't you design clothing as a job?" Peter asked.

Imogen shook her head. "Not very often. There are other designers at Tour de Force and the stuff I design isn't really suited to the label."

"And what about this young man?" Grandma asked, indicating Christian. She'd relaxed her hold on Imogen's arm and was less teary.

"Christian is my boyfriend."

The older woman turned to him. "Do you take care of her?" she demanded.

"I try to, ma'am," he said. "I haven't been doing too good a job lately but I'm going to improve."

She harrumphed. "See that you do."

Imogen forced down a smile. She liked her. "What do you do for fun, Grandma?"

"Well I go salsa dancing on a Monday, play cards on Tuesday, help in the church community group on Wednesday, wrangle one or more of the children or grandchildren over for dinner on Thursday and have singing lessons on Friday."

Imogen grinned. "Sounds like you're busy."

"Got to keep active at my age or I'll wither and die." She was matter-of-fact.

"Mom, I think the others are keen to meet Imogen," Peter said.

She nodded. "Just one more thing." She became serious and took both of Imogen's hands. "I said some truly awful things when you were born. My only excuse was I was grieving for the loss of my only daughter and couldn't move past that. It is horrific to lose a child, no matter what age they are.

"I don't blame you for your mother's death – I never did. It took me a long time to stop blaming your father, but I eventually did that too. Life is too short to hold onto your anger." She took a breath. "I am so very sorry my grief prevented you from knowing your family, from meeting us. I won't ask for forgiveness, but perhaps you will be able to understand." Her grandmother's hands shook as she squeezed Imogen's hands.

There was no hesitation for Imogen. "Of course I forgive you. As you said, life's too short and I want to get to know you all." She hugged the woman.

"You are so sweet," she said, her voice shaky. "Now, go and meet the rest of them and give me a few minutes to myself."

Imogen was hesitant to leave the woman alone, she sounded so upset, but Peter gestured her to follow him.

The voices from the back of the house were still loud and Imogen clutched Christian's hand for support.

Peter entered the kitchen, which held a man her age feeding a baby in a high chair and a couple of women, preparing lunch. The scent of the food wafted around Imogen and her stomach grumbled. It smelled very much like fried chicken and some type of spicy Mexican dish.

"Ingrid, Sadie and Trent, I'd like y'all to meet Imogen and Christian," her uncle said as walked in. He turned to Imogen. "The little one is Kristy."

Her aunt, Ingrid, wiped her hands on a dish towel and hurried over. "Lovely to finally meet you," she said and gave Imogen a hug.

Trent gave a wave. "Howdy." He kept feeding his daughter and Sadie, with her hands covered in batter, grinned and said, "I would hug you but ..." She held up her hands.

Imogen smiled.

"Can I get you both a drink?" Ingrid asked. "We've got wine, beer, coke or iced tea."

"Iced tea, please," Imogen said and Christian asked for a beer.

"Have a seat," Ingrid said as she indicated the table next to Trent and baby Kristy.

"Do you need a hand with anything?" Imogen asked.

"Oh, no. Today you're a guest," Ingrid said. "Next time is soon enough to get you working." She laughed.

Next time. It meant a future with her mother's family. Imogen grinned.

"Just don't volunteer for the fried chicken batter," Sadie suggested.

Imogen relaxed as they chatted casually about what they did, how the different sports teams were doing – this was something about which Imogen knew nothing but Christian was able to partake in some friendly arguing – and one by one the different members of the family came in from outside to meet Imogen.

She suspected they'd organized it this way so as not to overwhelm her, as the moment someone went back outside, another person took his or her place, ostensibly to get another drink, or check on how lunch was going.

Grandma came back into the kitchen not long after Imogen had and she went outside to join the others and to 'tell them about their cousin.'

Imogen's nerves faded as it became obvious these people genuinely wanted to welcome her as part of the family. They didn't treat her like some kind of oddity but wanted to know more about her. By the end of lunch, she'd forgotten she'd only met these people today.

She insisted on helping with the dishes while Christian went out in the backyard to make up the numbers for a three-on-three game of basketball they were playing to work off all of the food.

"Imogen, you will come to my house for dinner on Thursday?" Grandma asked from where she sat at the kitchen table.

"I'd love to," Imogen replied.

"Good. I'll take you through the photo albums. You can bring your young man too if you like."

"I'll ask him."

Grandma nodded in satisfaction.

Before she left Imogen swapped numbers and email addresses with her uncles, Cece, Sadie and her grandmother. Her male cousins didn't do correspondence.

She walked back to the car, hand in hand with Christian.

"How are you feeling?" he asked.

"Happy," she said. "Exhausted, overwhelmed but happy. They're all so nice, aren't they?"

"Yeah."

"Thank you for coming with me," Imogen said and turned to him as they reached the car. She wrapped her arms around him. It felt right to have Christian next to her. He'd slotted in with her new family without a bump.

"You're most welcome."

As Christian started up the car he asked, "Where to now?"

"How about your place?" She didn't want to go home yet. Didn't want to run into her father until she worked out how she was going to tell him she would be spending time with her mother's family. Because she was determined he wasn't going to stop her.

"Sure."

***

The next morning Imogen left early in order to meet her father for their usual Sunday brunch at Chateau Fontaine. She'd debated all the different ways she could tell her father about meeting the Ryders and still wasn't sure which one was the best. She had to make sure whatever she said was about her needs and was nothing her father could turn and make about him.

At the guesthouse she showered and changed before walking through the garden to the chateau. The garden was one thing she was going to miss about moving to the new place, but she was determined she would make something from the plot of land she now called her own.

When she walked up the terrace her father was not yet outside, but Mrs. Povey had set out plates and cutlery. Imogen took a seat and waited. It wasn't long before her father joined her, and Mrs. Povey brought out coffee for them both.

"How was your day yesterday, *ma bichette*?" her father asked.

"Lovely, Papa. How was yours?" She wanted to gauge his mood before she went into any detail.

"Oh, so so. There is much to do before you fly out to the fashion shows."

That was a subject to deal with another day.

"Papa, I want to tell you something but I don't want you to get angry at me."

Her father raised an eyebrow. "I can never be angry at you, *ma bichette*."

Imogen tried not to let her frustration show. "Papa, I'm serious. Will you promise to listen to everything I say?"

"Of course, of course." He took a sip of his coffee.

"I told you I discovered Mama had a family," she began.

Her father's expression went from relaxed to hard in an instant. Imogen put a hand over his.

"I met with them yesterday. All of them. They're very nice people and they were very sorry for what went on after Mama died."

"Did they tell you what they said? Did they tell you what they called me?" His voice was tight and he removed his hand from under hers.

"Yes, Papa. Grandma Ryder said she regretted the words every day since she'd said them."

"You are already calling her *grandma?*" His outrage was clear. "Words cannot be unsaid."

"No, they can't," Imogen agreed. "But they can be forgiven, or at least moved past so life can continue."

"They called me a murderer. They thought I had killed the one person I would have died for." Raw emotion filled his voice and his hands clenched the table.

It had been twenty-nine years and yet her father sounded like it had happened yesterday. Wasn't the hurt supposed to fade? "They did. They were grieving for the loss of Mama just as you were. It doesn't excuse the words they said but it does explain them."

"You wish to associate with people who would react this way?"

"Papa, I have cousins my age. Cousins who were babies or not yet born when Mama died. I'd very much like to spend time with them."

His hands relaxed marginally. "Blake was a sweet boy," he said. There was some warmth in his tone. "He loved his Auntie Frances."

Imogen focused on the children. Her father couldn't possibly blame them. "He's a scientist now. His brother Trent is married and has his own baby, Kristy, who is cute as a button."

"Their mother was a bitch," her father said, his words sharp and the tension returning. "Always making Frances feel like a failure because she couldn't conceive."

Imogen disliked her without even meeting her. "Allen divorced her some years ago."

Her father nodded, satisfied. He hesitated and then asked,

"What about little Cece?"

"She's an architect. She works for George's dad, Hank."

"The man who examined your house?"

Imogen nodded. "Peter has two other children, Sadie and Connor."

"You have not mentioned your grandfather," Remy said.

"He died several years ago," Imogen told him.

There was satisfaction on her father's face but Imogen ignored it. She didn't know what had gone on between the two men and it didn't matter now.

"Papa, I'm going to keep seeing my family," she said softly.

His face hardened again. "I am your family," he said. "I raised you, I took care of you, and I loved you when they did not." His voice rose. "They are not your family."

"Papa ..." Imogen wasn't sure how to diffuse the situation.

"*Non*. You will not see them again. They do not deserve you."

The situation was rapidly getting out of control. "Papa, I would like to get to know them. Cece and Sadie are really nice." She focused on her cousins, kept her voice gentle.

Her father's face trembled with a series of emotions but then settled on unforgiving. "No. If you see them, you will not see me. I will have no association with those people."

"Papa, please don't do this." She hadn't really believed he would make her choose. "You don't need to meet them."

His gaze was steady, uncompromising. "Them or me."

Imogen blinked back tears. How could he do this to her? How could he rip away the chance to have more family now, when she'd only just met them? She had to hope he would back down. She had to hope he was bluffing.

"I will have you both," she said her voice as neutral as she could make it.

"*Non*." He stood up. "If this is your decision, I expect you out of the guesthouse by the end of the day." He walked away.

Chapter 15

Imogen sat on the terrace, tears blurring her vision.

Was this more of his theatrics? Was he counting on her to back down as she'd done dozens of times before?

Anger slowly built in her chest. She was tired of it. She was tired of his threats, tired of living her life to suit him. He might be bluffing but she would call him on it. She got to her feet and strode across the garden.

If he wanted her out of the guesthouse, she would be out of the guesthouse.

She needed a bunch of boxes, a big car and a place to stay. She picked up the phone and debated who to call. She couldn't very well invite herself to stay at Christian's: he might freak out. She dialed Piper's number.

"Can I stay at your place for a few nights?"

***

Piper had declared a packing frenzy. Imogen called Christian, Piper had called Libby and Christian had called George. They'd arrived within the hour, bringing with them boxes and a van George had borrowed from his father.

If Remy had noticed all of the cars arriving he didn't come to investigate.

The moment Christian arrived he strode over to Imogen and gave her a hug. "It didn't go so well?" he murmured.

"No. I can't understand it." Her heart ached especially when she saw all the boxes. She really was leaving her home. Her father was kicking her out.

"He'll come to his senses, and in the meantime you're staying with Piper." He seemed relieved she had somewhere to go.

Imogen was being foolish, but part of her had hoped he would ask her to stay with him. But really, their relationship wasn't at that stage yet.

She invited everyone into the living room, explained what had happened and her father's reaction.

Christian sat next to her, with his arm around her, giving her strength.

"There's not a lot that needs to be packed," Imogen told them. "Everything in my sewing room, my clothes and a few knickknacks around the place. The rest was here when I moved in." She had chosen some of the furniture but her father had insisted on paying for it so she wasn't going to risk him accusing her of theft.

"Where are you going to store it?" Libby asked.

There wasn't a lot of space at Piper's apartment. "I'll find a storage company tomorrow," Imogen said.

"You can store it at my place," George said. "The renovations are only just finished. I've got spare rooms I haven't filled yet. There's plenty of space."

"That would be great. It's just until I get the keys to my house." It was such a relief to have friends to support her. She was so lucky.

"And you make the house livable," Christian added.

Imogen didn't contradict him. He didn't need to know she was thinking of moving in straight away. She didn't want to be a burden on Piper and she wasn't entirely sure if her father would fire her from Tour de Force. She had to watch her money from now on.

She took Christian, George and Adrian into her sewing room.

The men glanced around the rows and rows of storage in her room. "This is all fabric?" Adrian asked, his eyes wide.

"Epic, isn't it?" Christian commented.

"I was thinking obsessive," George said with a grin and shook his head in disbelief.

"It's not only fabric. There are also sequins, beads, fringing, buttons and thread," Imogen told them. "I'll pack up the table and the machines."

"Are you sure you trust us with this stuff?" Christian asked.

"Of course. Be methodical. Everything is sorted in its own drawer. Put the drawers in order in boxes and you'll be fine."

She smiled and left them to it. Piper, Libby and Kate were in her bedroom, examining her walk-in robe.

"That's a lot of clothes," Kate breathed.

"I've packed a suitcase of what I should need in the next couple of weeks. The rest can go into boxes. Don't worry about creases or anything. I can press it later."

"I've been dying to get my hands on your wardrobe for years," Piper joked.

"What are you going to do?" Kate asked.

"I'm going to pack up the knickknacks." There weren't many but only she knew which ones they were. "Do you want to help?"

"Sure."

Imogen made up a box and went from room to room pointing out the things that were hers and Kate helped her wrap them and put them in the box. Each time a box was filled, it was labeled and put into the van.

It only took an hour for Kate and her to finish and by that stage Libby and Piper were almost done in the bedroom.

Imogen and Kate wandered into the sewing room, where the men were hard at work.

"I didn't know fabric came in so many colors or types," Adrian said.

"I didn't want to know," George grumbled.

Imogen laughed and packed up the items strewn across her table.

"This is so cool," Kate said, looking around. "Is this where you made my dress?"

"Yep. I made all the dresses here."

Kate wandered around, poking into drawers and cupboards. Imogen was happy to let her, not to mention happy she had so many friends who would cancel their Sunday plans to help her.

"How are you feeling?" Christian asked as he came over to her.

"Sad," Imogen replied. "But kind of relieved as well." She tried to explain. "I was going to be moving out soon anyway. Papa's reaction just sped up the process. And I'm sure when he realizes I'm serious about this, he'll come around." She wasn't nearly as sure as she pretended and she thought Christian knew it because he wrapped her in a hug.

"He'll come to his senses."

She hoped so.

***

By mid-afternoon Imogen felt like she was getting her life back under control. She wandered around the house, checking drawers and underneath cushions to ensure she hadn't left anything important behind.

She was going to miss this place: not only the house but the grounds as well. Especially her secret garden.

"Kate, do you want to check out my tree house before you leave?" she asked. They were all gathered in the kitchen, having a drink.

Kate glanced at Adrian and back at Imogen. "If I'm allowed."

"You can all come," Imogen said. "You might not get the chance otherwise." She smiled as she said it but the others understood what she meant.

They walked out along the path. Imogen held Chris's hand and brushed her fingers over the foliage that edged the walkway. She'd spent hours in this garden, inventing games to play with imaginary friends, following Mr. Barker around so she could have company, tending to her little patch of soil.

She pushed through the gate and brought her friends into her secret garden. Piper had been there before and of course so had Christian but the others stared up at the tree house.

"Oh. My. Gosh," Kate said, staring up at the wooden structure.

"It's just like I remembered," Christian murmured in her ear.

"Do you think we'll still fit?" Piper asked.

Imogen nodded. "I was up there the other day. Do you want to go inside?"

"Yes, yes, yes," Kate said, her eyes wide.

"Follow me."

She climbed up the ladder and pushed the trapdoor open. She went across and opened the bay window to admit some light as Kate climbed in.

"This is amazing," Kate said, turning slowly around in a circle.

"Come upstairs."

Imogen showed her upstairs and then the slide that ran around the trunk of the tree.

"Can I have a go?"

Imogen hesitated. "I'm not sure if it's been cleaned lately," she said.

George poked his head into the room. "I'll give it a go!" His grin was wide.

"It might not be structurally sound," Imogen said. The last thing she needed was to have someone hurt themselves.

"Let me check."

He peered out of the hatch and tested the slide. "It's been maintained. No spider webs, no leaf litter, no dirt."

Then the gardener *had* been maintaining it.

"Hey, Ade," George called down to Adrian on the ground. "Does the slide look secure to you?"

Adrian walked around the trunk of the tree before returning. "Yeah."

"Get ready to catch me if I fall," George joked and, before Imogen could stop him, he swung himself down the slide.

Imogen waited for the crack signaling the slide was going to break but all she heard was George whooping all the way down.

She laughed.

"Can I have a turn?" Kate asked, hopping from one foot to another.

Imogen stuck her head out and George gave her the thumbs up. "It's all good."

"Go for it."

Kate needed no further encouragement and she squealed all the way down.

Imogen smiled. She hadn't heard sounds like that in her tree house since she and Piper were teenagers.

"Move over, it's my turn."

Speak of the devil. Piper pushed her out of the way and went zooming down the slide, laughing all the way.

Christian was right behind her. "It hasn't changed at all," he said. "That's where I sat and wanted to kiss you," he said, pointing to a beanbag.

"And that's where I sat, hoping you were going to kiss me." Imogen pointed to the beanbag next to it.

"Want to rewind time?" he asked, pulling her over and down on to the beanbags.

Imogen laughed. "Absolutely." She threw her arms around his neck and kissed him.

With a growl he pulled her onto his lap.

"Whoops, sorry!" Libby's voice came from over by the door.

Imogen broke the kiss and glanced over. She grinned at Libby and then noticed Kate behind her, an expression of shock and hurt on her face as she stared at Christian in disbelief.

Kate pushed past Libby and ran for the slide, her eyes already tearing up.

Imogen realized the reason for the tears as Kate disappeared down the slide. "Oh no." She got to her feet, shaking off Christian's attempt to keep her on the beanbags.

"What's wrong?" Libby asked.

"Kate saw us kiss," Imogen told her.

"She knows what kissing is," Libby said.

"Yes, but she's got a crush on Christian."

Both Libby and Christian stared at her as if she'd grown another head. "I saw the expression on her face. I need to go and talk with her." Imogen slid down the slide and looked around for Kate. She was disappearing through the gate.

"Kate, wait!"

Imogen trotted after her. When she reached her, Kate was in tears.

"I'm so sorry, sweetie. I didn't realize you liked Christian."

"It's just like Libby was with Uncle Ade, except he liked her back. Chris likes you instead of me."

"Chris likes you too."

"He bought me flowers," she cried. "But it didn't mean anything to him."

"Of course it did. It meant he was thinking of you." Imogen paused. She wasn't sure how to phrase the next bit.

"But not in the same way. He doesn't like me the way he likes you," Kate said.

"No." She couldn't lie to the girl. "Christian and I have known each other for years. We have a different kind of relationship."

Kate sniffed. "I'm too young, aren't I?"

Imogen didn't think so: she'd been obsessed with Christian since she'd been a teenager. "Christian's too old for you, but you are plenty old enough to know your own feelings."

"I'm such an idiot." She turned to Imogen. "He's going to think I'm a silly little girl."

Imogen held out her arms to hug her. "I'm not sure he realized you were upset." She made a note to tell Christian. "I noticed your reaction and then you were down the slide so fast I don't think he saw your face."

"You won't tell him?"

"Not if you don't want me to."

Kate shook her head and wiped her eyes with her sleeve. She gave a big sigh. "How do I look?"

"Why don't you go back to the guesthouse and wash your face? It's time we left anyway." They needed to unload her boxes before it got dark. "I'll go and get the others."

Kate nodded and wandered back along the path.

Imogen felt sorry for the girl. It was hard liking someone who didn't like you back.

She pushed open the gate and found the others waiting at the bottom of the tree house.

"How is she?" Libby asked.

"She's all right. I told her Christian didn't see she was upset and she's happy about that."

"Shouldn't I say something to her?" Christian asked.

"Best not," Imogen said. "She'd be mortified if she thought you knew. I've sent her back to the guesthouse to wash her face but we should all be going."

"I've locked up the tree house," Piper said.

"Thanks."

The others walked out, giving Imogen some time alone. She glanced up at her tree house. She'd spent many days up at that window, pretending to be a princess and hoping her prince would come and rescue her from her boredom.

Then one day Christian had come, like a knight in a fairy tale, and after a perfect couple of weeks, disappeared again.

And it had been her father's fault.

He'd prevented her from having friends and taken away the one friend she *had* made.

Anger mixed with her sadness as she turned away from her garden. She had to live her own life; she couldn't continue to let him rule over her.

She walked back to the guesthouse, where the others were waiting for her. "I'll return the key to the house and meet you at George's," she said.

Christian stepped over to her. "Do you want me to wait?"

She did, but she also wanted to do this on her own. She didn't want to go from allowing her father rule her life to letting herself rely on Christian. She smiled her thanks. "No. You go with George. I'm hoping by the time I arrive, you'll have done all the heavy lifting."

He smiled but he was still concerned. She kissed him. "I'll be fine."

She waited until they had all left before getting in her car and driving down to Chateau Fontaine. She parked behind the house and went through the kitchen door. There was no one in there so she made her way through the house to her father's wing. At this time of day he'd probably be in the library. She found him sitting behind his desk and she knocked on the door.

He looked up, but said nothing.

"Papa, I have moved my things out of the guesthouse, as you requested," she said, nerves building in her stomach as he continued to look at her coolly.

She forced herself to move forward and put the keys to the house on the desk in front of him.

He didn't touch them.

"I'll be staying with Piper for a few days and then I'll move into my own house." She put the piece of paper where she'd written the address in front of him.

He stayed silent. It was as if he'd turned to wax.

Was this the treatment she deserved after a lifetime of obedience? The hurt outweighed the anger.

"Papa, you've truly disappointed me," she said, looking him straight in the eye. "I love you and you've always been there for me, but the first time I want to exert my independence you shut me out.

"I know you loved Mama, I know you still grieve for her and I know her family said some horrid things to you, but that doesn't give you the right to keep their existence a secret from me." She embraced her sorrow. "I may not have known better at the time, but as a child I was desperate for cousins I could play with. I can only imagine the mischief Cece, Sophie and I would have got up to in my tree house."

Her father continued to stare at her, unblinking.

The anger stirred. "I hope it won't take you thirty years to talk to me again." She turned and walked out of her childhood home, her heart cracking as she did so.

Chapter 16

Imogen walked in to work the next morning as uptight as if she was walking into a minefield. After her father's lack of response yesterday, she wasn't sure how he was going to behave today, in front of all of his staff.

She slipped into her office and stopped still, her heartbeat speeding up.

There was a box on her desk and everything else was spotlessly clean. There were no coats on the coat rack, no papers on her desk, and the few little mementos she'd had on her shelves were gone.

Taking a breath to prepare herself, she walked over and peered in the box. All of her things were in there.

There was a knock on her door and Imogen turned to Abigail. "What's going on?" she asked.

Abigail blinked. "Your father said you'd found another job and asked me to pack your things for you."

Imogen's legs went weak so she leaned up against her desk. "When did he ask?"

"Yesterday evening." Abigail hesitated and then asked, "Is everything all right?"

No, it wasn't, but she didn't want to drag Abigail into it. "It's fine. I wasn't expecting Papa to be so quick," she said with a smile. She walked over to Abigail and held out a hand. "It was lovely working with you."

"Same here."

Imogen walked back and took the box off the desk.

"Imogen, if there's anything I can do to help ..."

Imogen suspected Abigail knew what was going on, but she wouldn't be able to help Imogen without upsetting Remy.

"Thank you for the offer." Imogen walked out the door, carrying her box of possessions. Jacques's look of shock when he saw her made her pause. "Looks like you might get to go to one of those shows, Jacques," she said and continued on her way, out of the door and to her car. Keeping herself on autopilot, not allowing herself to feel or think, she drove back to Piper's place. Luckily Piper had already gone for the day.

She carried her box of possessions inside, put them on the kitchen table, made herself a cup of tea and sat down.

Then she allowed herself to think. To feel.

Her father had disowned her.

After decades of talking about his undying love and support for her, he'd turned on her the first time she'd done something he didn't agree with.

She'd been expecting sorrow, she'd been expecting tears, but when the emotion came through, all she felt was anger.

Red-hot burning anger.

The intensity of it scared her.

She'd loved her father unconditionally all of her life, given in to him time and time again, accepted he knew best for her, even when she'd disagreed. And it had all been for nothing.

She'd thought he'd loved her the same way but there were conditions on his love. She had to dress his way, design his way, live where he chose, date who he chose, socialize with whom he deemed appropriate.

And only then would he love her.

Well to hell with him.

He could love her as she was, as she wanted to be, or not at all.

She had other family now: people who'd loved her instantly for who she was. She had wonderful friends. She didn't need him. She didn't want him.

Just like he didn't want her.

Her angry walls came crashing down and the tears flooded

out.

***

It took until midday for Imogen to recover from her crying jag. When she had no more tears, she'd crawled into bed and slept until her stomach woke her complaining of hunger.

Though the last thing she felt like doing was eating, she opened a packet of nuts and sat down to contemplate her life.

She had a house, even if it wasn't quite livable. She should get the keys by the end of the week and she still had the money to do the renovations. What she didn't have was a job.

Now her father had disowned her, she could continue with her plans to build her own label, but it was going to take time and money, perhaps more than she could spare now she was unemployed. Of course, there was nothing stopping her from getting a job.

Her father had already told Abigail she had one so no one would be surprised to find her working somewhere else. With that in mind, she gave Simon a call.

"Imogen, to what do I owe this honor?" Simon asked when he answered.

Imogen bit her lip. She should have considered how to phrase it before she'd called him. "Is anyone hiring at the moment?"

"Hiring? You know someone who wants a job?" he asked.

"Yes." She took a deep breath. "Me."

There was deathly silence. "What happened, pet?" Simon finally asked.

She kept her voice light. "You were right. Tour de Force doesn't need me and it's time to try something a bit different."

"Why not your own label?"

"I'll do that eventually, but I need something to keep the money coming in."

Simon was intelligent. He could read between the lines. "Did you have an argument with your father?"

Imogen sighed. "Sort of." She didn't want to tell him details. "Do you know of any vacancies?"

"Chantelle was telling me the other night she wants to hire a production manager. She's grown to the stage where she can't do it all."

Imogen closed her eyes in relief. She would enjoy working with Chantelle, if the job was still available. "Thanks, Simon. I'll give her a call."

"You tell me if you need any help, pet. And when you start your label, you come to me and I'll put you in contact with all my suppliers."

"I will," Imogen promised. She hung up. She wasn't alone in the world. She had plenty of people who cared for her. She needed to remember that.

She dialed Chantelle's number and crossed her fingers.

***

By the time she hung up, Imogen felt a whole lot lighter. She was starting at Chantelle Vision in the morning.

Her phone rang. It was Christian.

"I'm sorry I didn't call earlier. How was your father this morning?" he asked.

"He fired me," Imogen said and was able to laugh at Christian's exclamation. She explained what had happened. "I'm all right. I've already found another job. I'm going to be Chantelle Vision's production manager."

"I knew the woman had good business sense," Christian said. "I'm not sure what time I'll be finished tonight," he said. "Do you want me to come around afterward?"

She wanted to see him, but it wouldn't be fair on Piper if he came around late. She didn't want to take advantage of her friend's hospitality. "I'm fine. I think I'll have an early one. I'm pretty exhausted."

"All right. Call me if you need me." He hung up.

Imogen ended the call and fired up her laptop. She wanted to review her business plan and check if Hank had sent through her house designs yet.

To her excitement, he had. He must have been working on them all weekend. She made a note to send him something in appreciation.

She needed every boost she could get.

Examining the floor plan from every angle, she considered how she wanted to use the rooms, where she needed additional power, and planned a little for the future, for if she should ever have children. Yesterday, when she'd dropped her boxes at George's house, he'd shown her around and explained all the extras he'd put in – things people often forgot about; plenty of power points in the theater room, or in her case the sewing room; LED lighting, network connections and outdoor power. She'd made notes of the things she liked, glad of his advice. Then she sketched up how she wanted her sewing room to be set out and what furniture she would need for it.

While she was thinking about that, she wrote a list of the minimum furniture she would need for the whole house.

There was a lot.

She was going to have to be careful with what she bought, because she now seriously needed to think about setting up her own label. It was a strange feeling. For the first time in her life she had to consider her budget. She'd been incredibly privileged until now.

Luckily Imogen and Piper had discovered some great thrift shops and consignment stores around the city when Piper had first moved out.

After finishing her list, Imogen arranged a meeting with Hank during the week to discuss the materials she wanted in her bathrooms and kitchen.

Then she turned to her business plan.

It had been a while since she'd read it. She would be clear about her future with Chantelle. It wouldn't be fair to be working on her own label and leave her friend in the lurch when she was ready to launch, but Imogen was fairly confident the older woman would be supportive.

She examined her male and female lines. Without her father's financial backing there was no way she could do both at once. It made sense to concentrate on the male line. Adrian and Kent wearing the clothing was a big deal. *Get the look of the rock star without the cost.* It made smarter business sense. But Chantelle Vision was all about men's clothing and that would mean going into competition with the woman who was helping her out. Though Imogen's range wouldn't be focussing on the high end of fashion like Chantelle's did.

Imogen sighed. It was difficult. She had to talk to Chantelle and perhaps concentrate on women's clothing.

Whatever happened she was determined to move forward with her life.

And be a success.

***

The week flew by for Imogen. It didn't take her long to settle in at Chantelle Vision. There were only the two of them in the small warehouse the label rented. Imogen had always known Chantelle was a savvy businesswoman and she was impressed by the level of organization and professionalism. Everything was filed and correctly set up and there were documents outlining exactly what needed to be done in each stage of the process.

Chantelle had some great contacts in the manufacturing industry and Imogen was able to use some of her own as well.

On Wednesday Imogen collected the keys to her house. In celebration of the event she invited everyone around for pizza dinner on the floor. She'd already arranged for the utilities to be turned on so they had electricity and water, if no other creature comforts.

Chantelle had declined the invitation but had allowed Imogen to leave work early in order to pick up the keys and arrange dinner.

Imogen pulled in to her driveway and sat there for a while. This was her house, this was her driveway, all of this was hers.

The giddiness bubbled up and out of her as she giggled and hugged herself. Getting out of the car, she noticed one of her neighbors arriving home from work. She waved and then waited as the woman walked over to her.

"Hiya. Are you our new neighbor?" The woman was in her forties, had thick, short, brown hair and was wearing a gray skirt suit.

"Yes. I'm Imogen."

"Natalie. Pleased to meet you. You've got your work cut out for you with that place. Or are you going to knock it down?"

Imogen was horrified. "Of course not. My house is beautiful."

"Glad to hear it. It would be a shame for her to go. Old Mrs. Smithers loved that place and hated the fact it was falling down around her."

"I'll do my best to bring it back to life."

"You got any family?"

Imogen's heart twinged. "I have some friends who are going to help."

The woman smiled. "Well, good luck to you. I'll see you around."

Imogen unlocked the front door, her smile getting bigger as the lock clunked open. Then she pushed open the door into her home.

The smell was a combination of cleaning products. Imogen inhaled it. Her house would smell like a lot of other things until it was ready for occupancy. She walked in, the floorboards giving the occasional groan or squeak as she walked along them. She moved up the stairs, running her hand over the banister as she climbed. This was all hers. Every square inch.

She would make it a home.

Her home.

Where everyone would be welcome.

A knock came from downstairs. "Imogen, you in here?" Piper's voice.

"I'm upstairs," she called down and Piper soon joined her.

"How are you feeling?" Piper asked.

"Happy. Sad. Excited."

Piper nodded in understanding. "This place is going to be wonderful when you're finished," she said.

Imogen smiled. She hoped so.

"Wow! Check out this place." Kate's voice came floating up from downstairs.

Imogen shared a grin with Piper. "Let's go down and show the others," she said.

***

George had arrived right behind Libby, Adrian and Kate, so Imogen took them on a grand tour of the house and garden.

"Dad said you'd got a steal and he was right," George said. "This place will be great when you've done her up."

Imogen beamed at him.

"When are you going to start?" Adrian asked.

She didn't want to rely on Piper for too long. "This weekend."

"We going to have a demolition party?" George asked, rubbing his hands together eagerly.

Imogen hesitated. "I don't feel right asking people to come and do so much work."

"Nonsense," Piper said. "We all want to."

"You made all my wedding dresses for nothing," Libby said. "I'd love to be able to do something to help you in return."

Imogen didn't think it was quite the same thing. She'd been doing something she loved to do making the dresses. This would be a whole lot of hard work.

"I'll borrow some of Dad's gear and we should be set," George said. "A weekend of demolition."

The others were nodding their heads. Giving in, and relieved her friends were so understanding she said, "That would be great."

Her cell rang and she answered it.

"Imi, I'm so sorry. I'm still at work." It was Christian.

She could hear the stress in his voice. "It's all right. Do you think you'll make it for dinner?"

"No." He sighed. "I've got a brief to prepare for tomorrow. But I'll be there as soon as I can, I promise."

Imogen couldn't help the twinge of disappointment. This was a big moment in her life and he wasn't here for it. But then he had been there when she'd decided to buy. She had to understand the demands of his job. "I'll see you then."

She ordered pizza and when it was delivered they spread out picnic rugs on what would be the dining-room floor and ate and talked.

Imogen showed them her plans and they made up a list of things to do on the weekend.

She was positively buzzing with excitement by the time they were finished. It was really happening.

By the time the others were ready to leave, Christian still hadn't turned up. Piper turned to her, concerned. "Are you sure you want to stay here tonight?"

Imogen was positive. Even if Christian wasn't able to come, she was going to spend the night, camping out in her house.

She'd borrowed a sleeping bag and blow-up mattress from Adrian.

When they had all left, she made up her bed in the front room. She debated whether she should call Christian to check if he was still coming but decided to leave him to it.

Too excited to sleep, she climbed into her makeshift bed with the book she'd brought with her. She would read until she got tired. If Christian didn't turn up, it didn't matter. She wasn't going to live her life based on the demands of a man again.

She was perfectly capable herself.

She was content as she was.

***

It was midnight before Christian left work. He was exhausted and angry. He'd made it clear to his boss that he had plans for the evening but it didn't matter. The brief was too important and Samuel had suggested if Christian wasn't committed enough, he would find someone who was.

But that commitment meant he had missed Imogen's housewarming party.

Would she still be up waiting for him? He'd promised he would be there and he really wanted to be with her. Getting in his car he decided to drive past.

There was only her yellow sports car in the driveway when he arrived and the house was dark. She was inside, sleeping alone in a strange house.

He didn't want to scare her by knocking on the front door but he didn't want her to be alone either. Chris sent a text, figuring if it woke her, she could let him in.

A minute later, the light came on in the front room. He breathed a sigh of relief and, grabbing his overnight bag out of his car, he trotted up the front steps.

The front door opened and she was standing in the light, wearing purple flannelette pajamas and a matching cotton singlet. Her short hair was mussed and she had a sleepy look in her eyes. She was beautiful.

"I'm sorry I'm late."

"I'm glad you made it." She smiled and opened her arms. He stepped into them.

Holding her in his arms balanced his world.

"Work needed me to do something urgently – "

"It doesn't matter," Imogen said and led him into the room where she'd set up her bed. "You must be tired."

He was. Imogen climbed back into bed and Christian stripped off and joined her, chuckling as the air mattress bobbed to get used to the extra body. This is where he should be. He snuggled into Imogen, intending to apologize some more, but instead fell asleep.

***

In the morning Christian woke to sun streaming in the window. Imogen was not in bed with him, but how she'd managed to get out without waking him, he didn't know. He sat up, groaning at the stiffness in his back. Imogen walked in, fully dressed and looking like she was ready to start the day.

"Good morning!" she said. "I didn't want to wake you, but I wasn't sure what time you needed to be at work."

"The usual time," he said and fumbled with his phone to check the time. Seven o'clock.

"I wish I could offer you coffee but I didn't think to bring any cups or a kettle or anything."

She was so bright and cheerful and he felt like crap. He'd missed an important moment in her life and she didn't seem to mind.

"There's a towel in the bathroom for you and some hot water." She laughed. "I think the hot water system is going to need replacing judging from all the banging and clanging it did."

He hadn't heard a thing. He'd obviously been tired. Getting to his feet he said, "Imi, I'm sorry I missed last night."

She took him by the hand and led him to the garish pink bathroom. "It's fine. You had important work to do."

But that was the problem. It hadn't been important work, at least not to him. It had been stuff his boss had insisted he do.

She kissed him. "Have a shower. I noticed a deli down the road. I'll race down and check if they're open and get something for breakfast."

Before he could say anything she was gone.

Sighing, he turned on the shower taps and winced at the

209

clunk and bang in the pipes. Imogen would definitely need a plumber to have a look at it.

He showered quickly, using the rose-scented body wash she'd left in the shower, and then got ready for the day. By the time he was dressed, Imogen had returned with two take-away cups of coffee and a couple of muffins.

They went out to the back porch and sat on the steps while they ate. It was peaceful there. A few birds flittered from tree to tree and occasionally there was the sound of a car going down the street, but it was generally quiet. A nice neighborhood.

"Will you still be able to come to Grandma's for dinner tonight?" Imogen asked.

He'd forgotten about it completely, but there was no way he was going to fail her two nights in a row. Her mother's family was lovely but going through photo albums was likely to be very emotional for her. "Absolutely. I'll pick you up at five-thirty."

"Great." She got to her feet. "I need to get to work. Chantelle let me leave early yesterday and I don't want to take advantage of her."

Chris stood up and followed her inside. "How's it going?" He'd made more of an effort to call her this week but they hadn't had the chance to properly chat.

"Really great. Chantelle has a strong business and it's interesting learning about the differences between a large brand and a smaller one." She packed up her bedding and grabbed her overnight bag.

Chris hurried to help her and carried both bags out to their cars. He waited while she locked up her house. He felt he should say something else – he didn't think his apology had been enough but she didn't seem to mind.

Shouldn't she be mad he'd not been there, that he'd put his work before her?

Or should he be relieved she was so understanding?

Imogen walked over and kissed him. "I'll see you tonight." She got into her sports car and drove away.

Chris climbed into his car, still uneasy. Was she not as invested in their relationship as he was?

***

Chris was halfway out the door at five that night when Samuel hailed him. He wanted to pretend he hadn't heard him but it was pretty sure Samuel wouldn't let him go. He was supremely pissed at the man. When he'd arrived in the morning ready to proceed with the brief he'd stayed back to prepare last night, Samuel had told him it wasn't needed, that the issue had been delayed. So he'd missed Imogen's housewarming for nothing.

He wasn't going to miss dinner at Grandma's.

"Chris, I forgot to tell you. The Australian branch has another issue with the partners. I thought since you are familiar with their operations, you could review the information. I've sent it through to you. They'll be in their office in two hours, expecting a response from us."

Chris kept his facial expression neutral but inside he was seething. The man had had all day to tell him this. "I've got plans for this evening."

Samuel blinked. "You are aware this job requires you to work the hours needed. If you're not interested, I'll find someone who is."

Chris heard the underlying threat. If he didn't do this, he wouldn't be given another chance. He'd be relegated to the group of lawyers who plugged away doing mundane local tasks, never given the opportunity to move up to senior ranks.

But he wanted that. It was far better to be overworked than to have no work at all. Remy had shown him that.

"I'll get right on to it," Chris said. He walked back to his office, pulling out his cell to call Imogen.

He hoped she'd understand.

***

Imogen wasn't sure how to respond to Christian canceling again. She knew work kept him extremely busy, and he'd been busy almost every day since she'd met him, but shouldn't there be a work/life balance? Shouldn't there be a time when he could say no, he had plans?

Or was it that his work was more important to him than she was?

It didn't make much sense because he was never happy when he discussed it. He was always dismissive of it.

Imogen drove to her grandmother's place alone. She couldn't help being nervous. She'd only met the woman once and there was so much to learn about her family.

She pulled up at the address at the same time as Cece. Relieved she wasn't going to the only person at dinner, Imogen smiled and greeted her cousin.

"Hiya, Imogen. You're in for a treat tonight. Grandma's making her honey-bourbon glazed ham."

"Sounds great."

Cece let herself in, calling out, "Grandma, we're here."

Imogen's grandmother came bustling out of one of the rooms. "Lovely." She gave them both a hug and kiss and then asked Imogen, "Where's that young man of yours?"

"He had to work."

Grandma tutted. "There's more to life than working." She gestured for them to follow her. "Come through. Dinner's ready."

She led them through to the kitchen, where a small dining table was set for four. "Take a seat."

Imogen sat and inhaled the aroma of the glazed ham. It smelled divine. Her grandmother placed a full plate in front of them both and then sat with her own. After she said grace, she asked, "What have you been up to this week?"

Imogen didn't want to tell them about her father disowning and firing her. Instead she focused on the positive in her life. "I got the keys to my new house."

Grandma grinned. "Tell me more."

So Imogen told them both about the house, about how she'd fallen in love with it even though it needed a lot of work. "Hank Jones is helping me with the renovations," she told Cece, remembering she worked for the company.

"That's great. You're in good hands with him. He's a magician," Cece said.

"When do you begin?" Grandma asked.

"Saturday. We're having a demolition party. George Jones insisted on it."

"He would have," Cece said, grinning. "He likes to knock things down."

"What do you do at the company?" Imogen asked.

"I design the houses. I meet with the clients and find out what they want and make it all fit for the budget they have."

"Sounds challenging."

"It's great fun."

Here was someone who obviously enjoyed her work. Imogen thought of Christian, wishing he could have the same enjoyment.

"Let's leave the dishes," Grandma said when they finished. "I want to go through the photo albums."

She dismissed Imogen's offers to clean up and took them both through to the living room where there were a number of photo albums already on the coffee table. She handed one album to Imogen. "This one is for you." She indicated Imogen should open it.

The first picture was of her grandparents on their wedding day and the rest of the pages took Imogen through a photographic history of her family. There were pictures of her mother as a child playing with her brothers, pictures of Remy and Frances's wedding day, even a picture of Frances holding a baby. The caption next to it said *Franny & Imogen (1 day old)*. Her mother was gazing at her with an expression of awe and happiness.

Imogen sniffed.

"I wasn't sure what photos you had, so I made copies this week," Grandma said.

"Thank you," Imogen choked out. She hadn't seen many pictures of herself as a baby and none of her mother with her.

"I've got some home movies buried somewhere," she continued, "but I haven't been able to find them. I'll have a movie night when I do."

Imogen couldn't form any words. In less than a week she'd discovered more family than she'd ever dreamed of, she'd learned where she'd come from and viewed pictures of her mother she'd never seen before.

She hugged her grandmother, blinking back her tears.

"There are times when the family moves me to tears too," Cece said with a smile and added, "Usually tears of frustration."

Imogen laughed, appreciating Cece's attempt to cheer her up. With the mood lighter, she went through the other photo albums with them both, watching her cousins grow up in photos of vacations they'd gone on together. She couldn't help the envy when she saw them all posing at some beach. She might have flown to Paris or London or New York for vacations but they had never been much fun. They had been filled with fashion shows, museums and plays. Imogen had enjoyed them but she had always wished she had a sister she could share it with.

When the evening was over, Imogen promised her grandmother she would come again next Thursday and arranged to meet Cece for coffee during the week.

More content than she had been all week, she drove home to Piper's apartment.

Chapter 17

Friday morning Chris didn't go in to work. He knew if he did, he wouldn't leave, and today was his pro bono day. He drove instead to the building that housed the legal aid offices and walked in the door as his phone rang.

It was work.

He debated not answering but that wouldn't help matters. He knew the argument he was going to use and he was fairly certain Samuel wouldn't disagree.

"Morning, Samuel," he said.

"Where are you, Chris? The UK merger is hotting up."

"I'm at the pro bono offices, doing my community service. I know how important it is to the company to uphold our community commitments." Before Samuel could comment he added, "I've uploaded all my notes to the case file and I've kept you informed with everything that has happened. If you want me to tell Rosalie I have to leave now, I can …"

Rosalie ran the pro bono service and nobody messed with her. She had contracts with each of the companies that guaranteed a set amount of hours per month and she came hunting if anyone didn't fulfill them. It was her passion.

"No, it's fine. Be here early on Monday."

Chris hung up and sighed with relief.

"Tried to call you in, did they?"

He turned to Rosalie standing at the reception desk. She was only a few years older than he was and today she wore her usual jeans with a beaded purple top. Her dangling purple earrings were in the shape of a peace sign, and despite her flip-flops, which added to her hippy appearance, she was tough. He grinned and nodded. "You've sure got them running scared." He walked over and shook her hand. "I'm mighty grateful."

She laughed. "I've got a full day booked for you. You might not be so grateful by the end of it." She led him into the office and showed him the pile of client notes. "Some have written up what they need and others want anonymity."

It wasn't unusual for people to be cagey about why they needed a lawyer, worried about their privacy.

"I'll give you five minutes to read through and then send the first one in."

Chris settled at the desk, read through information from the first client, who wanted advice on a building contract. There was a copy of the contract with the notes and he started to read.

***

By the end of the day, Chris was tired but energized at the same time. He'd met with client after client and had lunch at his desk, but he was certain he'd helped each and every one of them in some way. That feeling of satisfaction was what was missing from his normal day.

Perhaps Imogen was right. Perhaps he should start thinking about a career change.

He shook his head. Even the idea made him tense. But why was that? He wasn't enjoying his job.

It wasn't just about the money. It was about proving he could make something of himself, that the money his father invested in him to put him through college wasn't wasted. It would be ungrateful of him to give up after all of the hard work his father had gone through, all of the things his father had sacrificed to give him this opportunity.

His cell rang. Unknown caller. He answered it.

"Chris, it's Cece Ryder, Imogen's cousin."

"What can I do for you?" Was she calling to tell him off for not attending Grandma's dinner the night before?

"Imogen told me about the demolition party tomorrow," she said. "I want in."

Surprised she'd heard when George had only filled him in that morning, he gave her what information he had.

"Don't tell Imogen. We want to surprise her," Cece said and hung up.

Chris sat back as an idea came to him. Maybe it was a way to make it up to Imogen for missing the dinner. The more people they had working on the demolition, the quicker it would be. He jotted down a few names, tallied up numbers and smiled.

Picking up his phone he rang his father first.

This weekend he was going to show Imogen how much he and others cared for her.

He wasn't going to let her down.

***

Imogen was full of nerve-tingling excitement as she and Christian drove up to her house early on Saturday. She'd wanted to get there before everyone else and take photos of every room before they started working, and since she'd spent the night at Christian's it made sense for him to come along. She was going to do a renovation album at the end of it.

As they went through the house she heard cars pull in to the drive. At Piper's call she yelled, "We're upstairs."

She checked out the upstairs bathroom, took the pictures and then caught Christian's reflection in the mirror. He looked particularly tasty in his work clothes; cargo pants, long-sleeved top and heavy-duty boots. Who knew she had a thing for working men? Or perhaps it was just Christian.

"You done taking photos?" he asked.

"Yep. Better go give the troops their tasks."

There was a lot of work to get through with only a few people but Imogen was happy to begin.

They walked downstairs together and out of the front of the house.

Imogen stopped and stared.

Her front yard was full of people, all dressed for hard work.

She scanned the faces. There were the people she was expecting, plus Christian's father, Piper and George's families and the whole Ryder family including Grandma, who was holding some dish of food.

Imogen gaped. "What's everyone doing here?" She glanced up at Christian and he smiled at her.

Cece walked up the steps. "You mentioned the demolition so I called Chris to find out if we could help. I figured many hands and all that, so we've all come."

"After Cece rang, I thought there might be others who would want to help so I made a few calls," Christian said.

He'd been so busy lately she was surprised he'd had time to organize anything. A glow started in her stomach and she turned back to the crowd of people.

Everyone was waiting for her to say something. "Thank you all for coming." She was overwhelmed by their support. She had so many people who cared for her.

"This house ain't going to get done if we stand around all day," Hank called, coming up the steps. "I've divided people up by the jobs they think they can do." He showed her his list.

Imogen scanned it. "Looks good. Let's get to work."

There were cheers and everyone divided up into their tasks.

Mr. Barker was in the garden, pruning and cleaning up the rubbish. Grandma insisted on helping him where she could. Trent started fixing the picket fence out the front while Sadie, Connor and Piper prepped the outside of the house for painting.

Inside people split off to demolish the two bathrooms, George started up the floor sander in the bedrooms and Imogen, Christian and Hank got to work demolishing the kitchen.

It was true Imogen had never swung a hammer before, but it didn't take long to learn. Hank demonstrated what to do with the sledgehammer and then handed it to her. It was heavier than he'd made it look and she struggled for a moment to hold it the right way. She hefted it into the air and used the hammer's weight to crash into the cupboard. The cupboard cracked and she swung again. This time it came away and the elation that filled her was heady. She could really do this.

In what seemed like no time the big items were cleared out and carried to the dumpster she'd hired. Then it was on to the tile removal.

Hank had brought all his tools, so they were well equipped. Imogen worked on the wall tiles, with a hammer and chisel. It didn't take her long to work out she had to get the angle of the chisel right in order for the tiles to come off easily and she got stuck in. There was a kind of rhythmic quality to the work and she concentrated on the task. This was her house she was renovating. She would knock it back to its bones and rebuild.

She would make it a home.

A hand on her back stopped her mid-tile. Christian had brought her a bottle of water.

"Thought you might be thirsty."

She took the bottle and pulled down her dust mask. "Thanks." As she drank, she looked around. They were about halfway through the tiles. Hank had disappeared to help with another task so it was only the two of them in the kitchen and the thud, hum and grunt of the work in other rooms.

"This is incredible," Imogen said. "I can't believe how many people have come to help."

"They all wanted to," Christian said. "They all care for you."

How had she got so lucky? Only eight months earlier she had just had her father and Piper in her life. Now she had a whole group of people, including Christian.

He stepped forward and brushed some dust off her nose. "You're looking particularly adorable today."

She swatted him away. "I'm a serious demolition expert," she said and drank some more water. "We should have this done by lunch."

"Do you want to check out the progress in the other rooms?"

She did, she most certainly did, but she also wanted to finish the kitchen. "I will when we break for lunch."

Then she turned and got back to work.

***

By the end of the day Imogen was so tired she could barely hold herself upright as she waved goodbye to those that had helped during the day. There were promises to return early in the morning but Imogen couldn't think that far ahead. She was dusty, dirty and her muscles felt like they were made of lead. All she wanted was a shower and a bed.

"Busy day," Christian said, wrapping an arm around her waist.

She resisted the urge to flop against him so he could hold her up. "I don't know where everyone got the energy."

"They took breaks when they needed them," Christian told her. "I kept telling you, you needed to rest."

But she couldn't. Not while everyone was here, working so hard for her.

"Want to take a walk around?"

She did, but she wasn't sure she would make it up the stairs. "I might need a hand," she said.

He smiled. "Come on."

They went from room to room. Each one had some sign of work, whether it was the window frames being sanded, or the floors, or some other thing. Imogen spotted two floor sanders amongst the dust. The walls she'd flagged to come down were gone but the edges required patching. The wall she was putting in had its frame in place. Both the bathrooms were gutted and the front porch and back veranda had been repaired.

Outside all the trees that were staying had been pruned and everyone had been given bags of oranges and lemons to take home. There weren't a lot of plants that needed to be ripped out, and those that had to be, were gone. Mr. Barker had hired a turf cutter and was planning to rip up the remaining lawn in the morning.

Exhaustion settled around her and tears filled her eyes.

"What's wrong?"

"It's too much. I don't deserve this much kindness."

Christian brought her into his arms. "Imi, of course you do. You are the kindest, most generous person I've met. This is a way people can repay your kindness."

"Mama's family doesn't even know me."

"But they want to. Perhaps this is their way of apologizing for the past."

Imogen hadn't considered that.

"Come on. I think you need a shower and some sleep."

Because she was so tired and vulnerable she let him lead her to the car. He opened the door and helped her in, bending over to kiss her softly. In that moment, looking up at him, seeing the care in his eyes, Imogen realized she loved him.

She loved his concern for others, the way he made her laugh, she even loved his loyalty to the job he disliked.

She wanted to spend her life with him by her side. She could visualize him here, in her house – in *their* house – with children running around in the garden.

He moved away to lock up and she stared after him, her breath huffing out with the surprise. Her head was full of love mingled with fatigue, mingled with happiness.

This was a new beginning.

She was going to make the most of it.

***

The alarm buzzed Imogen awake and she moved before she thought better of it.

"Ahh," she moaned as muscles she hadn't known she possessed protested.

Next to her Christian chuckled. "I hear you." He stretched, groaning as he did so.

Imogen checked the time. Every fiber of her body wanted her to turn off the alarm and go back to sleep but all her helpers would be gathering at the house in an hour and she needed to be there to let them in.

She slapped off the alarm and carefully maneuvered herself into a sitting position. "I think I might have been run over by a truck last night."

Christian sat up behind her and massaged her back.

Imogen's eyes rolled back into her head. "So good."

He laughed. "Let's get you into the shower." He helped her up and she followed him into the shower. The hot water ran over her back, soothing her aching muscles.

"How am I going to do it again today?" she asked.

"There's not as much work. The heavy stuff is all done. It will be mostly sanding and scraping today."

That didn't sound like much fun to her, but it needed to be done.

And if the others could do it, so could she.

After the shower and the caffeine hit she felt more human but not enough to keep her eyes open during the ride to her house.

When they arrived, Hank and his wife, Marla, were already there working on the outdoor room that was going to be Imogen's sewing room.

"Morning folks," Hank called from on top of the roof where he was replacing some tiles.

"How can he be up there already?" Imogen asked.

Marla grinned at her. "He's the fittest person I know. You forget he does this every day."

Guilt hit her. It was supposed to be his day off. "He should really get some rest," she said.

"Nonsense," Marla said. "He hasn't been this excited about a project for a long time. You won't be able to keep him away. In actual fact he's talking about branching out to do more renovation work rather than just new builds. You've given him a new interest."

Her words made Imogen feel better but she wasn't entirely convinced. Before she could make sure George's father really was happy, others started to arrive. Hank came down from the roof to give them all tasks and then went back up with Christian to give him a hand.

Imogen was sanding when Mr. Barker arrived carrying a rolled-up tube of paper.

"Imogen, I wanted to show you my design for your garden." He gestured her over to the table.

Imogen couldn't believe he'd done anything. She'd only given him a vague idea of what she wanted yesterday.

He spread out the plans. "This is the front yard." He took her through the details, including paving the driveway and building a garage on the side of the house that would match the architecture.

It was a simple design and one that would be easy to manage. "Looks wonderful. Send me the invoice for all of this work next week and I'll pay it straight away."

He smiled at her and placed the other design on top. "This is the backyard."

The first thing Imogen noticed was the words *secret garden*.

She examined the drawing as Mr. Barker explained his vision. It was everything Imogen wanted.

When she was finished, she flung her arms around the man and hugged him tightly. "It's perfect."

When she let go, his face had gone beet red. "Well, ah, if you like it I could go to the nursery and get the plants for the front yard today. The back will need some structural work before it's ready for planting."

"Yes, please." She wanted to go with him but she couldn't abandon the house. "Call me when you've got everything and I'll give them my credit card number."

"It'd be better if you came with me," Mr. Barker said.

Ingrid was standing nearby and must have overheard. "Go on, honey. Buying plants is one of the most fun parts. We've got everything under control."

"I can't leave when everyone's working so hard for me."

"Of course you can. We wouldn't be here if we didn't want to help."

When Imogen still hesitated Ingrid added, "Do you want me to get Grandma to tell you?"

Imogen smiled. Her grandmother would tell her in no uncertain terms to go. "All right. Thank you. I'll take my cell in case you need me."

"We won't." It was said with a smile.

After telling Christian where she was headed, she joined Mr. Barker in the car.

At the nursery Imogen was enthralled by the number of plants and colors available.

"If you find anything you like, we can always change the plant selection," Mr. Barker said.

"Thank you, Mr. Barker."

The man smiled at her. "I think you're old enough to call me Ethan," he said.

"All right. Thank you, Ethan." That was going to take some getting used to.

They wandered through the nursery filling the cart. A few times Imogen spotted something she loved and added it. Ethan smiled and made adjustments to his notes.

When they arrived back at the house it was mid-morning.

The roof of her sewing room had been repaired and people were mostly sanding or scraping floors, window and door frames to prepare them for painting and sealing. The amount of work that had been done was amazing. As soon as the bathrooms and kitchen were finished she could move in.

Feeling guilty for going shopping, Imogen got straight to work planting. It was fabulous to get her hands dirty, dig through the soil and help her garden come to life.

By midday her front yard was complete, with the exception of the lawn.

Christian walked down the front steps of her porch and over to her. "Everyone's breaking for lunch."

Imogen turned to him and wrapped her arms around him. "It's amazing. How am I going to thank everyone for their work?"

"Come with me." Christian took her hand and led her out to the front pavement. They stood next to each other and looked back at her house.

The picket fence was freshly painted white, the garden was full of color and the front of the house, though needing a coat of paint, was well on its way to looking its best.

Imogen's neighbor Natalie came out of her house and walked over to them. "I can't believe the work you've done in a weekend," she said.

Imogen introduced her to Christian and then said, "I've had a lot of help."

"I'll say. Mrs. Smithers would be thrilled. When are you moving in?"

"As soon as I can. The bathrooms and kitchen need replacing first."

"Well good luck to you. I'm sure you'll both be very happy here. It will be nice to have a family there again." Natalie said goodbye and walked back to her house.

Imogen didn't comment on Natalie's assumption she and Christian would both be moving in.

She glanced up at him. She loved him, wanted him to be part of her life, but she had no idea how he felt about her.

His expression was thoughtful. She wasn't sure whether she wanted him to be thinking so hard about them, so she grabbed his hand. "Let's get something to eat."

He let her lead him around the back to where the others were gathered for food.

Grandma had outdone herself again and there was plenty to eat. Imogen piled a plate full and went to talk to Hank.

"How do you think we're going?" she asked.

"By the time we're finished this afternoon all there will be left is a little bit of sanding inside and the rest of the outside. I've got the kitchen and bathroom people booked to come next week. You should be ready to move in by mid next month."

Excitement fluttered in Imogen's stomach. She'd never imagined it would be so soon.

"One thing I would suggest is you pay someone to paint the outside of the house. Everyone's done a great job prepping the areas they can reach but you really should get some scaffolding up and the professionals in."

"Can you recommend someone?"

"Yeah. I'll email you the details tomorrow. He's a little bit pricey but he's the best."

Imogen had no idea how she could express her thanks to all of these people. They had done it for nothing, had worked extraordinarily hard on their days off to help her. Her father would have thrown money at the house but this way felt right for Imogen. She wanted to rebuild the home she'd bought, wanted to put her own sweat into it and make it shine. It was amazing.

The thought of her father made some of the fluttering stop. She'd not heard from him since they fought. Imogen needed to fix their relationship if she could. She wanted her father to be part of her life still. She wasn't going to let her father's resentment fester as it had with the Ryder family. Perhaps she'd invite him around to her house next week so he could see what she'd done with it.

"Right people, break's over. Time to get back to work," Hank called as he put his plate down on the table and moved back inside.

There were a few light-hearted groans but everyone did as he asked.

Imogen was putting her plate on the table when Grandma

stopped her.

"You haven't eaten enough," she said with a frown. "Finish what's on your plate and then you can get back to work."

Imogen didn't bother arguing. She picked up the plate and took a mouthful of the food.

"What's bothering you, lamb?" Grandma asked.

"Nothing." Imogen could hardly tell her grandmother she was upset her father wasn't there. It would seem selfish and ungrateful.

"Of course there is. Your mother got the very same expression on her face when something was bothering her."

Surprise flooded Imogen. "Really?"

Grandma nodded. "You're very like her." She patted Imogen's shoulder. "So what's wrong?"

"I was wondering what Papa was up to." That was the truth, though perhaps not the whole truth.

"Piper said he was busy with a show."

"Piper spoke to him?"

Grandma nodded. "She called to invite him to come."

Imogen didn't need to know what he'd said. The answer was as clear as his absence.

So he had known about the weekend. There was a lot that needed to be said between them but Imogen was determined to fix it. She wasn't going to spend almost thirty years estranged from her father because of their argument. They needed to come to an understanding.

She put down her empty plate. "I'd better get back to work." She gave her grandmother a kiss on the cheek. "Thank you for everything."

Her grandmother smiled and replied, "Off you go then."

***

Imogen spent the rest of the afternoon scraping and sanding the bedrooms. They were the most neglected rooms because the previous owner hadn't been able to get upstairs to tend them. Still, by the end of the day, all that was required up there was a new bathroom, a good clean and then the painting. She debated whether she could move in now. The toilet was working so the only thing really lacking was a bathroom to wash in. She considered washing using the hose in the backyard. A few cold showers wouldn't be so bad, would it? She could have breakfast when she got to work and she usually lived on take-away food anyway so that didn't have to change. If she moved in now, she wouldn't be a burden on Piper.

"You're deep in thought."

Christian's voice right behind her made her jump back from the window she'd been standing at.

"I was debating whether I could move in now," she said.

He frowned. "Why? The place is a mess and you don't have a bathroom."

Imogen sighed. "Piper's place isn't really big enough for the two of us and I hate relying on her."

"Why don't you move in with me?" Christian looked as surprised by his suggestion as Imogen felt.

She opened her mouth to say something but no words came out. Did that mean he loved her? Did he mean it only as a temporary measure – a friend helping out a friend? Did he actually want to live with her?

"I've got plenty of room and with work, I'm hardly ever there anyway. This way we can see each other at night even if I have to work."

Imogen's heart went splat.

He was suggesting the move as a convenience to himself. He wouldn't have to make the effort to arrange to see her: she'd be waiting for him at his place like a good little woman.

And what would it mean for her to move out from under the control of one man and be at the mercy of another man's goodwill?

She forced a smile. "Thanks for the offer, but no." She loved him but she would go into the relationship on equal terms.

Christian gaped at her.

"My place is almost ready, so it doesn't make sense to move everything twice." Not if he didn't actually care for her the way she loved him. God, her heart was aching as much as her body was.

Christian frowned. "Why not? It makes sense."

"Not to me." She kept her tone light though her thoughts

were dark.

"Isn't my apartment as good as if not better than Piper's?" His tone was confused, bordering on offended.

"It's not that. I want to spend some time living by myself. I don't want to go from living under my father's watch, to living with someone else."

"You think I'd be like your father?" He was incredulous. "I am nothing like the man. He's a selfish, egotistical, controlling bastard with no thought for anyone else's feelings but his own."

Imogen's breath caught in her throat. The dislike in Christian's voice couldn't be hidden. She had learned some hard things about her father of late, but he was still the person who'd loved and cared for her her whole life. She still loved him.

The only two men she'd loved in her life hated each other.

Before Imogen had the chance to respond, Christian said, "I guess we don't really know each other at all."

He walked out of the room.

Imogen stared after him, her chest seizing painfully. Was he leaving? Was this it? He was going to dump her for not wanting to move in with him?

Her first instinct was to go after him but she stopped herself when she reached the door of the room. Christian had already gone down the stairs and out the front. What was she going to say to him anyway? Was she planning on giving in, moving in with him, just to make him happy?

Was she going to behave exactly the way she had with her father? Giving in to keep the peace?

No.

The determination came out of nowhere. She wasn't going to rush after him and placate him. She'd give him a day to cool down and then talk to him, try to make him understand how she felt, try to figure out how he felt about her.

Not once had either of them mentioned the L word, but love him she did.

"Imogen, do you need a lift?" Piper's voice called from downstairs.

If Christian had left, she would need one.

She slowly walked downstairs, her hand running over the dusty banister. The dirt reminded her this wasn't an ending, no matter what happened with Christian.

She had a new job, a new house and new family. She didn't *need* any men in her life.

And the two that she *wanted* didn't want her.

Chapter 18

Chris backed out of the driveway, his thoughts going a million miles an hour.

Imogen didn't want him. He felt the same tearing pain in his chest as he had the day Remy had given him Imogen's letter. The same confusion, disbelief and shock. He was a teenager again, being told he didn't measure up.

He wasn't good enough for her.

What more did he have to do to prove his love to her? He'd organized the demolition weekend so she could finish her house faster and he'd not freaked out when Remy had found them in bed together.

He shook his head. How could she think he would be controlling like her father? She didn't understand him at all.

He didn't realize something like that could hurt so much.

He drove on autopilot, his mind racing. It was Remy's fault. He'd given Imogen the ultimatum, kicked her out of her house and her job, all because she dared to choose her own path. Because of the way he treated her, she was determined to prove she could make it on her own.

The implication of the thought pounded down on him. He slowed the car.

Imogen not wanting to move in with him had nothing to do with him. She wanted time to prove to herself she could succeed without her papa. And he'd been so hurt, so defensive that he'd lashed out, said things to protect himself.

He'd hurt Imogen.

He was as cruel as Remy.

He had to figure out how to make it up to her.

***

Imogen didn't want to go to work. When the alarm screamed at her in the morning, her entire body ached and her brain was cotton candy.

She'd barely slept despite her physical exhaustion, but she couldn't let Chantelle down. Imogen rolled out of bed and shuffled to the shower. The hot water soothed the ache out of some of her muscles but the steam crept into her head and made it even foggier.

When she was dressed, she went out to the kitchen where Piper was having breakfast.

"Here." Her friend passed her a mug of coffee. "I figured you could use one of these."

"Thanks."

"You look shattered," she commented.

Imogen scowled at her, annoyed at how well dressed and perky Piper was today. "Don't your muscles feel like they're made of lead?"

"A bit. I go to the gym, remember? My muscles are used to the work out." She took a sip of her drink. "So are you going to tell me what really happened between you and Chris yesterday?"

Imogen choked on her coffee. When she'd finished coughing she said, "What do you mean?"

Piper gave her the look. "You can't lie to save yourself."

So she hadn't bought the work emergency excuse Imogen had given her. "He asked me to move in with him, and I said no. He didn't take it too well."

Piper sat back. "Well I wasn't expecting that. Why did you say no?"

Imogen sighed. "Two reasons. I realized I wanted to discover the independent Imogen."

Piper nodded in understanding.

"And he said he was hardly at home anyway, so my moving in wouldn't affect him, and we could still see each other if he had to work late."

Piper stared at her in disbelief. "A convenience invite?"

Imogen nodded.

"Did he say how he felt about you?"

"Nope."

Piper sighed. "I gave him more credit than he was due. Idiot."

"He was right?"

"Absolutely. Don't you go thinking this was your fault."

"I could have explained it better." If he'd given her the chance.

"So what are you going to do now?"

"I'll call him tonight."

"He should be calling you."

Imogen shrugged. It didn't really matter. She would clear the air and wait for his response. She wasn't going to hold a grudge when she knew how damaging they could be. If he was still angry she would have to get on with her life without him. She wasn't going to be involved with someone who tried to control her. Not again.

But damn, the thought of it was a knife to her heart.

Piper checked the clock. "I've got to go. Call me if you need to chat."

Imogen nodded and waved goodbye.

Finishing her coffee, she got up and went to work.

***

After work Imogen debated going over to her house. She was exhausted, but she couldn't keep away. She drove around to find Hank's truck still in the driveway. She called out as she entered the house.

"In the kitchen," Hank called back.

Imogen walked down the corridor to the back of the house where her kitchen had been.

Where her kitchen was.

She stared around at cabinets neatly in place, exactly where she'd wanted them.

"What do you think?" Hank sat at a trestle table doing some paperwork.

"This is amazing. I can't believe it's been done so quickly."

"They had a last-minute cancellation so they slotted you in. I've come over to lock up."

The cabinets didn't have doors or a bench top yet, but she could visualize the final result. It was how she'd pictured it.

"They've started the bathrooms as well. Go and check it out."

Imogen didn't need any urging. She wandered into the downstairs bathroom, and ran her hand over the vanity. "Do the taps work?" Imogen called to Hank.

"Yeah. They're connected. Turn them on."

Imogen turned on the taps and water came gushing out. She laughed. Maybe she could move in. She could have a couple of days of sponge baths. Though she should probably organize a new hot water system too.

Turning off the taps she surveyed the rest of the room.

There was bright blue paint around the shower area, which she guessed was some kind of waterproofing. All that was left to be done was the tiling and the shower screen.

Upstairs was a similar story. It was the bigger bathroom and it had the vanity in place and blue waterproofing on the walls.

Hank looked up as she returned. "It's all working?"

"Yeah. What's next?"

He took her through the project plan for the week, which included electricians, plumbers and tilers all coming through on different days.

She was so glad she'd hired him to project manage the renovation. There was so much she wouldn't have thought of. She'd definitely give him a bonus at the end; she knew he was making time for her.

"Were you planning on doing any work tonight?"

"I've borrowed Piper's vacuum and was going to clean up some of the dust."

"Good idea. It'll take a few passes before you get rid of it all. There's no more demolition to be done and there shouldn't be a lot of dust with what's left. Start upstairs away from the bathroom and you should be right." He stood up. "I'm going to head home."

Imogen hugged him. "Thank you, Hank. I couldn't have

done this without your help. It means a lot to me that you're putting so much into it."

Hank hugged her back. "It's my pleasure. This house is a gem and if you hadn't bought it, I would have. I've wanted a different project for a while now."

She walked him out the front and waved goodbye. As she was turning to go back inside, a car pulled into her drive.

It was her father.

Surprise washed over her. What was he doing here?

Imogen hesitated on the front porch, wanting to run down to him, but unsure what his reaction would be.

He got out of the car and she realized he was as uncertain as she was.

Giving in to her instincts, she waved and trotted down the steps. "Hi, Papa. Do you want to come inside?"

His posture relaxed only a minuscule amount but it was enough for Imogen to realize he had been expecting a different reaction from her. "It's old."

She laughed. "It is. You should have seen it last week. We've done the garden, the fence, and fixed the porch as well." She took his hand and rattled on, pointing out the things they had changed.

"You did all of this?" he asked.

Imogen hesitated. "I had help." Would he ask who and walk out?

"It is very kind of people to help."

"Yes." She opened the front door and led him inside.

He sneezed.

"There's a lot of dust still. I was going to clean it this evening."

Her father said nothing but followed her upstairs, where she took him for a tour, explaining the work they'd done and what she was going to use the rooms for. He made minor comments but he was obviously thinking. Imogen wasn't sure whether it was a good thing or not, so she kept talking, showing him downstairs and to the new kitchen.

"You have no sewing room," her father said when she was finished.

"It's outside," she said. She flicked on the yard lights and took him over to the outside building. "I haven't done anything here yet but I'm planning on installing cupboards and getting a big table."

"It's a good space. I started Tour de Force in a space smaller than this."

Imogen wasn't sure how to take his comments. Did they mean he was encouraging her to set up her own label, or was he just making conversation?

"I didn't know that."

"There is a lot you don't know about me, *ma bichette*." He took her hand. "We should talk. Is there somewhere we can sit?"

Unease washed over her. Her father did not talk like this. Something was wrong. She led him to the back steps and sat. "What's wrong, Papa?"

He shook his head. "The question should be who is wrong, and the answer would be me."

"I don't understand."

"I have spent years telling myself everything I did was for you, that I was protecting you, caring for you, making sure the world was not as cruel to you as it had been to me. But I realize now, I was punishing people for being cruel to me."

"Grandma is so sorry for what she said."

"No. It was before that." He patted her hand. "I have always told you I was an orphan. It is not true. I was a foster child. My parents did not want me and neither did anyone else."

Imogen put an arm around his shoulder and he leaned into her, showing vulnerability she never knew he had. Her father had always seemed like Superman to her. She had certainly never imagined him as a small, unwanted child.

"I ran away from the last foster home when I was sixteen. I changed my name, moved to Paris and found a job in the fashion industry."

Imogen didn't know what to say, didn't know what to think. She stood up, walked a few steps away and turned back. "Why?"

"I wanted to leave my past behind. I had no happy memories of Nancy, where I grew up, and I didn't want anyone to find me."

"Did Mama know?"

He nodded. "She was the only person I ever told. She was the ray of sunlight in my world and I would have done anything for her, including moving to America."

Imogen couldn't quite work out what was going on.

"When Frances died and her family accused me of killing her, it was like being a child all over again, not being accepted or loved. I would have left America altogether if not for Chateau Fontaine. So much of her went into that house that I feel she is still with me when I'm there."

So much of her father's behavior was starting to make sense. "You didn't want me to experience the same hurts as you," she said.

He nodded. "But I was also very selfish, wanting you all to myself. I did not realize how much I had done until you stood up to me."

"Does that mean you forgive me for meeting Mama's family?"

He nodded.

She walked over and hugged him. "Thank you, Papa."

He hugged her back and then pushed her gently away. "You are far too forgiving, *ma bichette*. I have more to say. I must apologize to you."

Imogen opened her mouth to speak but he held up a hand.

"I did not listen to you when you wanted to design your own clothing. I did not want to consider you leaving Tour de Force. I did not want your wonderful designs going out to people who would not appreciate them. I wanted to keep you all to myself."

Imogen's breath caught. He thought her designs were wonderful?

"By trying to keep you by my side I have pushed you away. Can you forgive me?"

"Of course." She was certain she wanted her father in her life, but she had to make a few things clear. "But I'm not moving back home."

He glanced around. "I can see."

"I'm going to continue seeing Mama's family."

"I would like to talk to them myself."

Imogen stared at him. "Really?"

"Yes. I have been foolish. It is time we buried the past."

"They would like that." She took a breath as she said the hardest part. "I'm not coming back to Tour de Force either."

He closed his eyes and sighed before opening them again. "Would you reconsider if we did a new label for you?"

Imogen hesitated. Not long ago she would have said yes, but now … "I'm working for Chantelle. I can't let her down when she helped me out." Plus she wanted to find out if she could do it herself. It was a challenge, not unlike her house, and she needed to know she could do it.

"You are a good person and I'm a foolish old man. It is my own fault for losing you."

Imogen sighed. "You're not losing me. I'm exerting my independence. Most kids do it as teenagers – call me a late bloomer." She hugged him. "Let's go inside. It's getting cold."

They walked in and Imogen locked the door behind them.

"You've done a lot of work. You are looking tired."

"It's been hard work, but it's almost done. Hank has organized the bathroom and kitchen people and I've got to clean the house."

"I will hire someone. You should not be on your hands and knees cleaning."

Imogen tried for patience. He always had to interfere. "Papa, I want to do it. It's my house."

"And I am not allowed to contribute? You have all these people helping you for two days and I can't give a little bit of money?"

Buying things was his way of showing he cared. Remy wouldn't necessarily pick up a hammer, but he could help by paying for things. He'd had the kind of childhood she could barely imagine – could she blame him for trying to spare her? She swallowed down her instinct to say no. "That would be wonderful, Papa. I'll ask Hank if he can recommend a cleaning agency."

They walked out the front of the house and Remy looked up at the outside as Imogen locked the door.

"You are going to paint the outside?"

"Yes. Hank's arranging it for me."

"I will pay for that as well."

Imogen didn't bother to argue. "Thank you, Papa."

"Shall I take you to dinner?"

With a smile she looped her arm through his. "That would be grand."

Her father wasn't likely to change his ways very much, but it didn't matter.

All that mattered was she had her father back.

***

Chris was at the end of his tether. He hadn't left work until after ten o'clock on Monday night – too late to go and see Imogen – and today was shaping up to be a similar situation. He had to talk to her today, before too much time had passed.

"Chris, they won't deliver dinner. You'd better go pick it up." Samuel stuck his head in Chris's office. "Then bring it to the boardroom."

It was after seven at night, which meant all the administration people were long gone. Samuel's statement pretty much summed up where Chris was in the pecking order. Right at the bottom of those at the top. "Samuel, I've got to go home."

His boss turned back and frowned at him. "Why?"

Chris debated what to tell him and decided on the truth. "I've got to fix things with my girlfriend."

Samuel's jaw dropped. "We've got a half-billion dollar merger happening and you want to go home because you've had a fight with your girlfriend?"

He didn't know why he'd hoped Samuel would understand. "I've been working eighty-hour weeks and I've missed too many big moments in her life."

"Welcome to the big leagues, kid. We've all missed moments. Why do you think I'm on to my third wife?"

The very idea horrified Chris. So the workload didn't get any lighter the higher he climbed. He didn't want to spend the next twenty years of his life this miserable at work, and he most certainly didn't want three wives. He wanted Imogen.

The uncertainty he'd been experiencing for the last few week suddenly cleared. He needed to be happy in his job, and happy in his personal life. This job would give him neither.

Chris stood up and shook his head. "I'm sorry. I have to do this now. I'll be back early tomorrow."

"You are paid to do the hours necessary to complete your job. This job is not finished."

"I know, Samuel, but I'm not willing to lose the love of my life over a merger." He smiled suddenly as he realized it was true. He did love Imogen, with all of his heart.

Samuel was quiet for a long moment. "Be in at six," he said, and walked out of the door.

Chris gathered up his things and almost ran to the elevator.

He had to tell Imogen how he felt.

***

Pulling up in front of Piper's apartment, nerves wheedled into his stomach. He took a deep breath and got out of the car, hurrying up the path to the door.

Piper answered his knock and crossed her arms when she saw who it was.

"Can I speak to Imogen?" he asked.

"No."

"Please, Piper. I need to talk to her."

"She's not here." There was nothing welcoming in her voice.

"Where is she?"

"Give me one good reason why I should tell you after the way you treated her."

Frustration broke through the nerves, but he kept it down. He needed Piper on his side. "I've got to apologize. I've been an idiot."

"Yes, you have been." She glared at him and then sighed. "She's moved into her house."

He'd missed another big moment in her life. She'd said she was going to move in as soon as she could; he just hadn't expected it to be so soon.

He needed to fix everything now.

"Thanks." He turned and raced back to his car. He hoped she would be willing to listen to him.

***

There was a light shining in the front room of Imogen's house when he pulled into the driveway.

This time he climbed slowly out of the car and walked up to the front door. He'd said some hurtful things to her and he couldn't take them back. Perhaps he should have stopped and bought her flowers.

But that would probably seem insincere.

He knocked on the front door and it took forever to open.

Imogen stood there as beautiful as ever, but her eyes were ringed with dark circles. She looked tired and as if she'd lost some weight.

"Christian." Her voice was music to his ears but her tone was pure exhaustion. God. Had he caused it?

"I'm sorry for not returning your call." It was the first thing that came to his head. "Work was insane …" He shook his head at his own excuses. "It doesn't matter. I'm going to find a better balance or a new job."

"Why are you here?"

"To apologize. For saying things about your father, for thinking those things about you. I realize it was my own insecurities making me so defensive. I didn't hear what you were saying."

"I forgive you." She put a hand on the doorknob.

Relief flooded through Christian's body, only to evaporate at Imogen's next words.

"If that's all, I'm tired and want to go to sleep."

She still stood in the doorway, guarding her threshold. There was no invitation in her body language whatsoever. Perhaps she misunderstood.

"Imi, I'm sorry for what I said, sorry for not understanding you needed your independence. You don't need to move in with me."

"No, I don't."

Chris was missing something vital here. There had to be something he could say to make her want him again. He reached out to touch her arm, but she moved it away.

Desperate now he stepped in, forcing her to either touch him or step back.

She stepped back.

"Imi, if I could take back those words, I would," he said.

Her face showed her fatigue. "Which words?"

The question made him pause. What had he said? He didn't really know. He remembered being offended at the comparison to her father, remembered saying awful things about him. But he'd already apologized for that.

It had all begun when he'd asked Imogen to move in with him. He'd been so scared of her rejection that he'd tried to make it sound like a casual thing, like he didn't care whether she stayed.

But he did.

And she didn't know it.

"Imogen, I love you. I wanted you to stay with me so much that when you said no, I reacted badly."

Imogen's eyes widened. "What did you say?"

"I wanted you to stay with me – "

She shook her head. "Before that."

The light bulb glowed so brightly in his head he was amazed he hadn't seen it before. "I love you. You're the light in my day."

She stepped forward, wrapping her arms around his neck. "I love you."

Her kiss was like the elixir of life, sweet, energizing and so completely right.

Chris hugged her closely to him, afraid to let her go.

She stepped back and ran a hand over his cheek. "I didn't think you cared. Your offer to move in together was like one for a friend."

"I was scared of your response."

"I understand now." Her eyes turned serious. "I'm still not going to move in with you," she said, waiting for his reaction.

She needed time for herself; he understood that now. As long as he had her in his life, he would be fine.

They would work through any issues together; he would get his work life under control, she would find her independence and they would support each other.

There was no rush.

As long as he had a whole lifetime with her.

"Do you want to see my new bedroom?" Imogen asked with a wicked little grin.

He took her hand. "Would I ever."

They laughed as they went upstairs.
It was a new beginning.

Epilogue

Imogen adjusted the flower arrangement on her outdoor table and smiled as her phone rang. She hurried inside to answer it.

"Imogen, it's Elle. I'm sorry, I won't be able to make it to your housewarming. Toby's not well."

"I hope it's not serious," Imogen said, instantly concerned. Elle had called her to thank her again for the haircut and they'd kept in contact. Imogen had been looking forward to introducing Elle to her friends.

"It's not. My next door neighbor's daughter just had a head cold and she's passed it on to Toby."

"That's a shame. Tell him I hope he feels better soon."

Imogen hung up. She worried about Elle, who appeared to have no one to help her. She'd never mentioned any family or where Toby's father was, but Imogen didn't know her well enough to pry.

Christian walked into the kitchen carrying two bags of ice. "Where do you want these?"

"There're two containers outside," she told him, and held the door open. Her heart swelled with pride when she saw her back deck and neat garden. The garden wasn't completely finished yet, but the tree house was there, as well as a swing. This was all hers.

But her house wouldn't be nearly as complete as it was without so many people helping, so she was having a housewarming party as thanks. She'd spent the whole day cooking and hoped that everything tasted all right. She'd had Mrs. Povey on speed dial the whole day.

Her one worry about the evening was that her father would be seeing her mother's family for the first time since Imogen was born. She had no idea how that would go.

She pushed the worry aside as Christian walked up to her and wrapped her in his arms.

"You've done an amazing job, Imi," he said.

"It was a team effort." And there was still work to be done. The kitchen and bathrooms were complete, but most of the other rooms still needed a coat of paint. She had prioritized her bedroom and the sewing room, and this week she'd set up her living room. The rest of the rooms were getting done after work or on the weekend, when she had the energy to pick up a paint brush. Though she was getting much better at it.

The outside had a fresh coat of paint and the plans for her new garage were waiting to be approved by the authorities.

Her doorbell rang and she squeezed Christian. "They're here." She hurried through the house and opened the front door.

"Happy housewarming!" Kate yelled, handing her a bouquet of bright flowers.

Imogen grinned. "Thanks, Kate." She greeted Adrian, Libby and Piper and showed them in. Before she could close the door, George pulled up.

"Do you want to be the greeter, or the hostess?" Christian asked her.

She was keen to show off her house to those who hadn't seen it. "Hostess." Christian knew everyone who was coming, so he could show them through to the backyard.

"Wow, check out the kitchen." Kate's voice floated down the hallway.

Imogen hurried to show them through.

***

Imogen was coming down the stairs after showing George's and Piper's family through the house when the doorbell rang. She answered to find her father on the porch.

"Hi, Papa. Thanks for coming." She hugged him and kissed his cheek.

"I see the painters have done the outside," he said.

"Yes, and the cleaners you hired were fantastic at getting rid of the dust." She glanced behind him and saw her grandmother and uncles. Nerves appeared instantly. She ushered her father inside and turned to her grandmother.

"Grandma, I'm pleased you could come." She hugged her and then turned to where her father was standing. She wasn't certain how to break the ice.

"Julie," her father said. He hesitated. "It is good to see you again."

Her grandmother nodded her head. "Likewise, Remy."

Remy greeted Imogen's uncles and aunt and they stood in the hallway, a little awkwardly.

"Would you like to see the house?" Imogen asked.

"I can't wait to see what you've done," her grandmother said.

Imogen led the way upstairs and Remy offered his arm to Julie. She took hold of it and smiled cautiously. Imogen let out the breath she'd been holding. They were both trying to bridge the gap. It would take some time before they were comfortable with each other – if they ever were – but Imogen was happy they could at least be civil.

When the last guest had arrived Imogen clapped her hands to get everyone's attention. It was a balmy spring night and they were all sitting outside.

"Thank you for coming tonight. I really appreciate all of your help and support with my house. There's a little way to go, but it doesn't feel so hard. I feel blessed having so many wonderful people in my life."

"We're blessed to have you," Piper called out.

Imogen smiled at her. "I've prepared a four-course meal for you all to enjoy, which I hope goes to show some measure of my appreciation for your hard work." She gestured to the appetizers she'd placed on the table. "I hope it's edible."

There was laughter as everyone began to eat.

***

Chris wandered over to his father who was at the back of the garden checking how the new plants were faring. "You're supposed to be relaxing and enjoying the evening," he said.

"This is my way of relaxing." His father turned to him and smiled. "How's work been?"

Chris hesitated. He'd been avoiding mentioning work to his father, worried about the reaction he was going to get. "I'm actually thinking about finding a new job."

"Aren't you happy there?"

"No." He'd never told his father the truth. He hadn't wanted to disappoint him. "The hours are getting a bit much."

"I don't know how you've put up with it this long," Ethan said. "I would have packed it in long ago."

Chris stared at his father. "You never give up."

"Changing direction or realizing something isn't what you thought it would be, isn't giving up. Why do you think I went into garden design after leaving Chateau Fontaine? I knew I didn't want to just maintain people's gardens, I wanted to build them."

"That's not the same. I'll have to take a pay cut and the new job may not be as prestigious."

"What does that matter? Didn't I teach you not to care about what other people thought?"

Chris's gaze found Remy, who was talking with Peter. Remy had actually spoken to him earlier, asked him about his work and been civil. They were both making an effort for Imogen's sake.

"I know what Remy did to you and Imogen all those years ago had an effect," Ethan said. "But you can't let it continue to rule the way you live your life."

Chris turned back to his father, frustration stirring. "You sacrificed so much to put me through law school," he said. "I owe it to you to be as successful as I can be."

His father's mouth dropped open. "You don't owe me anything. I willingly spent that money on your education because I thought that was what you wanted."

"It was. It still is." Chris ran a hand through his hair. "But if I change jobs I won't be as successful." He needed to make his father understand.

"Success is different things to different people," Ethan told him. "Do you think I'm successful?"

"Of course."

"So do I. I'm not the most sought-after landscape architect in Houston but I love my job and I earn a good living. What is success to you?"

The words sunk into Chris's consciousness. He'd always equated success to being number one. Had he got it wrong?

"I want you to be happy," Ethan said.

Were happiness and success the same thing? What would make him happy at work?

The joy and satisfaction he got from the pro bono work sprang immediately to mind. He also wanted regular hours so he could be there for all the important moments in Imogen's life. And he needed to earn enough to get by. His current work only provided one of those things.

Ethan clapped him on the shoulder. "You need to live your life for yourself, not for anyone else."

The final issue that had been weighing Chris down lifted from his chest.

He hugged his father. "Thanks, Dad."

***

Imogen closed the door behind the last guest and sighed. It had been the perfect night. She'd celebrated her new home surrounded by the people she loved. She was so incredibly lucky. Her job with Chantelle was better than she could have hoped and she was still working on her business plan in her spare time.

Christian walked over. "Shall we go upstairs?"

"In a second. I'm just enjoying the moment."

"So you should. You deserve all of this and more."

Imogen wrapped her arms around him. In the couple of weeks since their fight they had talked more, sorting out the issues that had been bothering them. Christian had spoken with his work about reducing his hours, but Samuel hadn't been keen on the idea so Christian was looking for another job. Imogen was pleased, but she hadn't pushed him either way. He had to be happy with whatever decision he made.

They spent as much time as they could together. Some days

that meant she stayed at his apartment, other days he stayed with her, and there were still days when they didn't see each other at all, but they always texted, emailed or called. She wasn't ready to take the next step of moving in together just yet, she was content to see how things went.

She took his hand. "I love you."

He grinned and kissed her quickly. "I will never tire of hearing that. I love you, Imi."

She squeezed his hand, more content than she had ever been. "Let's go to bed."

Thank you for reading!

I hope you enjoyed the book. It would be super awesome if you could leave a review wherever you bought it, because I love to hear what you thought of the story (yes, even if you didn't like it!)

If you've only just discovered the Texan Quartet, make sure you check out Libby, Piper and George's stories too. The next story in the series is where George finds love in Under the Covers.

Acknowledgements

There are many people who helped me with this book. First of all, Bethanie Christie, who came up with the idea of Imogen making Libby's wedding dress. Thank you for brainstorming with me and coming up with the perfect tie-in.

Thank you to the members of the West Houston Romance Writers of America chapter who were kind enough to answer my never-ending questions about the differences in terminology between Australian English and American English.

To my uncle, Ian, who helped me with medical issues and didn't seem the least bit perturbed when I rang and said I needed a way to kill a character – thank you!

To my mum, whose sewing 'treasury' inspired Imogen's sewing room.

Finally, and as always, to the wonderful team at Momentum – Joel, Patrick and Tara, as well as my editor, Kate, and cover artist, Jon. Thank you for your enthusiasm for my book and for helping me make it shine.

What Goes on Tour

The Texan Quartet # 1

What if the one time you didn't want love was when you truly needed it?

Forced to flee her abusive ex, alone with no support, Elle is determined to rebuild her life and protect her five-year-old son. Not one to take the easy road, she opens a bookshop café, but opening day almost ends in disaster. In the midst of this chaos, the last thing she needs is a man as charming as George Jones getting in her way.

George has always been a sucker for a damsel in distress, and Elle ticks all the boxes. But Elle's not interested in being rescued by anyone, especially not him. She knows her taste in men can't be trusted, but fighting George's charisma is harder than she expected. And George, who is not one to ignore an itch, has found there's something about Elle that's got under his skin.

When Elle's ex turns up to cause trouble, George must overcome his boyish flirtatiousness if he's to convince Elle to trust herself and let him into her life. But can Elle put her past behind her before it overwhelms her present?

http://www.claireboston.com/books/the-texan-quartet/

Under the Covers

The Texan Quartet # 3

What if the one time you didn't want love was when you truly needed it?

Forced to flee her abusive ex, alone with no support, Elle is determined to rebuild her life and protect her five-year-old son. Not one to take the easy road, she opens a bookshop café, but opening day almost ends in disaster. In the midst of this chaos, the last thing she needs is a man as charming as George Jones getting in her way.

George has always been a sucker for a damsel in distress, and Elle ticks all the boxes. But Elle's not interested in being rescued by anyone, especially not him. She knows her taste in men can't be trusted, but fighting George's charisma is harder than she expected. And George, who is not one to ignore an itch, has found there's something about Elle that's got under his skin.

When Elle's ex turns up to cause trouble, George must overcome his boyish flirtatiousness if he's to convince Elle to trust herself and let him into her life. But can Elle put her past behind her before it overwhelms her present?

http://www.claireboston.com/books/the-texan-quartet/

Into the Fire

The Texan Quartet # 4

Piper Atkinson uses the truth as a weapon, but her latest interview candidate is more than just a headline.

Piper wants to be the kind of journalist who makes people sit up and take notice of the issues, and in Houston, Texas, there are plenty to go around. In the city's high-end restaurant world, reclusive Native American chef Taima Woods is discussed in reverential whispers, so when the opportunity to interview him arrives, Piper jumps at it.

But getting to Tai is tougher than she expected. He has a deep mistrust of reporters, and a private life he'd prefer to keep hidden. There are two passions in Tai's life – his cooking and his tribe – and he means to keep it that way. But the closer Tai gets to Piper, the closer he comes to conceding a third.

Through Tai, Piper discovers a world she knew nothing about – a damaged and ostracized community in need of a voice. But the more Piper wants to help them, the more Tai understands that to love Piper is to turn his back on his people.

Will Tai reject the one woman who's ever understood him? Or can Piper show him that hardening his heart helps no one?

http://www.claireboston.com/books/the-texan-quartet/